Kay D Johnson

First Page
Last Page

Johnson, Kay D
First Page Last Page

ISBN 978-0-9952658-3-7 (pbk)
ISBN 978-0-9952658-4-4 (ebook)

GoMe! PUBLISHING

First Page Last Page

Nitra Zupan was on a deadly mission. She was heading to Memorial Park to kill off the one obstacle in her life that was causing endless hours of grief. It kept her awake at night. She couldn't eat because of it. She had to put an end to it. To her, it was a nuisance that needed to be obliterated from the face of her earth. Nitra Zupan had made up her mind; she was finally going to kill off her stubborn writer's block.

It was a typical autumn morning, with warm sunshine and pale blue skies, but she didn't care about those positive aspects, she was preoccupied with the one lone cloud that slowly crept across the horizon. That singular grey anvil cloud worried her. Even from that far off distance she could feel its tension charging the air. Despite the weather man's earlier warning that the weather could possibly turn nasty, Nitra decided she'd take the chance anyway. She hoped that the storm would hold off long enough for her to get some crucial writing done. As she walked through the park, she deliberately crushed dried leaves under her boots. She scanned the park for signs of other humans. There were none — just the way she liked it. She had to be completely alone; doing that deed was a solitary task. It had to die by her hands.

Composing in the great outdoors had its own set of hazards. Problems such as extreme temperatures, talkative passers-by and eye straining sunlight, were all distracting nuisances. But the greater problem was the two enemies of paper — strong winds and pelting rains. Both could wreak havoc within seconds, causing months of work to be destroyed forever. And by the looks of that one distant storm cloud, it held the potential to inflict such a destructive misery. Unfortunately for her, she had no choice; she had to do it today. Her editor imposed deadline was slowly creeping up on her and she was tormented by a serious case of writers block. She understood that the weather would either hold and she could get a few pages scribbled down, or it could turn into a severe storm, shattering her creativity completely. It was a risk she had to take. Today she was determined to sit in the park and go over her notes, no matter what the wretched weather man said.

After a fast five minute walk, she finally arrived at her favourite slate blue bench. She preferred it over all the others in town, its heavy ornate Victorian style made her feel special, as though she was royalty sitting upon her throne. There was that, plus the fact that it was in a secluded section of Memorial Park. Solitude was her creative companion. She plunked herself directly in the middle of it sturdy seat. She had learned over the years that if she sat on one end of a bench, an uninvited person would come along and sit at the other end. And that meant they'd eventually start talking to her, breaking her perpetual train of thought. She came to the park to write in an alternate atmosphere, not for pointless chitchat. The change of scenery freed her of her writer's block. Today she was in one of those comatose moments and she needed the parks help in destroying it.

She let out a long deep sigh, relieving herself of her angry tension. She closed her eyes to concentrate on her task, letting go her self-imposed hostility. Opening her eyes to the bright sunlight, she methodically organized her writer's tools. To her right she spread out her empty lined paper, her pencil, and a stack of crumbled up scraps of paper. On her left she placed a tidy pile of neatly hand written pages. The paper was manufactured specifically for her. The red lines and heavy weight was ideal for her rapid style of writing. She patted those gently, lovingly as though they were her offspring. Nitra preferred to write with pencil and paper. For her, the computer's constant spell and grammar checking, distracted her from the flow of her ideas. At the end, when she was totally satisfied with all of the many rewrites and corrections, she'd then transfer the manuscript to her computer.

On the pages there were red notations penciled in the margin, some with big arrows that pointed to heavily slashed out words. Others scribbles were ideas that were to be incorporated later in the plot line, creating the unexpected twists she was so famous for. Letting out another heavy sigh, most of the burning knots departed her stomach. Nitra was starting to relax. From inside her oversized tote bag she pulled out a thick sandwich wrapped in white paper. Peeling back the one corner, she bit into it, then moaned with ecstasy. Black forest ham with mayo and Dijon mustard on light rye bread, even the crust had been removed for her. Nitra inhaled deeply with the satisfaction of the moment. After her sandwich she intended to go through her pile of scribbled notes, hoping she'd find a block breaking inspiration on one of those filthy, wrinkled pieces of paper. She was always writing things down. On napkins, the back of paper placemats, even on the tags off of clothing she found in the bottom of her tote — any type of small blank space where a few words could be jotted down quickly before they left her mind forever. Character sketches, one-liners from a conversation or a mini plot line that would pop into her head out of nowhere. She was blocked and in that pile, she hoped was her un-blocker. She chewed the last mouthful of her sandwich while feeling the heat of the sun on her chilled face. Autumn was definitely setting in. Coloured leaves were scattered everywhere.

Tucking away her empty sandwich wrapper, she set her mind to work. She picked up the unruly stack and began the task of deciphering their scribbled language.

Tall but small, not intelligent, but very smart
Blonde with black moustache — Tabby's

She smiled at the memory it evoked. He was a handsome man, very suave, but he ruined the illusion by speaking. She put it on her left. The next one read quite differently.

Pink tight see-through dress
A user, big breast, big ideas, big greed
God protect the men from that one — Tim's b-day party

She added that one on top of the first one. She took the next hunk of paper off the pile. She had to hold it up to the sun to read its faded letters through the smeared paper.

4

The Smile — Through the mayhem, he calmly went about his business, all the while retaining his customary half-grin. And that's what made him so incredibly sexy. His quiet self-confidence made her wonder what was really going through his mind.

She remembered that lad. It was in the middle of a very hectic award ceremony that this fella, in his twenties, was calmly working away with this sexy contented smile on his face, the smile a person has after having a great night of sex. She closed her eyes, picturing his face and body movements. She muttered to herself while placing it in a separate spot beside the other two, "That one might work?"

Just then she noticed that the leaves were starting to dance along the ground. Her face felt a sudden breeze that wasn't there the second before. Where had the sun gone? She was now sitting in the shadow of that large anvil cloud.

Then it hit.

The wind instantly gathered speed, blowing the leaves up into a flurry of fall colours. She tried to hold everything down with outspread hands, but she was too late, it did the same to her papers. With one forceful wind gust, they exploded, sending everything into the air. She jumped to her feet, franticly grabbing at what pages she could reach while on their upward spiral. She managed to catch one, then another, but it appeared pointless, they were everywhere. She watched as they were sucked up into the strong swirling air. At that exact moment, the wind halted for just a mere second, releasing some of the pages so that they fell towards the earth. She scrambled after them, scooping them up as fast as she could, cramming them down the front of her sweater. When the second was over, the wind returned, pushing the other pages even higher. Then the rain hit, depositing blurry drops on her glasses that made it impossible for her to see where the pages were or where she was going. As quickly as the rain came, the same sudden down pour stopped.

Soaked to her skin, she hopelessly watched through the one dry corner of her glasses as her work floated completely out of sight. They disappeared over the horizon and were gone. Nitra's heart sank. In a matter of seconds, her work had vanished. Eight weeks of work gone. All she could do was cry. She let herself go, releasing the pain and the frustration. She swiped her glasses on her wet sweater. The papers inside crinkled, reminding her that not all the pages were taken away, they were still there. She shuffled to the wet bench and sat in the seat's puddle — it didn't matter, she was wet anyway. Sitting numb, she blew out a heavy pain filled sigh, her gut knots were back. Eight weeks work gone! She held her forehead in her palm. What was she going to tell her publicist? William had already been on her back about meeting next month's deadline. This was going to infuriate him and that meant he'd take it out on her at a later date. Another deep sigh helped relieve the crushing pressure on her chest. Slowly she pulled out a page from her sweater. She smoothed it out against her chest, and then placed it on her lap. It was page 5. She did that for each of the remaining pages tucked in her sweater. In the end she had recovered 15 of the 34 pages. She restacked them in numerical order, determining she had pages 2, 4, 5, 9 to 12, 15 to 18, 22, 25, 32 and 33. The rest were gone, including her precious scribbled notes.

Before she left, she scoured the park's fence lines and shrubberies, hoping to find just one more page. But all she found was two of her soggy scribbled notes and plenty of garbage. Even while distraught, she made a mental note to talk to her neighbour's brother, the mayor of Hamlin, about the cleanliness of his town's parks. Nitra returned to the truck only to realize that she had also left the window partway down and the front seat was drenched as well. She let out another gloomy sigh. It was just not her day. Angry, she purposely slammed her bottom on the seat with leathery 'homolog' sound. "God damned wind. God damned rain. God damned wet underwear crawling up my butt!" She yanked it out of the crack in her behind. Starting the truck, she set her jaw, and headed for home.

Nitra sat at her desk, trying desperately to rewrite the first paragraph of the first page. It was most important paragraph of the entire manuscript, the hook as it was called in the publishing world — it was vital. For most readers, the hook determined whether they purchased the book or not. If it wasn't worded just right, the chances are that the reader would return it to the shelf and walk away. No matter how hard she tried, the exact words wouldn't form on the page in front of her. They weren't the same. She mumbled to herself, "Oh damn it! Was it — *'a blend which allowed each strand to gather power from light, both solar and lunar, that made it shimmer with vibrant energy."* Or was it — *"a blend that made his jet black hair shimmer in the sun along with its exotic scent and energy."'* She couldn't remember. "Crap!" She slammed her fist on the desk. From there, she sunk her face in both of her hands and let go a deep grunt in her throat. It was agony. The words she had written previously were perfect. They said exactly what she wanted them to say. They painted a perfect picture, her perfect picture. The words on the page in front of her weren't working and it was evident that it was hopeless to attempt to recapture the feeling of her original words. There was only one thing left to do. Find those lost pages.

She paced about the cottage. First, to the kitchen for a cup of tea, then back to the writing room where she sat in her computer chair staring at the screen. How was she going to get those pages back? They went in every direction, including up. Way up. This was even more frustrating than the rewriting. She blew out a heavy frustrated sigh. That sigh flicked the newspaper clipping on her bulletin board — that's when it came to her. She jumped from her chair and rushed to the recycling bucket in the back hall. Paper flew in all directions. She squealed when she found it. The local news rag. She flew to the kitchen table, laid it out in front of her, smoothing out the bent back corners. She flipped it over to the back, opening it to the second inside page. But it wasn't there. She flipped back one more page, then another and another, until she found it. There it was, in small print in the upper right hand corner, the address and phone number for classified advertisements. She scribbled down the phone number on the palm of her hand. She started to rise to her feet, heading for the phone, but stopped half way up. She sat back down with a hard futile plunk. What was she going to put in her ad? How was she going to word it? Lost papers - please return to Nitra Zupan. No, that wouldn't do. What about; writer seeking lost pages of book. Please contact Nitra Zupan. Nope, that still wouldn't do. No name. Including her name would be disastrous, she'd have every lunatic calling her like last time. Maybe a fictitious name? What would she call herself? Several names ran through her head, making her laugh at her own imagination. But silly names like Rose Bud or Ima Queen wasn't helping her in find her lost pages. Getting serious, she got out her preferred tools — her mechanical pencil and sheets of red lined paper.

She scribbled, then erased and scribbled some more. In deep thought the pencil bounced off her bottom lip before capitalizing the first word. She smiled at her success.

REWARD. Lost pages of manuscript.
Blew away in Tuesday morning's windstorm
Will pay $20.00 for each page returned to author.
Call 555-1287 between Noon – 6 p.m.

Twenty dollars per page seemed fair. For twenty dollars people would make the effort to find and return the pages. It was definitely worth it to her to have them returned. She had a deadline coming up at the end of next month and it wasn't nearly close enough to being finish. And that was *before* she lost the pages. She'd be sunk without them.

With the newspaper in hand she headed for the phone. Out of the blue she was sideswiped by Gemma, her 15 pound cat. She was on one of her 'chase the nothing' runs and happened to connect with Nitra's ankle.

"Holy Christ Gemma! You trying to kill me?" She had to do one of those funny little jumps so she wouldn't step on her paws. "Stupid cat! Get out of here!" With that, the feline scurried around the corner & out of sight. "Stupid dumb cat," she muttered it again, furrowing her forehead. Nitra plunked down in the over-sized arm chair by the window. Pulling the phone onto her lap, she poked at the keys that matched the numbers smeared on her palm. She got to the third number 5 when she realized something, how was she going to pay for the ad over the phone. Credit card? No way was that happening. She was dead set against '*plastic pay-for-it-tomorrow*' cards. In her opinion those companies robbed you blind while you give them permission to do so by signing a tidy little contract. Only foolish people gave away their money for the privilege of being compulsively greedy. Nitra Zupan was no one's fool. She returned the phone to its designated spot. Letting out a heavy sigh, she knew what was coming next, another trip into town.

She hated going to town — with the exception of her occasional visits to the park. It was always the same. She'd have to be careful where she went and where she parked her truck. Generally, it would be as close as possible to the building she had to go into. She liked being a well known writer, but not that part of it. The royalties were wonderful, the book signings were tolerable, but the harassment during daily life had made her visits to town out-and-out miserable. The people meant no harm, they only wanted to meet a celebrity or have one of her books signed by her. In her head, she knew she should be grateful that they liked and remembered her. The day would come that they would stop and she'd somehow miss it. But right now it made going about her private life very stressful.

According to those who knew her, that was why she had basically become a recluse. Most of her friends had given up on her. They were tired of declined invitations to large dinner parties or evenings on the town. They also realized her being shot at, didn't help matters either. Nitra had narrowed down her socializing to private functions at their homes or quiet dinners at hers. That way, she avoided the scrutiny of the public eye or the possibility of intruders. Even the local press gave up, a decision she was relieved about. No more worrying about what she wore or what her hair looked like. She could be herself — her real self — like she was on Tuesday morning. Just being able to sit quietly in the park and soak up its atmosphere.

Nitra folded the paper in half, tucking it in her beaded tote bag and grabbed her truck keys. When she reached the back door, she hollered up the stairs, "I'm going to town. Do we need anything?"

"No. We're good. I did groceries the day before last." The man's voice was more businesslike than friendly. After all, Wallace McPhee was Nitra's housekeeper, not her roommate.

"Okay, see you." She let the screen door slam hard behind her. Sometimes it bothered her that he wasn't her close friend, yet other times, it was a blessing. Like when she brought home a male friend from the city. He kept his nose out of it. Nitra preferred her men to be from the city. In her opinion they were exciting, intelligent, and more over, they didn't care for farm equipment or car racing. But it had been a long time since that had happened. Since Christmas she'd been afraid to go to the city. The other dilemma was that her face was well-known to too many men. Sometimes she hadn't been sure if a fella actually liked her or whether his intention was to brag to his buddies that he had screwed a writer. That was the joy and the curse of being a female writer. She climbed into the truck and headed into town.

Nitra parked four blocks away in front of King's Drugstore. It was as close as she could get to the newspaper office. People nodded as she went by. She smiled in return. The seat of her truck was still slightly wet and now so was her ass. Large dark blue ovals showed exactly where she

11

had been sitting, making everyone look at her butt as she walked passed. Hearing the whispers she knew they were looking; but she was there and she'd do what she came to do in spite of wet spots or what they thought. Opening the door of the newspaper office, she found the local Chief of Police, Harry Palmer leaning against the counter. Nitra tried to stop her grin. She still couldn't look at the man without giggling about his name. What on earth were his parents thinking when they named him? *It would be cute!* The word that came to her mind wasn't cute, but more like cruel.

"Well this is an honour. How you been Miss Nitra?" he walked toward the door to greet her. "Why I haven't seen you in almost nine months. Not since that 'fan incident' back around Christmas time." His face flushed a little. Inside he hoped she didn't bring it up, nevertheless he felt it necessary to offer the opportunity, "Things good your way?"

She swallowed down her memories, "Things are good. Nice and quiet, just the way I like it. And how's things with you and your family." She knew better than to ask about his job. When she first moved to Hamlin she had made the mistake of asking for some details regarding an unsolved robbery that had happened the year before. Officer Palmer made it perfectly clear that his department did not give out information about crimes committed in his district, especially to a nosey writer from the big city. It was still a minor sore spot between the both of them.

"My oldest is getting married." His grin was proud, "Next May."

Nitra had heard that his son Mark was marrying a doctor — well a veterinarian actually. "That's wonderful. Bet your wife's happy."

"Not as happy as me. One down and one to go. Then I can retire, so me and Marianne can go travelin'. Like down to Florida in the winter." They reached the counter, "You ever been there?"

"Oh yes, last year for a book signing. But it was in the summertime, too damned humid to really enjoy the visit." She blushed a bit at admitting she was somewhat famous and traveled extensively because of it. "So, how's that daughter of yours? When's Tammy getting married?" From the corner of her eye she saw Bernice wave wildly behind Harry's back. It was her way of saying *'don't go there'*. But it was too late; Nitra's foot was already in her mouth. She had completely forgotten that Harry's daughter was gay and may never be getting married, at least not to Harry's way of thinking. "I mean … when's she moving out?" Again Bernice's hands flapped like an angry seagull. Apparently, she'd done it again. Trying to save the situation, she asked one more question, "I mean … is she done college yet?"

Bernice's eyes rolled back in her head before she stepped in to save Nitra from the pit-of-doom questions she was wallowing in, "Harry didn't you say you had paper work to do back at the station? And Nitra what can I do for you? I'm kinda backed up with my own paper work, no time for chitchat. So what do ya need Honey?"

Grabbing the offered opportunity, she stepped right passed Harry to stand directly in front of Bernice. "I want to put in a lost ad." She noticed by the expression on her face that Bernice didn't understand what she meant and reworded her statement. "I lost some papers this morning in the wind storm and I want to put in an ad for their return." She pulled out her folded paper and started to hand it to Bernice when they both heard the front door close, meaning Harry was gone. Nitra relaxed the tension in her shoulders. "Do you think twenty dollars a page is enough of a reward?"

Bernice's pretty blue eyes nearly fell out of her head, "Are you serious? Twenty bucks a page! Hell Honey for that kinda money, I'd rummage around in the ditches myself." She yelled over her shoulder, "Hey, Chris you hearing this out here."

From the backroom came a higher than normal soft male voice, "No. What's going on?"

"She's offering twenty bucks a page to return her papers she lost this morning. Twenty whole damned dollars!"

Chris waddled his way around the corner, "Yah, so? Sounds about right to me."

Bernice's mouth fell open, "Wait, you're not surprised by this." She waggled her finger at him, "which tells me that you've seen this happen before. I'll be damned. Spill it Sugar, I want the details." Bernice used little pet names like Sugar and Honey. Nitra couldn't figure out why though, she was born five counties over and nowhere near the South. It did however go well with her over teased red hair and frilly dresses.

"There are no details, silly. It's just common sense. Simply put, if I was Miss Nitra the writer here, and knowing her annual income," he looked over the top of his glasses at her, "and I do know your annual income, I'd say shelling out twenty dollars a page is quite a bargain for her. Am I right Nitra?"

She hated when he used his know-it-all face. It was essential that she straighten him out regarding his little theory. "Not quite. You're basing my future financial status on my past financial status and as you know, in the writing world, they either like you or they don't. So although you're right, you are also very, very wrong."

He had been corrected and he knew it. He bowed to her slightly, "Well played."

Bernice piped in, "Say Chris, don't you think this would make a great story?"

At the exact same time both Chris and Nitra hollered, "NO!" sending Bernice leaning backward on her seat.

Nitra spoke up first, "No way, I'm not doing it. I don't want every God damned idiot fan at my doorstep wanting crap from me." By now she was practically yelling at Bernice and stabbing her finger into her own chest, emphasizing the point that she didn't want any part of her idea.

Chris took another route. He yelled at the air and waving his arms around, "And I don't want the headache of having every big ass city paper busting my chops about our town's little treasure here."

The word 'treasure' caught Nitra completely off guard. She turned to smile at him, "Why thank you Chris. That's the nicest thing anyone in this town has ever said to me."

"Yah, yah. Don't let it go to your head. I only meant that compared to the rest of the village idiots, you're the closest thing we got to a celebrity. Hell next in line to you is Harold and his dancing dog. It's slim pickings, if you know what I mean."

Nitra should have known better than to think someone from Hamlin would give her a sincere compliment. "Oh," was all she replied.

Bernice caught it. In Nitra's eyes was the sting of being rejected yet again by the people of Hamlin. She knew that feeling first hand. She had moved to Hamlin fifteens ago and still got the same treatment. Sympathising with Chris's dismissal of Nitra, she changed the topic immediately, "So you got all written up what you want to put in the paper?" With her eyes she shot imaginary daggers into the side of Chris's head. It partially satisfied her nasty urge for revenge, but a lot more than that would be needed for complete gratification.

Nitra handed her the unfold paper, "Can you get it in today's paper or am I too late?"

Bernice nonchalantly tilted her head left in order to look around Nitra's body toward Chris, "Don't know. *Is* she too late Chris?"

He checked his watch, "It's after one o'clock. The deadline is one o'clock."

He folded his arms tightly to enforce his arrogant authority.

First, the insulting of Nitra's talents and then his superiority bullshit — Bernice couldn't stand it — he had to pay. In retaliation Bernice crossed her arms as well, "Are you going to make me call your mother?" She pretended to reached for her phone, "I'll do it, and you know I will." It was a threat she delivered with a pleasant yet malicious smile.

That made his smug face drop. He waved his hands to stop her, "No ... it's okay. In fact, I'll run it down to the ad department right now." He stuttered a little, "Mm-m-myself. It'll be there in ten seconds." He reached for the paper, but Bernice held it tight with her well manicured fingers.

"Hold your horses. I've gotta check it for mistakes first." Her bubblegum pink lips moved slightly as she read it word for word, dragging out his wait. "Yep, it's good." She slammed it in Chris sweaty palm, "There you go Sugar."

16

They both watched as he scurried down the steps to the basement. Bernice giggled, "Lord, I love making that man squirm."

"Is he really *that* afraid of his mother?" She tried to hide the pleasure she took in seeing him panicky and jump when told to, but Bernice saw it in her face.

"No, not really." She started to write out Nitra's bill. "Just ... just when it comes to you." Her handwriting was as frilly as her clothing.

Nitra only tilted her head, she didn't understand her meaning. Why her?

"Oh come on, are you trying to tell me you don't know?" Nitra just shrugged her shoulders in response. "Oh my God, you don't know!" Bernice looked her square in the eyes, "Honey, his mother is your biggest fan." She waved her hand over her head, "Christ the moon sets and rises on you. She calls here every day or two to find out if you've been in town and what you did while you were here."

A chill ran over Nitra's body. It was one of those moments when a writer either felt flattered or fearful, "Oh, *that* kind of fan."

"No, no. She's actually a sweet old broad. Loves you to pieces. But I think it's mostly on account of the fact she use to be a writer herself."

"Really?" That fact turned his mother from weird to admirable.

"Yah. She only had one book published though. The rest got rejected." She handed her the bill to sign and took her money. "Broke the poor thing's heart." Bernice had a caring soul; this wasn't gossip, just kind-heartedness.

Nitra had to ask, "Have you read her book?" Bernice nodded while she counted out her change. "Was it any good?"

"I'll say." She leaned across the counter to whisper, "To tell you the truth, it was spicy as hell. Full of lust and half-naked lovers. I couldn't put the damned thing down."

"Really?" Nitra's mind churned. She smiled wickedly at her, "You think you could get one of those rejected manuscripts. I think I know someone who'd be mighty interested in them."

"Piece of cake." In her sultry way, Bernice strolled over to Chris's desk, stuck out her slim round butt, pulled out the bottom drawer and took out a stack of carefully bound manuscripts, "This enough for you?" Her face was just as mischievous as Nitra's.

"Holy shit! There's got to be … what ten of them there?"

"Twelve." She handed them over to Nitra. "But just take one. That way Chris won't notice that any are gone. If it gets rejected, no harm done, right? If it gets picked up and published, I'll take the blame. Deal?"

She laughed at her. By blame, she really meant praise. "Deal." She flipped through the titles. One caught her eye, "This one. He'll flip for this one." Bernice tucked the others back in his desk while Nitra slipped her chosen copy in her tote bag.

Just then Chris came running up the stairs, panting with a red face. He glared at his secretary, "It's in. You happy?"

Bernice gave a little chuckle, "Yep."

"Me too!" poked Nitra. That made him grunt before exiting for the backroom, closing the door behind him.

"Let me know what happens. Mara's a great lady." She pointed over her shoulder with her thumb, "Even though she raised that creature, she's still all right by me." The phone rang. "Oh hell, I gotta go. Bye Honey."

Nitra waved bye and left the office. When the newspaper office was out of sight, she opened up the manuscript for a closer inspection. Reading while walking proved to be a problem. She stumbled into a mailbox on the way back to her truck, scraping her elbow on its top. Bernice was right, it was good. Sizzling hot, with juicy mini-plots. William was going to love it. He would crave more. Out of curiosity, she checked the date on the original submission sheet — 1972. That explained everything. In those days this would have been considered pornographic, now it was simply a hot romance novel. As she slipped the book back in her tote bag, she wondered what it would be like to not write. She thought about what she'd do if William dropped her as a client. That terrified her. Anxiety swarmed in. She had to get those pages back and finish the book or he just might do exactly that. In the meantime the spicy surprise manuscript would appease his royal-highness, distracting him from her current disaster — if only temporarily.

Chapter Two

Nitra squirmed in the old wooden chair. Her back hurt from tossing and turning for the last two nights. She slept on and off, never really reaching a state of true solid sleep. When she did sleep, she dreamt of floating blank pages, followed by a very irritated William. But it was the recurring sound of the bullet that woke her up, leaving her covered with sweat and scared. It had been two days without any calls. Instead of panicking, she stayed rational by telling herself that it was too early for anyone to call. The ad was printed the afternoon, in the day before yesterday's paper and most people wouldn't have had a chance to read it until last night. So sooner or later, she should hear something today — she hoped. The damaged sciatic nerve in her lower back sent sharp spiky pains down her leg, forcing her to shift in her antique chair again, making its spindled legs creak.

Through his teeth, Wallace grunted out, "Will ya please stop squeakin' that chair?" His Irish temper was difficult to control sometimes.

20

"Sorry. My back's bugging me." She shifted her right cheek as she said it. The legs creaked again, sending a shiver down Wallace's spine. "Sorry."

He bent over to pull out the first batch of bread, while sliding in the next. She snuck a peek at his delightfully round firm butt over the rim of her tea cup. The heavenly perfume of fresh baked bread filled the kitchen. That was his specialty — baked goods. That's why Nitra hired him in the first place. It certainly wasn't for his housekeeping capabilities and it certainly wasn't his pleasant disposition. The truth was it was his rustic rosemary-olive focaccia that got him the job permanently.

Nitra's original housekeeper, Mona, was rushed to the hospital one morning after she complained of chest pains. Mona was not only her housekeeper, but her best friend. When Nitra heard the words chest and pain in the same phrase, she insisted she go to the hospital by ambulance, straight away. The next day Mona's daughter delivered the bad news; Mona had suffered a mild heart attack and would have to retire from the housekeeping business. During one of her many visits to Mona, she suggested that Nitra try out a man name Wallace McPhee for the position. He had a good reputation in the town and she thought he'd work out well with her. At first Nitra was hesitant. A man in *her* house? Doing the cooking and cleaning for her? It was hard to imagine a full grown man walking and working in her space. It had always been a female domain from the first day she moved in. But Mona convinced her otherwise. She insisted that Nitra give him a two week trial period. If it didn't work out, no time was lost. But if he did, and Mona was sure he would, they were ready to go. After umpteen phone calls, Nitra persuaded Wallace to the two week trial period, by offering a tidy bonus for his time if it didn't work out. Then on the third morning, she woke up to the sweet scent of fresh cinnamon buns filling her nostrils, she knew Mona had delivered her an angel. But it was his rosemary-olive focaccia that got him hired. She asked him to permanently stay through a mouthful of that warm buttered paradise. That was five years ago and to her delight, he still made fresh bread every second day.

He placed two freshly toasted slices in front of her, "Worrying won't make them come any faster."

"Easy for you to say, you don't have your life's work riding on them." She slathered on a thick layer of strawberry jam. It too was homemade.

His Irish accent added a tone of mockery, "Oh, don't I? May I remind ya that if ya don't get paid, neither do I." He tossed another fistful of cubed beef into a shallow ceramic bowl.

"Oh, shut up! I don't need to hear that right now. There's enough pressure on me at it is." Sometimes it felt as though they were married, a feeling she didn't particularly like at that moment. So to remind him who was paying who, she added instructions, "Today I will require some miniature muffins, small scones, and tiny quiche. If people are coming here to return my pages and get their money, I should at least be hospitable about it."

He stopped dicing the onion, spun about to stare at her, "You've got to be kidding me?" He pointed to the floor with the knife as though it was the exact spot they would come to. "You're expecting them to come here?"

"Yes." She managed to say through a mouthful of jam and toast.

"You want them to drive twenty miles to get twenty dollars. Are ya daft Girl? It'll cost them a fiver in gas alone."

He shook his head at her, "Nitra darling, you'll have to go see them. It's only logical."

She swallowed down hard on the lump of toast. That was the last thing she wanted to do. She didn't do well with strangers as it was, but to do this outside of her home meant she couldn't even escape when it got too much for her to handle.

"Oh Christ Girl, not that again?" He pulled out a chair to sit across from her. "It was just one bad t'ing, that's all. Ya gotta let it go Ni. If ya don't, it's gonna eat ya alive." He reached across the table to pat her hand, but she pulled it away.

"Just let it go. Just like that. Just like it was no damned big deal." Within ten seconds, she went from fragile to downright furious. "Easy for you to say. You weren't the one who damned near got her head blown off. Oh no, that was me, wasn't it?"

"That was an accident and ya know it. Harry couldn't see 'cause of the fallin' snow. And ya did come out in the same direction the lad went in. How was Harry supposed to know ya weren't the lunatic? Ni, it was a mistake ..."

She cut him off, "Some fuckin' mistake? Missed my head by six fuckin' inches." She was nearly screaming at him, "And it's not Harry that I'm scared of, it the fuckin' nut-bar fans that worried about." Nitra only swore when she was truly angry and at that moment, all the anger she had been holding inside rushed out at once. "I'd be fuckin' stupid to do that again. No sir, I'm not meeting people by myself. You'll have to come along."

His face fell, "Nitra, ya can't keep dragging me along to every little event and meeting. It's not right."

"Who gives a shit if it's right? It's what I need. And you're coming." She crossed her arms, signalling the discussion was done.

A signal he understood all too well. He was about to convince her otherwise when the phone rang. She didn't budge in anyway, which meant he was the one getting it.

"Hello?" He listened for moment. "Yes. That's right, twenty dollars." He paused again. "Yes. This morning would be fine. She'll meet you at Gladys' Diner." Nitra waved franticly in the background, but he chose to ignore her. He peered at the clock, "Yes. Ten o'clock is fine. She'll see you then. Bye." Hanging up the phone, he formulated in his head what his answer would be.

"What the hell are you doing? They were supposed to come here." The veins in her neck popped out, "Christ! Was I talking for nothing?"

He tucked his hands behind his back, taking a hard military stance before speaking, "So, ya want strangers coming to your home ... to find out where ya live, as opposed to meeting them in a very public place?" He pointed to the phone, "Oh ya, that sounds so much safer, having them come here."

Her mouth fell open. She couldn't argue with him, he was right. It was best that she not bring people out to her house and leave herself wide open to more problems. "Oh, fine. I'll go. But you're coming with me."

"Nope." It was his turn to cross his arms in defiance.

She insisted, "But you have to."

"Um ... no, I don't. I'm your housekeeper, not your bodyguard. And I'm not be doin' it. And Ni, I'm doin' this for your own good. You need to face this problem head on. Ya need to get over it. Now, if you'll pardon me, the washin' is

24

done and I need to turn it over to the dryer." With that, he promptly turned on his heels and walked away.

She had no choice, but to sit there and watch him vanish out of sight. However she could still yell after him, "Get back here you idiot, I'm not done talking to you."

"I can't hear ya," was the only annoying reply she got from the other room.

The clock on the kitchen wall softly chimed the half hour. It was halfpast nine. That made her jump into action. It was a twenty-five minute drive into town and if she didn't hurry, she'd be late. And Nitra Zupan was never late for a meeting. Never!

To her luck she found a parking space right in front of Gladys' Diner. Gladys — that name always made her smile. It reminded her of a bully she had to contend with in the sixth grade. For months Gladys picked on her until one evening Nitra mentioned to her Mother that the girl was still tormenting her. Her Mother quietly remarked, "So call her Happy Bum," adding no other remarks. It took Nitra awhile to figure out what her mother was trying to say. Eventually she realized the play on words, Gladys – glad ass – happy bum. It was the perfect ammo against her ugly bulky enemy. The next day, Nitra waited until a large crowd had gathered to watch her being teased by Gladys. At an optimum hushed moment, she let Gladys have it. She calmly declared, "You got it ... Happy Bum." It took a few seconds for the smarter kids to get it. They quickly explained it to the others while laughing and pointing at Gladys. The bully suddenly appeared as not so tough and controlling, but rather ridiculous and clumsy. For the first time in Nitra's life, she had triumphed over a nemesis. It felt good. A sensation she never forgot. The name Gladys still made her smile.

The worst part was she had left the house not knowing who she was meeting. And there was no way she was going to give that son of a bitch Wallace a chance to gloat. So she just left. Walking through the door, she scanned the customers, trying to figure out which one it was. In the third booth by the window sat a man with a semi-crumbled page lying in front of him. It had to be him.

She cleared her throat, "Hello. Are you the one who called about the reward?"

With a sweeping hand jester, he offered her the other side of the booth, "Yes, please take a seat. Would you like some coffee?"

"Um … no. I can't stay that long." She mentally went through the list of lies she made up on the way there and found the perfect one, "Unfortunately, I have another appointment across town in ten minutes. But that was very nice of you to offer, thank you." She looked him over quickly. To her surprise he was quite a handsome man — older, but still quite youthful.

"You're welcome. Well, to the point then." He slid the page across the table, "Is this one of your pages?"

She picked it up to skim through it visually, "Yes it is. It's page 19. I was hoping for page one. It's the page I need the most."

He took a casual sip of coffee, not saying anything. He was waiting for her to offer up the reward.

Realizing the silent awkwardness, she spoke up, "Oh yes … the money." She rifled through her tote bag, producing a twenty dollar bill. "Here you are, twenty dollars as promised." In turn she slid the bill across to him. "Um … just out of curiosity, where did you find it?"

"Stuck in my front fence." He tucked the money in his coat pocket.

"And how far away is that from Memorial Park?"

"I'm not sure. I live on the corner of Main and Tanker Avenue. So that's ..." he got cut off.

She kind of squealed it out, "Eighteen blocks away! Wow, they did travel far."

From the booth in front of her, a head popped up over the seat, "Hey, are you the one looking for those lost papers?" Nitra nodded yes. "Then we're both lucky asses 'cause, like I've got three of them right here."

She couldn't believe her ears, "Fabulous! Let's see them?"

In the booth behind her, the heavy set woman turned her ear closer to Nitra's booth so she could hear every word of the conversation clearly. She needed as many details as possible.

The fella was in his early twenties, dressed in a rather tattered black leather jacket. He pulled out a doubled up wad of papers. Unfolding them, he grinned from ear to ear, "Dude, like sixty bucks. I'm getting drunk tonight." He followed that with a high pitched *Wahoo!* Several people in the diner turned to look at him, including the older waitress.

Nitra took the pages and scanned them like before. There was a problem. Only two of them were hers, pages 13 and 14. The other one was a typed list of office errands. "What's your name?"

"Sid, Sid the kid." He let out another *Wahoo.* This time the waitress shushed him.

"Okay, Sid. These two are mine, but this one is not." She pointed at her pages, "So I'm only paying for these two."

27

"What? Hey lady, are you trying to rip me off? 'Cause if ya are, that sucks." To emphasize his meaning, he waved a three fingered hand sign that metal rockers used.

"I'm not trying to rip you off. It's not mine, so I'm not paying for it." She handed him back the odd page.

"But Lady, you said you'd give twenty dollars a page and there are three pages." He was starting to get frustrated with his lack of understanding.

The man sitting in her booth jumped in, "Look at the paper. It's not handwritten like hers are." He held one of Nitra's papers next to the one in his hand. "And it's on a different kind of paper. Hers has red lines. That one doesn't. See? So why would she pay you for something that's not hers?"

"Dude, you're right. It's not the same." He got quiet for a second, then he lit right up, "But hey, I'm still getting my forty bucks, right?"

"Absolutely! And here you are, forty dollars." Nitra held out the two twenties for him to take, "Have fun tonight." Morally she hated handing out money to someone who was going to buy beer and maybe drugs with it, but a deal was a deal and she always honoured her words.

"Ya, like thanks." He stretched them in front of his face, crumbled them in his fist and punched the air along with another loud whoop.

This time the waitress yelled at him, "Sid, get to hell out of here before I call the cops."

The word *cops* caught his attention with a head jerk in her direction. He did a little nervous leg shifting dance, "Dudes. Gotta go. Catch ya later." After a one finger salute to the waitress, he disappeared out the door.

"Damn it!" Nitra muttered to herself.

"Why damn it?" The man was still sitting there watching the whole thing.

"Oh, I'm sorry. It's just that I didn't get the chance to ask him where he found these." She rearranged them in an orderly pile.

He tilted his head in curiosity, "Why on earth would you want to know that?"

"Because if all of them don't come back; I'll have to go there myself to find them. I need every one of these pages back. All of them." She tucked the pages into her tote, "My, my, look at the time, I must be going." She stuck out her hand, "Thank you for your help with Sid. It could have got ugly."

"Anything for a damsel in distress." His eyes twinkled at her as though he actually meant what he said.

The words came out of her mouth before she could stop them, "What is thy name, oh knight of mine?"

"Tom." He smiled at her in a way that made her knees slightly buckle, "Tom Harper." He took her hand in his, gently kissing the back of it. With his face still tilted down, he looked up at her, with a sinful gleam in his eyes, "My lady."

A hot rush washed over her body, pooling red in her face. "Oh my! I do need to go and now." She slipped her hand out of his and backed away slowly. Her words came out in a sultry sigh, "Thanks again."

Once outside she began to chastise herself, "Thanks again? Smooth, real smooth." She flung open the truck door, climbed into the seat, slammed the door and jammed in the keys, "Brilliant, absolutely friggin' brilliant!" Then she was startled by a knock on the window. It was him. She inhaled deeply to calm herself.

Through her rolled down window, he proudly announced, "The corner of Third and Palmer."

He had caught her off guard, "What?"

"Sid found them in the bushes on the corner of Third and Palmer Drive." His deep blue eyes twinkled proudly at her again.

At the exact same time they said it, "That's ten blocks away!" making them both explode with laughter.

Nitra pulled herself together, "How do you know that's where he found them."

"I asked the girl that was sitting with him. Taffi was 'like totally awesome about her baby-dude'" He mimicked her behaviour which cracked Nitra up again. "Anyway, that's where he found them." He waited until she was fully paying attention to him again. "Um … and if you'd like, I could come help you look for those pages."

The offer came so out of the blue, she wasn't sure what to say. All she could do was to stare at him.

"Okay." Thinking he had bombed, he looked at his feet, "Well, nice meeting you anyway."

He turned to leave, but she stopped him, "Tom wait! I'd like that." She batted her eyes to let him know exactly what she was saying, "I'd like that very much."

"Good. Here's my card. Call me when you need *help*." He handed her his card. He let his fingers linger on it so that they were connected if only through the cardstock.

She couldn't pull her eyes away, nor could she manage one spoken word. All she could do was nod and smile.

Not sure how to take her silence, he decided it was time to go, "Okay, well I should let you go to your appointment."

"What?" She'd forgotten all about her little fib, "Oh yah, my appointment."

He was walking away, "So I'll see you later, right?"

She yelled behind him, "Right. Yes. Definitely. Bye Tom."

"Bye … hey wait, I don't even know your name." He was still walking backward and was getting further away.

"Nitra, Nitra Zupan." She almost added 'the author' out of habit, but stopped herself. Apparently he didn't know who she was and that suited her just fine.

"Okay! Bye Nitra Zupan." He waved one last time before he disappeared around the corner.

Stunned, she stared after him. Did what happen, really happen? She couldn't be sure. The mind can play tricks on a person when they're in that lovely state of goofiness. She ran everything through her head, the words, the facial expressions, and the lingering card – every last detail. Then she ran it through one more time to be completely sure. Her conclusion: Mr. Tom Harper had just asked her out on a paper hunting date. And by God, pages or no pages, they were going. It had been a long time since she'd seen that kind of twinkle in a man's eyes that was aimed directly at her and she wanted to see a more of it. She read his business card, Tom Harper – Antique Restorations, 14 Quinn St., Hamlin Ontario.

A horn beeped behind her bringing her back to reality. With no other spaces to be had, the man wanted her parking space. She pulled out of the space and headed back to the house — and back to a self-righteous Wallace.

Her mind bounced back and forth between Tom and Wallace. The misery of now facing Wallace and his told-you-so attitude, versus the curious daydreams of time spend with the unknown Tom. But as the laneway to her cottage came into sight, all her thoughts shifted to Wallace.

31

This wasn't going to be easy, but it had been a long time coming. While shifting the truck into park, Nitra made up her mind right there and then that today was the day Wallace McPhee would have to be put in his place. He was her housekeeper and she was his employer; a fact he apparently had forgotten. The question now was; how was she going to accomplish this daunting task? If she played it one way she would only get half of the results she wanted, but he'd still be reasonably friendly. But if she took the other route, she'd get what she'd want, but he'd be hell to live with. Turning the doorknob to the kitchen, she decided to choose her approach when the time came. He would be the indicating factor of her ultimate decision.

Dropping her tote on the floor, the beads clattered on the wooden floor. She hung her keys on the fourth hook. "I'm back!" she yelled up the stairs. No answer. "Wallace, I'm back!" She knew he wasn't far away, the stove had a pot of something bubbling away with big *blurps* and he never left his cooking unattended.

"Wallace where are you? Get in here, will ya?" Still no answer. Now annoyed with his behaviour she went searching for him. She opted to start in the living room then head upstairs. She flung open the heavy doors loudly muttering to herself, "That stupid friggin' man, who in the shit does he think he is, not answering me right away. Asshole! Why I should …" the words instantly faded from her lips. Before her, sat a tiny old lady and Wallace, they were having tea.

Nitra felt her face heat red. She apologized with her waving hands, "Oh my. I'm so sorry. I didn't know Wallace had company. Please excuse my vulgarity. It's been a trying day. I'll leave you and Wallace to visit. And again, so sorry for my foul mouth."

She turned to walk away when Wallace stopped her, "Nitra, this is Mrs. Hollander. She's actually here to see you."

"Oh." she swallowed down her guilty lump and made her way to her favourite chair.

Replacing her teacup, Mrs. Hollander's voice came across soft, but very clear, "I have something that you need. Just let me get it." Pulling a huge tote up into her lap, she rummaged around inside and took out a folded page. As happy as Nitra was to see the page, she was equally appalled by the old woman's tote bag. Not that it was ugly, it merely reminded her of her own tote bag. Was this the same visual effect her own tote bag had on other people? She quickly made a mental note — get rid of her tote bag – it's an old lady thing!

"I read in the newspaper that you lost some pages of your manuscript. So I looked around my yard and I found this." Her frail hand offered it to her. It was the first draft page on the Marion incident, the last sheet in the pile that blew away. "I hope you don't mind, but I read it. Curiosity is a strong power you know." Her pale cheeks pinked a little, "I liked it, but why does Marion need to be such a dimwit? Just because she's older and British, doesn't mean she has to be dumb."

There it was — criticism without knowledge. Once again she would have to defend her words. "Oh, but she does. You see, in this story I portray her as nonsensical for a reason. Because of her silly nature, she is easily manipulated into revealing information during a conversation without realizing she's doing it. It's important to have dumb people, as you put it, as well as intelligent and sinister characters. One balances out the other." She took the cup of tea Wallace offered her, "Please

33

understand, I do not think seniors are stupid nor do I believe that English people are silly. And Marion is an important part to the story. It's really not evident on that one page you have, but it's there."

"Mrs. Hollander, more tea?" Wallace was truly in heaven. He loved to fuss over elderly ladies. And they certainly enjoyed it in return. And why wouldn't they? He was six feet tall, with a runner's build and hazelnut eyes that made most female's hearts pound at the sight of them. And in a strange way it seemed to arouse Wallace to wait on them hand and foot. His eyes lit up and his face held a naughty grin as though he was performing some type of sinful act. She wasn't sure why, she couldn't put her finger on it and common sense told her not to ask either. Something should be left alone. Privacy was privacy and too much information was simply too much information.

"Oh, no thank you. I do need to be going. It's my friend's birthday today and we're going to have cake with ice cream and a bottle of twenty year old scotch." The word 'scotch' lit her face up. "She is going to be seventy-eight years old ... and I can't wait to remind her that I'm still a whole two years younger than her." She giggled at the delight of teasing her friend. "And never you mind about the twenty dollars. I'm just happy to help." She turned her attention to Wallace, "Oh my dear boy, if you ever get bored with your dusting and cooking, just give me a ring and we'll go out dancing. We'll paint the town two shades of red." She slipped her arms around his thick chest and buried her face into it. It was not a friendly hug, it was more.

That site made Nitra uncomfortable, almost to the point of queasiness. She had to stop the indecency of it. The recollection of the bubbling concoction in the kitchen was her answer. "Wallace whatever you have on the stove smells like its burning." Within two seconds he let go of Mrs. Hollander and vanished to rescue his *boeuf bourguignon*.

Nitra helped her on with her jacket, "Do you need a ride home?" Nitra hadn't seen another vehicle in the driveway of the house. If she had, she wouldn't have cursed a blue streak into the living room.

"Oh no, I'm fine. I came on my bike." She turned to wave a little good-bye, "Thank you for the tea Wallace."

"Bye now. And thank you for my page." To her amazement Mrs. Hollander donned a bright glittery red helmet before mounding her smaller, but rather impressive red motorcycle. She slipped an arm through the strap of her tote bag, started the bike with a stomp and roared down Nitra's laneway out of sight. No wonder she objected to Marion being portrayed as old, scattered and silly, it was everything she wasn't.

Back in the house she read the words on the 'Marion' page. Should she change it, making Marion a little less daft? The answer was clearly no. Those were her words and that was their intent. When it came to this section, she'd even fight with William to not modify it in any way.

From the kitchen came Wallace with a large tray. Stacking the teacups and pot on to it, he watched out of the corner of his eye until she was done reading before interrupting, "So how was the trip into town? Did ya get your paper?"

Nitra took it as another one of his barbed sarcastic remarks. She stared coolly at him for an extended second. She said nothing. Turning on her heels, she calmly walked to the doorway of her writing room and announced directly at him, "For lunch I will have another cup of tea with a sandwich." She showed no sign of any particular emotion while closing the door softly behind her.

Wallace stood, staring at the closed door. He wondered what in the hell that was all about. What he had done wrong this time? Sometimes he questioned why he stayed working for the woman. She was impossible to work for. He spent most of his time mottle coddling her and her fears. The rest of the time he cleaned up her messes, leaving the cottage spotless. In true male fashion, he shook his head at the door, shrugged his shoulders, and ignored it all. Apparently he *had* to make her a sandwich with a cup of tea. Walking pass the white tea cart, he smiled to himself. That should work just fine. He'd leave it outside the door satisfying her majesty's testy request while making his point at the same time.

Chapter Three

Gemma scratched at the door until Nitra opened it. There in front of her stood the white tea cart. It held a small pot of tea, one dish of hand trimmed sandwiches, a silver tray of lemon cookies and a round bouquet of fresh rose buds. The sight of its perfection sent her into a fury. How dare he? He served her every one of her favourites, right down to the flowers in her much-loved crystal bud vase. "Bastard!" she screamed at the kitchen door. Quickly she clamped her hand over her mouth. If he heard her, he would know he won. Examining the cart, she pulled it into the writing room and closed the door tight. She found herself talking to the cat, "I'll show him. The son of a bitch! I'm gonna eat every last morsel on this cart just to piss him off." She lowered a bit of sandwich for Gemma, "Here, help me out, would ya."

It took some doing, but she managed to eat it all. Using the moisture of her fingertips, she pressed the last crumbs off the tea cart. "There! Take that you ..." the phone rang. "Hello?" she listened for quite a long time before she got to say anything. She tried, but she hadn't been allowed to get one word in. "Okay, I'll be there in ten minutes. Bye." She shook her head and joked to Gemma, "Christ that woman can talk. This is going to be pure hell." Re-focusing her attention back to the cart, she opened the door, pushed it

37

back into place and quietly closed the door again. "That'll teach him," she mumbled to the cat again. Looking at her watch, she decided she better get going.

Nitra peeked around the corner of the doorframe. With no Wallace in sight, she made a bee-line to her keys and tote bag. "Damn it!" she had forgotten to change over her ugly old-lady tote for a slick sexy purse. Out the door and straight to the truck with still no sign of him. "Good, I didn't want to talk to him anyway." At top speed the truck roared down the road, heading north.

Remembering the mile-a-minute direction, she spotted the big brick house on the hill. The winding driveway led to a double set of massive oak doors. Parking the truck, Nitra had a feeling that it was going to be interesting to see what the woman looked like. By all appearances it looked as though she was well off. The landscaping was impeccably maintained, with large swathes of roses surrounded by lush lawns. Even the doorbell was ornate and chimed instead of binging.

Nitra waited. After a few minutes the door was opened by a maid who was wearing the most hideous uniform Ni had ever seen. It was a drab grey with navy blue piping at every seam, giving it lines that were not flattering to such a full figured woman.

The maid tilted her head, "May I help you?" Her tightly bound red hair didn't budge, but sat high on top of her freckled, ivory face.

Nitra recognised the voice immediately; she was the woman on the phone. "Yes, I'm here about the ad in the newspaper." She sounded much younger on the phone. Seeing her face to face she guessed she was about thirty five years old.

To Nitra surprise, the maid began to look her up and down. "Are you from an agency or here independently?" Her sharp green eyes inspected every inch of Nitra's appearance.

Feeling rather violated by the ogling, Nitra promptly explained herself — mostly to make it stop. "Um … I think there's some kind of mistake. I'm here to pick up a page from my manuscript that was lost two days ago."

She watched as the maid quickly scanned the hallway behind her. Leaning in closer to Nitra she whispered, "I know that. But if my boss sees me with you, she'll yell at me. My name is Katie." She leaned upright again and with a semi-smile, she barked the order, "Come with me to the kitchen. And be quick about it!" She gave Nitra a friendly wink letting her know it was all a harmless ploy to avoid trouble from her boss.

Nitra winked back. Enjoying the wacky game, she added a slight curtsy, "Yes ma'am." Pretending to be obedient, Nitra walked two paces behind Katie, something she had witnessed many times at the dinner parties of the wealthy. For more authenticity she hung her head and kept quiet like a good little servant should. Katie pushed open a narrow white door and motioned for Nitra to go inside. Again Katie scanned behind her for any signs of her boss, then quietly closed the door.

"I'm sorry about that. And thank you for being such a good sport." Her whole body demeanour changed. Relaxed, her shoulders fell freely forward, her rigid spine curved and the hard lines in her face dissolved into a pleasant smile. "You're early. You said ten minutes. I meant to meet you in the driveway before you came to the door."

"Um … it's a thing I do. I'm generally early for everything, meetings, dates, deadlines …"

"Oh deadlines, yes." She pointed a finger in the air motioning to hold on for a minute. Katie rummaged through a bottom drawer of a cabinet, pulled out a paper and handed it to Nitra, "I believe this is what you came for?"

"Yes, it's page 27. Thank you." While she rifled through her tote bag, she asked the same question as before, "Out of curiosity, where did you find it?"

Katie cleared her throat and looked around. She whispered her answer, "Outside my friend's house. You see, I was in town running errands and stopped by a friend's for coffee." Her head drop down in discomfort, "I shouldn't have, it was on paid time. And after I left the apartment, I saw the page sitting in a pile of leaves. So I scooped her up and called you." Her face was a vivid display of mixed emotions. It was red with embarrassment, combined with fear while smiling happily.

"Well thank God for that! Or you wouldn't have found it for me." She handed her the twenty dollar bill.

Just as Katie's fingers touched the money, the narrow door swung open. In stomped a grey haired man carrying a tray, "Fuckin' old bitch. I hate her rotten guts."

Katie cleared her throat. "Isaac, your language please, we have company."

Isaac pointed with his nose, "What's with the money? And who are you?" There was no smile on his face or kindness to his voice.

Contempt was the word Nitra used to describe his demeanour. For that reason Nitra didn't answer. She wasn't exactly sure who Isaac was and didn't want to cause trouble for Katie.

"None of your business. That's what." She snapped the bill from Nitra's hand and stuffed it down her uniform front.

"Well, thank you for coming. I'll walk you to the door." She hastily guided Nitra by the arm passed a scrutinizing Isaac, through the kitchen door, down the hallway and out to the front steps. Katie's face was crimson. Her words spilled out as rapidly as they had on the phone, "I'm very sorry for treating you this way. It's just that if Mrs. Reinhold starts asking Isaac questions, he'll sell me out. For a tidy bit of money no doubt. Then I'll get fired … or worse, get deported." Her face darkened even redder. "And I don't want to go back to Ireland. It's dangerous back home."

Ireland! She was Irish. The red hair, freckles and green eyes fit the Irish profile, but Nitra would have never guessed it by her spoken words. She used no Irish vernacular nor did she have even a hint of an accent. Wallace's brogue was sometimes so heavy that Nitra couldn't understand his words and made him repeat himself several times before she understood him, much to his exasperation. Truth being, sometimes she did it on purpose. She enjoyed ticking him off, just for the fun of it.

From inside the house they heard the sound of heels clicking on the marble floor before a female voice screeched, "Katie. Where are you? I've been ringing for you for the past five minutes. Come … here … NOW!" The pitch was high, harsh and demanding.

Panic and apology swept across Katie's face at the same time, "Please, I'm going to have to ask you to leave."

"Say no more, I'm already gone!" Nitra turned and headed straight for her truck. "Thank you! Goodbye!" She watched as Katie disappeared into the house. Her heart sank for her. She couldn't stand the thought of someone living under those conditions.

41

On the short trip home she ran Katie's situation through her head. She decided that Katie's working conditions had to be changed. She'd ask Wallace for his input on what to do about it. He'd know who to call or what to do next. She wondered if they already knew each other. Since they were both true Irishman and Hamlin was a small community; they may have met each other through some type of ethnic gathering.

As she came closer to her driveway, she noticed a mid-sized grey car parked on the side of the road, about 500 yards from its entrance. The peculiar part was that as she passed nearer to it, the driver slumped over into the passenger seat. That action set off an alarm in Nitra's gut. She twisted in her seat to see who the person was. Did she know the person? Was the person male or female, young or old? She couldn't tell. They remained hidden down inside the car. The next best thing to seeing a face was seeing a licence plate number. But that too was obstructed. A heavy layer of mud covered the plate and bumper of the car. It splattered pattern revealed that it was not there intentionally, but rather naturally, as though it came from the recent storm. "Damn storm!" Concentrating on the grey sedan, she wasn't paying attention to where she was going. She turned her head forward just in time to see an enormous pothole directly in front of the truck. She tried to swerve to avoid it, but it was too late. The tire pounded into it, throwing the steering wheel loose from her grip. She grabbed it again, only this time with the hold of a pit-bull. Cranking the wheel to the right she managed to veer around the ditch. This unfortunately sent her in the opposite direction, heading to the ditch on the other side. The words of her driving instructor boomed in her mind,

'Don't over compensate. Aim for the place you want your vehicle to go.' And that's what she did. Nitra turned the wheel slightly this time and aimed for the entrance to her driveway. Reaching the straight portion of the lane way she slammed on the brakes, jerking everything on to the floor of the cab. The truck stalled out. She let out a long shuttered breath. Then the adrenalin rush hit her. Emotions of anger and fear streamed out at once. "Stupid fuckin' pothole!" she angrily slapped the steering wheel with the heel of both hands, "Fuckin' stupid Wallace! I told him to get that fixed. Jerk!" She shook her fist at the cottage. In the rear view mirror she caught a glimpse of the grey car race by. Spinning her head about, she craned her head to see past the roof support. She watched miserably as it disappeared around the bend in the main road. It was gone and she still couldn't tell who was driving it, which made her even madder. "Damn it!" Then the anger gradually changed back to fear. The question still remained in her mind – who was it and what did they want?

Tap, Tap, Tap. The startling sound behind her made Nitra jump and squeal. Whipping her head around to the window she was confronted by Wallace's face jammed into the window, "You okay? I saw it from the kitchen. Are you all right?"

At first the sight of Wallace comforted her. If he was with her, whoever it was wouldn't come back. She let out a held breath and straightened out her glasses. Finally feeling completely safe, her emotions immediately turned to anger. She abruptly rolled down the window to yell at him, "You God damned it idiot! They got away and it's all your fault."

"They — who's they? And what are you talking about?" Once again poor Wallace had blindly walked into a hornets' nest.

She threw her arms up in the air, "The car! The grey car." She pointed down the road, "He – she went that way. Did you see who it was?" She was so keyed up that her words came out in a long stream, "The car was on the side of the road and the driver dived into the other seat and the licence plate was covered in mud and the God damned pothole was there and I lost control and I didn't see who it was." She gulped in a breath, "And it's all your fault." She stabbed him in the shoulder with her sharp index finger.

Wallace pulled away from the finger, "Slow down, you're not making sense." That got him a death look, "What car?"

"The grey car that just drove by. Didn't you see it?" Nitra's face was desperate, "Tell me you saw it?"

He shook his head, "No, I didn't" He peered around the trucks windshield. "Um ... are you sure there was any body there?"

That hit a nerve, "Oh, so now I'm crazy. Seeing things, right?" Nitra couldn't hold it in, "I'm not crazy. There was a grey car and it was parked on the side of the road. And why would the driver hide when I drove past? Oh no, not this time. I'm not imagining it. That car was there." She twisted the key in the ignition, but nothing but an *RRR-RRR* sound come from the engine. "Oh great! You let me down too." She slapped the steering wheel again. Discouraged, she hung her head for a moment; then decided that it was best she get away from the whole situation before her temper got the best of her. She grabbed her tote, shoved the door open just missing Wallace. "Get out of my way, damn it!" She stomped half way up the drive before turning around.

44

To the confused Wallace, she yelled. "Well just don't stand there, bring my truck up the house."

He simply crossed his arms and narrowed his eyes at her. That display of defiance meant that he'd do it, but Nitra had to do something else first.

"Oh for Christ sake," She rolled her eyes in her head, "Oh fine … please." The tone of voice was more mocking than polite.

"Thank you," he yelled condescendingly back to her.

Nitra stomped her way to the door, slamming it behind her. Hearing the phone ringing, she ran to pick it up, "Hello?" She waited for a response, yet none came. "Hello?" she listened to the voice on the line "Yes, that's me." Again she said nothing while the person spoke. From outside she heard the sound of her truck pull up to the house. "Yah. That would be great. I'll see you shortly. Bye." She let out a large sigh as she hung up the phone. It was another call about a page from her manuscript. Nitra sat quiet for a minute, gathering her thoughts — and her strength. It meant another trip to town to meet yet another stranger. It was taxing on her, both physically and emotionally. Thoughts of the car still lingered in her mind; making her wonder if it was safe to go on her own. But what choice did she have? None. Wallace had made it perfectly clear that he wanted no part in the recovery of her pages. She'd have to do it herself. But what if this was a lunatic? Wallace wouldn't know where to send the police. So she scribbled down the name and address on a sticky note, tucking inside his opened cookbook. Blowing out another tense breath, she headed outside to her truck. Nitra reefed open the front door to find Wallace hammering under the front of the truck.

45

Her first impulse was to yell at him some more. He was fixing her truck and she needed it now. But how could she be mad at him? He was a housekeeper not a mechanic. He was doing the best he could. For that reason she decided that the honey approach would work better than the vinegar one. She crouched down to his level, "What are you doing? Is it bad? Can you fix it yourself?"

He stopped hammering to answer the question, "No. Not really. It's mud." He returned to his hammering.

She stood straight up, "Mud? What do you mean mud?"

He stopped again, "I mean, you have mud caked into the radiator and half the engine." He poked his head out from underneath, "Go get the garden hose Girl? We'll get the dirt outta her."

Nitra had to think for a moment. It was not her normal habit to haul around hoses; that was the gardener's job. Then she remembered him asking for permission to have another spigot installed at the front of the house for easier access. "Coming right up."

From under the truck he watched her long legs scurry for the hose. Her full round butt made him ache again. He closed his eyes and reminded himself that he was not permitted to think that way about her. Nitra was his employer, not a woman. She was off limits. No matter how he felt about her.

"Found it!" She tugged the long stream of hose down to where the truck was. "Here." She bent over to hand him the hose.

The view of her gapping top flooded his mind. Her soft breasts cupped in her bright pink lace bra tortured him again. Trying to escape the tantalizing view, he distractedly stood up and slammed his forehead into the bumper. He collapsed, spread eagle on the ground with moan.

She yanked on his arm, "Come out from under there. And this time slowly."

He did what he was told. He slinked out and sat up straight on the grass.

"What are you doing? Trying to kill yourself?" Suddenly concerned by the dribble of blood running down his face, she knelt in front of him and leaned in closer to examine the cut. "Oh, you'll live. It's only a small nick." She touched his forehead lightly with her fingertips, "Does your head hurt? Can you see all right?"

Her breasts were directly in front of his face, again driving his heart rate up. "Oh, I can see everything just fine."

"Nothing blurry?"

"Nope, clear as a bell." He wanted to touch her just that once. He wanted to know what her skin would feel like in his hands. He imagined it would feel warm, soft and smooth against his own skin. Her scent was sweet, like honey and roses mixed with ocean air. He secretly inhaled her.

"Good." She leaned back on her heels. "Now, I don't think you'll need stitches, but if you want, I'll drive you into the hospital. And by the looks of it, there's going to be one hell of a bump around it in about twenty minutes. We should get it examined by a doctor, just to be safe."

"Get my head examined? Yep, that's a good idea." The joke for meant for him, not her. He was crazy for having those feelings for her.

She squinted her eyes at him, "Are you making fun of me?"

"No. I'm making fun of me." Wallace put his hand against his forehead and scrunched his eyes tightly. She was so damned tempting, he had to close them.

47

"It hurts, doesn't it? You want some ice?" She was beginning to get scared. She had never seen him in pain. To her, his facial expression seemed twisted and contorted as though he was in real agony.

"Ice … yah, that would be great." He watched as she jumped to her feet and hurried to the kitchen. Once she was inside, he mentally reprimanded himself, *Hold on there, lad. Don't be doing anything stupid, you'll regret later.* Then he pinched the inside of his thigh, creating a sharp excruciating pain. It was a self-inflicted deterrent to relieve him of the other sensation he'd been feeling in that area.

With another bounce, she knelt in front of him again, "Here." She slowly pressed the ice filled towel onto the slowly forming bump. "Can you still see clearly?"

Again her tender round breasts were at his eye level. He couldn't take it this time. He jerked his eyes and head away from her. "Ouch!" He closed his eyes again. He had to get away from her before he surrendered to his boorish urges and grabbed her right there on the lawn. "Give me that, so you don't hurt me again." He purposely switched to a nasty mood in order to drive her away. "Why don't you go do something else besides picking on me!" He got to his feet. He looked down to see Nitra kneeling directly in front of him. Her black hair framed her face emphasizing her olive green eyes. Another sexual rush swept over him. His mind flashed visual images of her pleasuring him. He couldn't control it any longer, he had to leave immediately. He also had to make sure she didn't follow him. That would only make it easier for him to get them both into trouble. He spun on his heels and headed toward the kitchen door. He yelled over his shoulder, "The truck still runs. You just need to wash away the mud from the rad so it doesn't over heat. I'm gonna lay down for a bit, so don't be bothering me."

48

He stepped inside the kitchen and closed the door. From behind the kitchen's yellow gingham curtains, he watched Nitra stand up and stare up at the house. In his heart he wondered what she was thinking at that moment. Was she thinking of him? Did she think about him the same way? His head throbbed, reminding him he had to call his doctor before he went to lie down, just in case there was a problem concerning a concussion. From the window, he spied on her while she washed away the caked mud. She looked up at the house one more time before she left in the truck. He'd wash away the clumps of mud she left on the lawn with the hose later, when he wasn't in so much pain.

As Nitra turned onto the main highway, she put Wallace out of her mind and focussed on the drive ahead. It was a long drive up the shoreline to the address he gave her over the phone. Mentally, she ran down which routes she could take. She eventually chose the longer route because it was more populated than the others. If her truck was going to break down, she wanted to be near people who would help her. The further she got out of town, the more something nagged at her gut. What she couldn't understand was why he was so far away? A page couldn't possible have traveled that far. Or could it? The wind was quite strong that morning. Her gut argued with her head – the gut won. She quickly came to the conclusion that it may be a good idea to double check the legitimacy of the call. Stopping at Hadley's Gas and Grill, she headed to the phone booth. She slipped in her quarter and poked out the numbers. It rang once, and then twice, he picked up on the third ring.

"Hello?" she waited. "I'm the lady you called earlier and I'd like to verify that the page you have is actually mine. It's a long drive to your place and I'd like to be sure I'm not

49

driving there for no reason." Listening to his question, she answered him with a tiny phrase, "Read it to me." If it was hers, she'd know right away. She listened to the words he was reading. After the third line she interrupted him, "Okay, you can stop now. It's not my work. I've never heard those words before." She waited while he voiced his opinion. "Yes, I'm sure. But thank you for your time. Good-bye." She immediately hung up the receiver so she didn't have to argue with him any longer. The smell of hot onion rings and grilled burgers wafted under her nose making her stomach growl. She simply followed the smell with her nose straight into the restaurant.

Hadley's was a national treasure. It was situated on one of the main highways that led out of Hamlin. The owner, Jed Hadley took great pride in serving both the locals and the tourist, fresh tasty food in a clean restaurant by pleasant waiting people. Something he and his staff had managed to do on a daily basis for over twenty-three years. Visiting Hadley's was like going to your grandma's kitchen, right down to the motherly advice. *You're looking thin. Are you taking care of yourself? Are you getting enough to eat? You need soup. Soup will fix you right up?* It wasn't a ploy to sell more soup — they just gave a damn. Something that was lost in big box fast food places.

Nitra pushed open the heavy glass door and stood by the, '*Please wait to be seated*' sign. While waiting, she scanned the restaurant for changes. There were none, it was the same as it had been since she lived here. The booths held pure white tables with red vinyl benches. The dividing walls were still tiled in a checkerboard red and white. The chrome railings gleamed under the stained glass hanging lights.

A waitress walked by with a tray filled to the brim with food and drinks. Nitra spotted the strawberry milk shake on the far side of it. Her mouth watered. "Honey, I'll be with you in a minute. I gotta feed some people and I'll be right back to get you a seat." With that she was gone. The people moan about how much food was on their plates as she placed them on the table. She asked the usual question, but no one needed anything else. She said the Hadley motto, "Enjoy the food folks and if you need anything just holler. One of us will come a running." She stashed the tray in its cubby hole.

"Hi ya Honey, sorry for the wait. It's mighty busy today." She smiled a genuine smile, the kind that said she actually enjoyed her job. Her name tag read Sarah. "You here by yourself or is someone coming to meet ya?"

Nitra blushed a little, "Nope, just little old me."

"No problem. We've got a section that's made for singles like you. Follow me." Sarah grabbed a menu off the pile and swished down the aisle.

Nitra wondered what she meant by 'singles like you' but followed Sarah anyway. Coming around the corner she quickly understood. In the south corner of the restaurant were several small round tables that held only two chairs, some only one. She guessed this was the 'lonely singles corner.' Most of the patrons were men, who at that moment, were checking out the new arrival. Nitra's stomach churned at the thought of having to sit amongst them.

"Now honey you pick out a table and I'll bring you your water." She offered Nitra a menu.

"No thanks, I already know what I'm ordering." Embarrassed by the 'singles tables', she leaned into her,

"Um … is it possible that I not sit here. I'd rather a booth if there's one available."

"Why yes. That's not a problem at all. I just thought that you'd like to meet the others … you know … singles." The grin in her eyes was innocent. She meant no harm, only a little match making — restaurant style. "This way. Got one right over here."

"Thank you." Nitra made a mental note to tip the waitress extra for her kindness. She followed Sarah to a smaller two seated booth by the front window.

"This more to your liking?" Nitra nodded happily. "Now you said you knew what you wanted. If I get it in now, we can beat that bus load of hungry people." Sarah pointed out the window with the tail end of her pen. "What would you like to drink?"

"Strawberry milk shake." A succulent smile slid across her lips, "An order of onion rings and a cheese burger."

Sarah looked down from her scribbling, "Everything on the cheese burger?"

"Lord No. Just mayonnaise and sliced dill pickle. Oh, and a little onion too. What the heck. Not like I'm gonna be kissing anybody." She tapped her finger on the table, wondering why she said such a stupid thing to a stranger.

"Okay, let see," Sarah read down the list to make sure the order was correct. "A strawberry shake, rings and cheese burger with mayo, pickles and onion. I'll be right back with that shake." A lot of her attention was on the bus load of people that had just arrived. That many people at once would mean chaos in many roadside restaurants, but not at Hadley's, they simply shifted into high gear.

Nitra watched as the people filed off the bus. The majority of them were seniors with the occasional younger family member tagging along. However Nitra saw

52

something else that caught her attention. It was Tom Harper talking to a slender blonde in a very slinky dress. Her heart raced for a moment. Who was she? And what did she mean to him? Was that his girlfriend or worse his wife? She was about to chastise herself for liking a man she hardly knew, when Sarah showed up with her very pink shake.

"Damned good looking ain't he?" she looked out the window at him. "If I was 10 years younger, he'd be in trouble right about now."

Nitra had to ask it, "But what about the girl?"

"You mean "the lady in red'? Hell honey, that's his kid sister, Tina. She ain't nothing but a freeloader. Chances are, she's hitting him up for money right now. Drugs are an awful burden — even for those who don't take them."

"She's an addict?" Sarah answered Nitra with a sombre nod. "Does he give her money for drugs?"

"Not anymore. He use to. But after he had sent her to rehab, Tina didn't stop using, so he cut her off completely."

"That's a harsh way to do it." It was upsetting to think that his sister was totally abandoned.

"Oh no, it's not like that. He told Tina that if she ever wanted to go back to rehab and try again, he'd cover the costs. And knowing Tommy, he'd probably take care of her after she got clean." Looking at the waiting area, Sarah added, "Oh honey, I gotta get going, the place is filling up. Rings and burger will be here in jiffy." Her pace doubled as she made her way to the lined up of seniors waiting for tables. In a half-chuckle, she called out, "Okay, who the oldest?" A frail female hand popped up in the back. "Fabulous, you get the good table." She made a swirling motion with her finger, "No point in wasting it on the rest of these youngsters." She got the laugh she was hoping for. "Follow me folks. Right this way."

From the looks of things, Tom was not having a friendly family visit with his sister. She watched as he crossed his arms and took a hard stance. His sister started to pace in a small line. He didn't budge. She yelled at him, but he only shook his head *No*. Her body language changed, she was begging him. Again he said *No*. Then Tina hit him. Nitra couldn't believe her eyes. She hit him in public for everyone to see. Apparently this was not new for Tom. He didn't flinch. He still said nothing. He stood perfectly still and waited while she continued to scream into his face. Nitra noticed that the people in the restaurant were watching them as well. Some accused him of abuse, while others took his side. But Tom's true self-defence was the fact that he did nothing. She, on the other hand, hit him again, this time in the face. It appeared that this time she'd gone too far. He turned on his heels, walked directly to the truck, climbed in and drove away, his sister flailing and screaming after him until he was completely out of sight.

Sarah carefully placed Nitra's plate on the table, "Damned if it don't hurt every time I watch it."

"That happen a lot?" She felt as though she was invaded his privacy even though it wasn't private after their public display.

"Oh, about every two weeks or so. She never quits and he never gives up. Family." She saw the deep concern in Nitra's eyes, so she changed the subject, "Honey, you need ketchup for rings?" Nitra shook her head no. "Okay. Gotta run. Old people get cranky if they don't eat on time. I'll be back when I can. Enjoy Honey!"

Nitra switched her focus back to Tina. She was pacing again. She recognised the characteristic erratic drug addict behaviour. The walking changed to talking. She was arguing with herself, shaking her head and smashing her fist into her thin thigh. It was hard for Nitra to watch, she was never exposed to such a degrading lifestyle. It was odd contrast, her elegant red dress against the hellish monster the drugs had created in her. A long white limo pulled in beside her. The heavily tinted window was lowered so she could lean over to talk to whoever was inside. She shook her head *No,* yet didn't walk away either. Nitra's curiosity got the better of her, "Sarah!" she yelled across the room, "Quick, come here!" her hand called at the waitress a mile a minute.

Sarah walked as fast as she could without running, "Holy Hanna, what's the matter?"

She pointed with an onion ring, "Who's in the limo?" She was talking with Sarah, her eyes never leaving Tina. She didn't want to miss anything. "Is she in trouble or something?"

Her tone was disapproving, "No. That's her boss."

"Boss? But I thought she was a drug addict."

"She is. She works to feed her habit." Sarah was becoming impatient was her nosiness, "Look, all I know is that she works for Stavros down at the strip club."

The red dress, of course! It was all making sense to her now. A thought occurred to her that she didn't like. "She's not a … a …" she couldn't bring herself to say the word.

"Hooker? No. Well, not that anyone's saying anyway. Look Honey, I gotta go. I've twelve tables and two hands. You know how it is?" Sarah was gone before she could say yes.

And she did. Nitra had served her time as a waitress and never forgot the hard work it was — demanding patrons, indifferent sweaty cooks, and aching swollen feet. These days, she made a point of leaving a hefty tip for servers who went the extra mile. She watched Tina talking to Stavros. At first she started to walk away, yet turned around and went back to the window. Although she was shaking her head *No*, she still climbed in the opened limo door. Witnessing Tina's reluctance and dependency, churned Nitra's stomach enough that she pushed away her plate. She thought about Tom. It must be heartbreaking to have a sister that was an addict and a stripper. She took a long sip from her shake.

"Hi. I don't mean to bother you, but aren't you Nitra Zupan?" It was one of the grey-haired ladies from the bus.

Nitra swallowed her mouthful, "Um … yes I am." She recognised the look in her eyes — she was a fan.

"I just want to say how much I enjoy your books. *Life on the Lawn* actually made me stop to think about my own life and my possessions. And look, here I am on a bus tour! Because of you, I sold an old chest of drawers that I didn't really care for anymore. I got fourteen hundred dollars for it. That's how I paid for my tour ticket." Her enthusiasm bubbled up in her face, "Anyway, I came over to say thank you and … um …"

Nitra knew the drill. People often wanted an autograph but were reluctant to ask for it. Over time she had learned to offer it to them, putting them at ease. "You'd like my autograph."

"Wow. Would you? That would be fabulous." She dug into her tote bag for a pen and note pad. There it was again, the dreaded old lady tote bag. Nitra cringed at the sight of it. The ladies grin persuaded her to forget about it. "What's your name dear?"

"Rosy Rutherford." Her face simply glowed with delight.

Inside the little note book she wrote down her usual friendly phrase; '*To Rosy Rutherford — my good friend and greatest fan ~ Nitra Zupan.*' Her name was scrolled in fancy autograph script, not her legal signature. That was a mistake another author had made, costing him $3,500.00 on a forged check cashed by dishonest fan. "There you go. I'm glad you enjoyed the book but that wasn't really my intentions. It was part of the plot line …"

She cut her off, "Oh, I know that silly. None the less, it was true."

From the front of the restaurant, a bald man yelled to Rosy, "Hey Sweet Cheeks! Come on! The driver's calling us to bus!"

Rosy blushed, "That's my new boyfriend. He likes your books too. We read them in bed every night." It was a mental image Nitra tried to block out, not to mention the name Sweet Cheeks. While heading for the door, she waved the signed note book in Nitra's direction, "Well, thanks again. Gotta run, bye."

Nitra gave her a gentle wave good-bye. It had been pleasant encounter, the kind she enjoyed.

Sarah came to give her the bill and clear away her dishes, "So you're a writer? Neat! What kinda books do ya write?"

"Fiction mostly." Reaching into her tote, Nitra pulled out a twenty dollar bill, "Here. That should cover it."

Sarah slid the money and the bill to the edge of the table to scoop it up with her fingers, "Yep. I'll be right back with your change."

"No need. That's good. Your service was first-rate and friendly, worth every extra penny." She slid out of the booth and quickly headed for her truck. She liked to do nice deeds, but didn't like to take credit for them. It was just her way.

Chapter Four

On the drive back to the cottage, she ran through the events of the day — her fight with Wallace; meeting Tom, Mrs. Hollander, and the accident after seeing the strange grey car at the side of the road. The car still baffled her, but not as much as Wallace's weird reaction from hitting his head on the truck. That was her purpose for heading home, to check on him. She worried that he might have a concussion. If he still had a head ache when she got back, she was taking him to the doctor's. Her mind wandered to her latest book. With only five of the nineteen missing pages returned to her, she was still worried about meeting her deadline. She had considered telling William that they were lost, but she knew that would bring on a long lecture about the necessary use of computers and backing up her work onto disks. She did utilize her computer for the finalization of her work, but felt it held her back creatively during the writing process. No matter how much he bugged her about it, she wasn't accepting the laptop he sent her. In fact, she had decided to send it back the following week. She'd make him wait a few days to allow his self-appointed gratification to peek before ruining it for him. That's what was so great about William being her boss, he was easy to torment.

Nitra turned down the roadway that led to her cottage. By then the sun was sitting low in the sky. It shone directly in her eyes, forcing her to squint, narrowing her field of vision. Focusing mainly on the road ahead, she slowed down the truck to a reasonable speed. The next half mile was comprised of corners and small knolls that were tricky to drive under regular circumstances. She managed the first corner by staying close to the shoulder. It was followed by the largest knoll of the road. Again she kept to the shoulder but far enough that she didn't sink in its soft gravel. The next stretch of road was straight, that she sped down it, trying to make up for lost time. Again, she slowed down when she approached the next knoll. When driving in the country it was always best to drive near enough to the right ditch so that others coming over the hill, they wouldn't collide with you when they forgot to share the road. Along the opposite ditch ran a towering ancient stone fence that hid the countryside from traveling onlookers. That was the southern boundary of Hansen's farm. Part way up the hill was the break in the fence line, the threshold for tractors and trucks that worked in the fields. Coming over its top, the sun beamed her in the eyes once more. She turned her head quickly to the left, skirting the painful sunlight. To her shock, when she refocused her eyes, she was face to face with a grey car. The exact same grey car she saw earlier in the day. She was sure of it. By then she had driven past the open section, so Nitra slammed on her breaks, screeching to a shuddering halt. Instantly she shifted the truck into reverse and stomped on the gas. She knew she was taking a chance, there could be another car coming up the hill and she would crash into the front of them. At that moment she didn't care, she needed to see who was in that car. She had to know who her enemy was, if she was to protect herself from them. What she didn't count on was the car pulling out into the same lane she was in. She quickly concluded that the driver was attempting to follow her. They nearly collided. Again, Nitra slammed on her brakes. In the same instant, the driver of the car swung her vehicle over into the left lane and floored it. With a flash Nitra caught a glimpse of the driver as the car rushed by. The person behind the wheel was wearing deep red lipstick, so presumably it was a woman. The woman's image quickly vanished as the car broke the crest of the hill. A loud horn blared and the car swerved into the right lane. A wide-eyed Mr. Tompkins was grabbing and twisting his truck's steering wheel, trying to avoid the car and then the ditch. Within seconds, his massive hands held the wheel firmly, swinging the truck's front end squarely back onto the road. Realizing that he was safe and out of her way, Nitra floored the truck and chased after the car. Mentally, the writer in her, named it the *'Grey Phantom'*. She raced over the knoll, then down its other side. Her truck was old with stiff steering, so slowing down was a necessity when it came to the next hairpin corner. That's where the *'Grey Phantom'* made its get away. It was far enough ahead that it was able to veer down a side road out of Nitra's range. Nitra stopped cross ways in the junction, watching the grey car vanish down behind the road's hill.

Her pulse pounded in her temples. Her breathing was shallow and rapid, causing her chest to hurt. "Damn it! Damn it! Damn it!" She slammed the steering wheel with both palms. Without warning a long high pitched beep came from behind the truck, making Nitra jump, twisting backward in her seat. It was Wallace pushing on his horn. It stopped. His horn turned into yelling, "What the hell are ya doing Girl? Get out of the way." His arm stopped flailing through the open window. "That is if you want supper on time. If not, well then take your time then."

She couldn't believe her luck. He was there, protecting her. Or was it luck? She had to find out. Nitra jumped out of the truck and raced to Wallace's car. It was her turn to yell, "Did you see her? It was a *HER*." Although her breathing returned to normal, her stomach still churned from the rush of adrenaline.

"Calm down Girly. What are ya ramblin' on about? What *her* are ya talking about?"

Nitra's words come out in one long gush. "The person in the grey car. The same car from earlier today. She came back. The driver is a woman. I saw her Wallace. She was wearing red lipstick."

"So because she was wearing red lipstick and driving a grey car that means she was trackin' ya?" His words weren't mocking her. He was trying to piece together her chaotic half-sentences. "Are ya sure?"

"She was waiting for me again. Think about it. If she wasn't, why did she speed away when I stopped?" She closed her eyes tight before swallowing the lump in her throat, "She was waiting for me to come home." When she opened her eyes, she looked to him for comfort. In those green eyes, he could see how much the incident had unnerved her. She looked down the side road again, "Oh Wallace, now I'm scared. That was too close." She lowered her head, her voice soft and shaky, "And I can't go through it again."

He understood Nitra had to be reassured that she would be protected, "We'll park your truck in the garage when we get back. From now on you're not to leave my sight. And I'm calling Palmer too. This time, I'm not waiting."

"You'll get no argument from me. Not after last time. God knows who that woman is and I ain't taking any chances." She let out a loud sigh, "Um … could you follow me home?" Her eyes pleaded with him not to leave her alone. Once the adrenalin had worn off, she found herself truly frightened by the whole ordeal.

He grinned and teased her with a laugh, "Good God Girl, I've been waiting on ya to get out of *my* way! So … if ya wanna get yourself moving, I can get on with makin' supper." He shifted the car in gear and nudged it forward a few inches.

"Okay, okay." She jammed her finger at his face, "But stay right behind me. Your job depends on it." She followed her order up with an anxious, "Please?"

"Yes boss. Whatever ya say, boss." He eased up the brakes once more, rolling it forward again. "But Girl, I'm still waiting on ya." He let it roll another few feet.

He was acting so juvenile that she decided to enjoy the rare moment by teasing Wallace right back. She caught up to the car and leaned in his window, "So what are you making me for dinner?" Unknowing its affect on him, she jokingly batted her eyes at him. "I hope it's something hot and spicy." She exhaled the last three words turning them into sexy enticements.

Wallace swallowed hard. She was doing it again. "Oh, I'll give ya something that'll set ya on fire." He stopped himself before he said what he really wanted to say. "But I can't do it from here, now can I?" He let the car roll forward, pulling her out of the window. "Come on Girl, get to your truck and drive like the wind." Then he beeped the horn repeatedly just to annoy her.

Placing the back of her hand across her forehead as though she was about to swoon, she called to him, mimicking a southern accent, "Why sir, you make a lady feel so cherished?"

He smirked her way and revved the engine. In retaliation she took her time sashaying back to her truck. Climbing inside, she started up the motor and waited for Wallace to fall in behind her. With all jokes aside, she kept an eye out for the grey car and the lady with the red lipstick.

Finally reaching her driveway, she let out her held breath, releasing her tense shoulder muscles. Wallace lifted the garage door. She carefully parked it inside and closed it behind herself when she left. He walked her to the door and waited while she unlocked its deadbolt. Once she was inside, he waited to hear the bolt 'click' into place. In turn, she listened for him to pull his car around to the back of the cottage. Nitra stood by the kitchen door waiting for him. Hearing a knock, she cautiously pulled aside the curtain to be sure it was him. A mistake she had made once and would never repeat again. She unlocked the door, allowing him to come in, but quickly slammed it behind him, sliding its deadbolt into place.

He hung up his coat, "Front locked too?"

"Yes. I'll check the windows next." She tried to slip her tote onto the floor, but her sleeve caught on one of the beads and she had to shake it free. She reminded herself to change it later in the evening.

"No, ya better let me do it. But ya can put on the kettle for tea. I'll start down here, then go up stairs." He was diligent about the task, closing each one, locking it and then pulled up hard to see if it would budge. With the lower floor secure, he thought he'd check on her before going upstairs.

63

He pushed open the door to find Nitra standing at the sink holding the kettle, which was overflowing with running water. She was silently crying. That was the way she was. She held things inside, not showing her weaknesses to anyone. His heart ached for her. He wanted to hold her, to comfort her, but he knew he couldn't. Instead, he quietly closed the door behind him and left for upstairs. By the time he got back downstairs she was sitting calmly at the kitchen table, stirring sugar into her tea.

With a silly little salute, he reported to her, "All hatches battened down, captain!" Getting her to smile, he relaxed his tense muscles. At the refrigerator he asked his standard question, "Are ya hungry right away or do I make food that takes a bit to be good." She had come to understand his odd Irish manner of speaking.

"A bit to cook is fine. Wait a minute. Didn't you make something 'beefy' earlier today?"

He pointed to the paper stuck to the refrigerator. The big green letters read, *Irish Community Dinner*. "It's in the freezer for next week. Taste's better that way."

She said nothing for a few minutes. By the expression on her face, he knew she was mulling over something in her head. He had learned not to disturb her when she was in 'thinking mode'. He simply waited for her to start talking when she was ready. Finally, her cheeks crinkled up around the eyes, "Do you think I'm in any real danger here?"

He shrugged his shoulders, "Personally, I don't think so, but that's a decision for Harry to make. He'll know what do."

She muttered under her breath, "Palmer's an idiot."

"True, but he's all we've got." He put the ingredients on the counter. "And ya need to let the past go. He didn't shoot at ya on purpose and ya bloody know it."

"Yah, yah, yah. Big bad mistake … blah, blah, blah. I've heard it all before."

Wallace held his aching head for a second before chastising her, "Now that's enough of that. Oh, and that reminds me — are ya calling him yourself or am I doin' it?"

"You do it. You're the one who thinks he's next to God." That's when she noticed he was rubbing his head. She changed her attitude into gentle concern, "Don't you think you should see the doctor about that?"

"I did. That's where I was when I came across ya in the middle of the damned road." The sound of beef sizzled in the skillet.

She blushed a little, "So what did he say?"

He was chopping the onions next. "*She* said it was fine. No stitches. But she did suggest that I be woken up every three hours during the night just in case." He turned to her, large tears streaming down his face. "So ya see we both need each other."

For a second she took him seriously, and was about to console him, when she realized it was the onions that were creating the melodramatic flood, not his breaking heart.

She lobbed her tea spoon at him, "You prick! That's not funny."

He simply ducked the flying object and laughed at her while wiping his cheeks. "Got ya Girl!"

"Oh, shut up you …" the phone rang. He watched as Nitra immediately tensed up. She gripped her tea cup so hard her fingers began to turn white.

Wallace picked it up, "Hello?" He watched Nitra's face while listening to the caller. "Yes sir, you've got the right number." He watched her taut face relax at hearing the word 'sir'. "Unfortunately I'm unavailable this evening, but any time tomorrow would be convenient. Is there a particular time that is better for ya than another?" He winked at Nitra trying to make her lighten up. "Yes, that will be fine. See ya then. Yes goodnight." He flopped the long phone cord across the floor and hung up the receiver. He added the onions to the skillet and stirred madly, but said nothing about the phone call.

Again her curiosity nagged at her, "So who was that?"

He pretended not to hear her by humming an Irish song. One in particular that he knew annoyed her a great deal.

She didn't fall for it though. She simply ignored him in return. She sashayed across the kitchen to her ugly old lady tote bag where she took out her red lined paper and mechanical pencil. She scraped her feet across the wooden floor until she reached the table. She slammed down the wad of pages, shifting continuously in her antique chair to make it squeak, while tapping her pencil on the tabletop.

To carry on the silent needling, he slowly stirred the ingredients in the simmering skillet and changed his tune to *'When Irish Eyes Are Smiling'* — a tune he knew she outright despised.

This lasted for almost fifteen minutes before he gave in, "Okay, ya win. Apparently a Slovenian *is* more stubborn than an Irishman."

"So answer the question." She tapped the pencil against her chin.

He removed the skillet from the heat and added the sour cream along with more fresh ground pepper. "Question?"

"You know the one — where did the universe come from?" He turned around to smirk at her, making her even angrier. She grunted at him, "No, you bloody idiot —who was on the God damn phone?"

"Patrick Spencer." He said it quick and blunt, not offering any explanation or details.

"That's it." She rolled her eyes at him, "Wallace please, I've no energy left for this. Just tell me why he called."

He took pity on her and let his shenanigans go, "He called about the ad. He says he has two of your pages."

Her face went from glum and tired, to excited and lit up, "Fabulous, let's go get them." She jumped to her feet eager, then her face turned suddenly serious, "You're driving though."

She got halfway across the kitchen before he stopped her with his arm, "Oh no, ya don't. Not tonight. Tonight, we're talking to Harry." He jammed his pointed finger in her face, "And don't ya be arguing with me Lass."

She opened her mouth to oppose him, but he held up a flat hand, halting her words. Infuriated that he was right, she stared directly into his face and angrily narrowed her eyes at him, "Oh, fine." Resentful, she returned to her chair, scraping it on the floor just to aggravate him.

"Now Ni, don't be like that. All fun aside, ya know it's for the best. Tomorrow it will be daylight with no fear of what's hiding in the dark."

She stabbed a pointed finger at him, "Ah-ha! So you *do* think I'm in danger?"

He closed his eyes and let his shoulder slump, he'd slipped up. He'd said exactly what he didn't want to say, "Oh, that's not what I meant and ya know it."

"*Where the tongue slips, it speaks the truth.*" It was one of his favourite Irish sayings and she delivered it with a smug yet sweet smile.

Knowing she'd caught him at his own game, he returned her quip with a line of his own, "'*Revenge is a dish*

67

best served cold.' Well done." He finished it off with a congratulatory bow.

"You still didn't answer the question." She stared directly at him, pinning him in place with her green eyes, accentuating each word, "Do you think I'm in danger?"

"Yes … no. I mean, I'm not sure. Ya might be, but then again ya do have quite the imagination on ya." As soon as the words came out of his mouth, he knew he was going to pay for saying them, so he went for broke, "Are you sure it was the exact same car as before?" He rubbed his throbbing temples again, "Or was it just another grey car that looked alike."

It took her two seconds to respond with ear-splitting yelling, "Quite the imagination! Oh, so now I'm seeing things again!" She smashed her finger into her chest, "I know the enemy when I see it. And that grey car is driven by someone who wants to do me harm. I can feel it! Admit it, you know I'm right and you're just as scared as I am. Why else would you lock all the windows and doors on the second floor?"

That hit a nerve. Wallace McPhee was afraid of no one, especially an imaginary one. "That's it! I'm calling Harry before ya lose your bloody mind." He stomped to the phone. He whipped a pointed finger toward the skillet and yelled back, "Stir that before it curdles and breaks."

She glared at him, but did what he said anyway. After all, his beef stroganoff was her favourite.

He punched in the last number and waited. "Hello? Yes, this be Wallace McPhee and I need to speak to Chief Palmer." She strained her ears to hear what was being said on the other end. "Yes, it is important." He twisted the cord around his finger, a nervous habit he thought he had broken himself of. "Hello, Harry. Wallace here." He waited for Harry's cordial response. "Oh, just fine. Listen Harry, Nitra's been having a problem with a fan again. Do ya think ya could come out here and talk to her for a bit? Get it all written down right away. Ya know, put her mind at ease." Nitra heard the words *'really busy'* and *'after dinner'*. "Well, if ya don't mind coming out now, I've got a fresh pan of beef stroganoff waiting to be eaten." He grinned from ear to ear, "Yes, that would be great. I'll set an extra plate for ya." He winked at Nitra, "See ya shortly then. Bye."

"Oh, that's reassuring. He won't come to help me, but he'll come for your cooking." At that exact moment her stomach noisily rumbled. Rubbing it, she silently smiled at him, "Although, I can't blame him, you are one hell of a cook. That's why I love you so much. I'll get out the nice bowls. You get the bread and butter. 'Cause we both know how much Harry loves his butter."

The word *'love'* stuck in his head. "Um … yah … bread." He couldn't trust what he heard. He ran her words back through his head. She had said it, yet he was sure she didn't mean it. But what if it was 'a slip of the tongue' and she really did mean it. He couldn't tell for sure. She was a confusing creature. Or was it him that was confused. His head throbbed as he sliced the loaf of home baked bread.

She placed the wide brimmed blue bowls on the table. "Do you think one loaf will be enough?" she laughed as she said it.

"It's gonna have to be, it's all I got and I don't bake again 'til morning."

Just then a car pulled up into the drive way. It was Harry.

"Holy shit! Didn't take him long?" Nitra peeked at her watch, "Thirteen minutes."

The cop knocked at the kitchen door. Wallace answered it, "Come on in Harry."

"Good evening Officer Palmer. Wow, you sure got here fast?" She took his jacket and hung it beside the door.

"Well, being a cop has its advantages. Sirens and light tend to get us where we want to go a little faster than average folks." He sniffed the air, "My God that smells heavenly."

Wallace took the hint, "Oh yes, please grab a seat." He motioned him to the chair that had the bread basket in front of it. "Piping hot stroganoff comin' up."

"I don't mean to rush you, but we've got that crowd down at the football game that'll be letting out around eight'ish and I've got to be there. Never understood why people get so riled up over a football game, but they do." He buttered a piece of bread and inhaled half the slice in one bite. "Mmm … you make the best bread. What's your secret?"

Wallace filled his bowl with noodles and ladled on a huge mound of stroganoff. He was about to answer when Nitra cut in, "Officer Palmer, I've been concerned about a particular grey car that I've seen twice today alone." He nodded as he shoved another fork full in his mouth. "Both times the car has seemed to be waiting for me. And both times the car was in the vicinity of this cottage."

"How close?" Harry mumbled through a mouthful of his heavily buttered second slice bread.

"The first encounter was 500 yards from my main gate and the second was on Hansen's Hill." She clutched her hands together over her chest, "Twice in one day is something to worry about — don't you think?"

70

"You get a good look at the driver?" She shook her no. "You get a licence plate number?" He shovelled another fork full in his mouth even before he finished the first mouthful.

Her stomach churned at the sight. "No. It was covered in mud."

"Okay, so tell me what you do know? I know you, and you've spotted something. You're always watching with that writer's eye of yours." He reached for his fourth slice.

Wallace grabbed a slice before Harry ate them all. "Tell him what you saw today."

Nitra recounted the whole incident to Harry who continually slurped noodles and stuffed his face with bread.

"Okay, but the interesting part is that I saw that the person driving the car was wearing red lipstick, so we could assume that the driver is a woman."

"Or a cross dresser." Harry pointed with his noodle entwined fork.

Wallace rolled his eyes, "Oh yah, there's so many of those in Hamlin. Come on Harry get bloody serious."

"Yah, you're probably right." He swallowed down his half chewed noodles and beef to ask the next question, "You notice anything else."

She ran it through her head again and that's when in hit her, "Mr. Tompkins! Why didn't I think of it before? Maybe he saw who it was."

"Andy Tompkins? He's got the farm next to here, right? He's on my way." He took a quick glance in Wallace's direction. "I'll go see him right after dessert. See what he's got to say."

Wallace couldn't believe it. The greedy mooch wanted dessert too. "All I've got is some stale vanilla ice cream. Nitra's not a big dessert eater so I don't usually make

71

dessert. Sorry." He lied. There were at least two dozen cookies, half a batch of brownies, and four slices of apple pie in the refrigerator.

Harry let out a disappointed, 'Oh'.

"If you find out anything, please call me immediately." She poked at her noodles, "Harry, I don't want it to get as bad as last time." She didn't look at him, she couldn't. It was an awkward subject, but it needed to be touched on.

"Nitra, I'll say it again, I'm sorry for shooting at you, but I thought you were him."

Her face had paled, "I know that. You were no more to blame than I was. Who knew he'd become obsessed after answering one fan letter. No one. It's just that I don't want any of us to go through another house invasion."

"Well, at least we know it's not him." Harry said it in jest, but it made Nitra sick to her stomach. "When a nut-bar's dead, he ain't anymore trouble."

Wallace watched Nitra close her eyes and squirm at the memory of the shooting. "Hey Harry, would ya like a coffee for the road? Just take me a minute to make some."

"Nah, doctor says I drink too much as it is. He says I need to cut out at least ten cups a day."

Wallace had to know, "Ten cups? Jesus, how many did ya normally drink in a day?"

"Some days fifteen, other days as many as thirty-five." Nitra's eyes almost popped out of her head. "Yah, that the same look I got from the doctor." He swallowed the last noodle down. "Mmm. Wallace, if you weren't a man, I'd marry ya." He studied Nitra for a second but changed his mind before saying it. "Well, I must be going. Old man Tompkins hits the hay really early and I've got that football thing." He rose to his feet and hiked up his belt passed the widest part of his currently expanding bulge.

Both Wallace and Nitra walked him to the door. It was Nitra that shook his hand, "Thank you for coming out here, Chief Palmer. I do appreciate your help. Again, let me know what Mr. Tompkins says."

"Can do. Wallace, thanks again for the grub. It was delicious." His face went dismal, "Sure wished the Misses could cook like that. Ain't no lovin' in her oven anymore."

"Well, if you'd like, Wallace could go to your house and teach Marianne his secrets." She couldn't resist. Harry had just bad-mouthed his wife and that infuriated her.

Harry looked Wallace up and down. Realizing he was a younger, handsomer man with an exotic foreign accent, he quickly declined the offer, "Oh no, that's okay. She's a busy woman, volunteering at our church and all that." He emphasized the word church to make the point that his wife was a good Christian woman and was not to be tempted by sinful flesh.

That show of jealousy satisfied Nitra's dislike for his disrespect, "We'll be up until about ten o'clock if you have any news. Thanks again, Harry."

Wallace had already opened the door and was waiting with an outstretched hand, "Yah Harry, thanks for coming."

"No problem. Happy to help." He slipped on his jacket, "And you keep all the doors and windows locked. I'll radio the station and let them know what's happened. And you call immediately if anything – and I mean anything — looks out of the ordinary. Don't wait like last time. You folks have a good night now." With that he headed for the cruiser and Wallace shut the door behind him, bolting it tight.

They both laughed out loud at the bazaar Harry-style evening.

73

"Now then, that went rather well. Don't ya think?" Wallace made his way to the sink and ran water for washing up the dishes.

Nitra brought him the dishes from the table, "Oh yah, fabulous. I feel completely safe knowing that Harry Palmer was out there right now protecting me from God knows who that wants to do God knows what. Yah, I'm feeling real safe."

Out of the corner of his eye, he watched her fidget around the kitchen. It was not like her to stay around when dishes were being done. She usually disappeared into her writing room, closing the door to block out the clanking sounds. Something was obviously bothering her. He knew what to do. "Um … I could use some help over here. Grab a towel and dry." That request usually chased her out of his way. To his astonishment, this time, she did it.

Opening the drawer, she chose a pale green towel then stopped still, "Wallace I've been thinking. What if this lady is another lunatic? I mean, what if she tries to come after me like Larson did? What am I supposed to do about it? How in the hell do I protect myself twenty-four hours a day, seven days a week? Or at least 'til she's caught?"

"Ya don't. Ya can't. It's impossible to do." He placed the clean skillet in the drain tray. "Look Lass, you're putting the horse before the cart. Let Harry look into the mystery woman and then we'll decide what to do then."

"That doesn't help me tonight, now does it?" She hung the dried skillet on its rack hook. "How am I supposed to sleep tonight knowing she's out there?"

It came out of his mouth before he had a chance to stop himself, "We'll just have to sleep together."

Shocked by the words, her head whipped around, "What?" Her eyes were the size of walnuts and fixed straight at him.

Seeing her reaction, he realized exactly what he had said and the implications of those impulsive words. Mentally he panicked. With waving hands, he tried to edit himself, "No not like that. I meant that we sleep together in the same room." He quickly amended those words too, "In separate beds ... I mean, different spots. Oh hell, ya know what I mean Lass." He drained pale white, then flushed red. Small beads of sweat formed on his throbbing painful forehead. As she stared at him, he felt his stomach churn. What had he done? What was she thinking about him?

Nitra simply blinked at him. She said nothing. He was absolutely red faced and visibly flustered. It was at that exact moment that she became aware of his feelings for her. Within seconds, it all made sense to her – the uncomfortable moments and odd actions slipped into place, forming a large puzzle, suddenly materialized into a grander picture. Words would not come to her. She had no idea what to say to him.

She told herself she had never really looked at him that way. She just assumed he was her housekeeper and left it at that. Then she stopped lying to herself — she had looked — just as he was looking at her. How could she not? He was a stunning male specimen. Tall, lean, with hazelnut coloured eyes that made her heart race and her knees melt. But she had never reacted on those lustful rushes. He was her housekeeper and to her, that meant he was off limits. She forced herself to stop thinking about him in that way. She switched her concentration to how they were going to get out of the tense awkward moment without creating future frictions between them. She knew she'd have to do it quickly. The poor man was coming unglued right before her eyes. She went with an impulse, "Boy, I could sure use a brandy right now. You know, to take the edge off." She immediately turned on her heels and darted directly to the living room.

Wallace let out a held breath he didn't know he was holding. He gripped the countertop's edge, closed his eyes and mumbled a reprimand to himself, "Ya bloody idiot? What are ya doing? Trying to get yourself fired?" From inside the living room he heard the china cabinet open. She really was drinking brandy, something she never did. It was Nitra's personal policy to only drink at social events. And even then only a maximum of three drinks. For her to drink at home meant she was upset. In his head he hoped it was because of the weird woman, rather than his stupid suggestion that they sleep together. Those same words echoed on his head. Again, the rush of her image whirled through his head. He cleared them out by shaking his head. "A cold shower, that's what I need." He pushed the living room door ajar, "Nitra, I'm going up for a shower, I'll be back in ten minutes."

Her only reply was a timid, "Okay!" As much as she wanted him away from her, she needed him near for protection.

He scurried up the stairs to a chilly shower and thorough self-chastising.

Downstairs she was scolding herself as well. Nitra knew he was right. The only way she was going to get any sleep was if he was close by her. He helped her feel safe. The thought of him sleeping in her bedroom was too overwhelming to consider. And in the same way, the thoughts of her sleeping in his bedroom were as equally as disturbing. She sipped brandy from her friendship glass. It was a single Czechoslovakian crystal liquor glass that was originally one of a set of four. The other three were each owned by her three best friends from college. On the last day they were together, they shared one last drink and toasted to their future. Each one kept the glass they drank from, vowing to always remember that night and each other. Currently, they were scattered throughout the world with careers and husbands, but kept in contact through hand written letters, a rare and precious form of correspondence. The delicately etched glass reminded her of their times spend together and of their times yet to come.

Down the steps pounded Wallace with his pillow under one arm and his comforter over his shoulder. "I was thinking that maybe it would be best of we sleep in here tonight. Ya can have the sofa and I'll take the love seat."

"That's a stupid idea." She savoured another long sip.

"Why not? It's a perfect solution for staying in the same room while we sleep." He plopped the bedding on the love seat.

"No, it's not that. You should take the sofa and I'll take the love seat. Wallace, if you haven't noticed the sofas longer and so are you. Besides, I'll feel better with my back against the wall." With her hand on the back of her neck, she twisted it gently to the right in attempts to relieve its tension.

"Good point. Okay, I'm on the sofa and you're on the loveseat. Got it." He switched his bedding to the sofa and laid everything out before climbing into it. "Ya gonna write tonight?"

"No. I can't think when my mind's like this." She had swallowed down the last bit of her brandy and was pouring herself another. "Would you like some?"

He almost said yes, but decided that strong alcohol and her in the same room would surely lead to trouble. "No, thank ya. I think I'll go straight to sleep. Tomorrow's gonna be a busy day with my baking and being your bodyguard." He tried not to think about the word body, but the images returned. "Well night then." He promptly turned over and locked his arms across his chest.

"Um … yah … goodnight." She tapped the empty glass on her bottom lip while deciding what to do next. Bedding, she needed her pillow and blanket. Quietly, she tiptoed up the stairs. She changed into her usual pink plaid flannel pyjamas. For the first time they felt different. She wondered if she was covered up enough. She buttoned up the top button to be sure. She told herself that she didn't want him to look at her that way — but her true emotions told her differently. Up until then she'd been avoiding what was really inside her. She didn't want to, but she did care for him. She sat herself down hard on the edge of her bed and convinced herself otherwise. She had to put an end to it before the whole thing got out of hand. Carrying her pillow and blanket down to the love seat, she made her bed and slipped inside. For some reason unknown to her, she purposely positioned herself to face him. She watched his muscular back rise and fall with each breath. She wondered how long he had felt that way. Right from the beginning or did it happen somewhere along the way? Half awake, she struggled to piece it all together — the times and the events that should have been obvious to her, but she somehow overlooked. Within minutes her heavy eyes closed, allowing her drained mind to finally drift off to sleep.

Chapter Five

Nitra was startled awake by the loud sound of shattering glass. Her body sat upright while her mind stayed asleep. It took her a moment to recognize the voice that was attached to the stream of cursing coming from the kitchen. The fragrance of fresh baked bread filled her nostrils, making her mouth salivate. Wallace was baking. The thought of warm buttered toast lingered on her taste buds. Then it sunk in, that was Wallace in the kitchen. The memory of the night before tied itself in a tense knot that lodged itself squarely in her gut. She flopped backward onto the love seat and moaned, "Lord, save me from my life."

The door flew open, "So, you're finally up? And it's about time too. It's almost eight o'clock. Half the mornin's gone already." He slid the tray on the coffee table, "Just tea and toast okay this mornin'? I kinda spilled the orange juice on the floor."

She sat upright again, "It's only eight o'clock? You're kidding me, right?" She flopped her head in her palms. "This is way too early for me. Let me sleep for another hour?"

He stuck his hands on his hips, "There'll be no doing that. We've got people to meet."

Her brain was still not functioning completely, so it didn't click in right away. "Who in the hell would I be meeting at this time of morning?"

He stabbed his hand into the air as though he was plunging a superheroes sword, "Sir Patrick Spencer — Guardian of the Pages."

"Oh Lord, yah, I forgot about that. I'll be ready in ten minutes." She flung back her blanket.

"Slow down Girl. Ya got an hour." He slid the tray closer to her, "So eat your toast. Damn, I forgot the jam." On his way to the kitchen, he yelled over his shoulder, "Ya want strawberry or peach?"

"Peach please." Her body relaxed once he disappeared behind the door, but tensed up again when he returned thirty seconds later with the tiny jam jar.

"I told Patti that we'd be at his place at nine o'clock. So be ready to go at ten minutes to." The oven timer bell binged in the kitchen. "Bread's done, gotta go."

She watched him leave the room while she lazily nibbled on her buttered toast. To her relief, they were both acting as though nothing had happened the night before. But she knew it was the day ahead that would test that theory. They would have to spend every minute of the day together.

At ten to ten, Nitra was standing by the kitchen door waiting for Wallace to turn up. She checked her watch again just to make sure she wasn't too early. It read the correct time. She pulled back the curtain to peek at the weather. It looked like rain. She scanned the outside for signs of Wallace, but he wasn't there either. Finally, she heard a sound from upstairs, she recognized that particular squeak, it was the one outside his bedroom door. She hollered up the back stairs, "Aren't you ready yet? Come on, it's nine fifty three. If you don't hurry up, I'll be late."

The sound of pounding feet came down the stairs, "First of all, It's *we'll* be late." He jammed his hand on his hip, "And do ya think we're actually gonna be late for anything that has to do with Patrick Spencer? Be late for him to do what? The man hasn't worked in three years."

"True." She turned about and yanked her keys from the rack.

"Um … what do ya think you're doing?" his eyes glared at her.

She didn't understand what he was asking her, "We're leaving? Aren't we?"

"But we're not taking your truck," his face was fatherly firm.

She still didn't understand, "Why not?"

He crossed his arms to emphasize his point, "'Cause the *Lipstick Lady* knows your truck, but she doesn't know my car."

She knew he was right – again. She loathed it when he was right too many times in a row, something that she refused to admit to, that early in the morning. So she change the subject completely, "*Lipstick Lady*? That's not her epithet. It's the *'Grey Phantom'*. Where on earth did you get such a silly name as that?" She hung her keys back in place.

He stepped around her to get his coat, "Oh, maybe because she's a lady that wears red lipstick? Besides, it sort of rolls off the tongue, alliteration wise."

She was surprised. He knew the word alliteration and what it meant. She was impressed. But what she didn't like, was that he was right again. It truly was a narrative name.

81

She was going to argue it out though, "No, I like *'Grey Phantom'* better." She stopped there, not adding any further explanation. It was a tactic she used to drive Wallace slightly crazy. She patiently waited for him to counter act her.

But he didn't. He simply opened the door, "Ya wait here Lass and I'll bring the car around."

She only nodded at him before he closed the door. In her head, she swore at him, *'You bastard. You were supposed to fight back. Well, we'll just see who wins this one?'* While she waited she formed her plan in her head. When the car pulled up to the doorstep and Wallace beeped the horn, she was ready to deal with him.

"Hurry it up, we'll be late." He grinned from ear to ear as she slid into the small bucket seat beside him. He revved the engine before he floored it. They flew down the drive way at neck whipping speed.

She held onto the door strap, "Holy Hanna! Where's the fire?"

He shifted gears, "Well, ya don't want to be late, do ya?"

As they came over the third hill, they came face to face with Chief Palmer's cruiser. He frantically honked at them, signalling that he wanted them to pull over.

Wallace pulled onto the shoulder and Harry pulled over on the opposite side of the roadway. Getting out of the car, he waddled his way over to their car, "Mornin' folks." Then he leaned over into the window, "How are you doing today? Any more problems your way?"

It was Wallace that spoke up first, "No. Everything's been quiet."

"Good to hear," His head bounced a hard nod.

Nitra jumped right in, "So Harry, did you talk to Mr. Tompkins? Did he see anything significant? Did he see her? Does he know her?"

Harry smirked before answering her questions, "Yes. No. No. And no." He was trying to be funny, but she wasn't in a joking mood. She told him so by frowning at him, so he said it properly, "Yes, I talked to Old Man Tompkins. No, he didn't see anything remarkably significant. He said he was too busy trying not to get run over. No, he didn't see her because of the same reason as before ... 'trying not to get killed by those two silly women' as he put it. And no, if he didn't see her, how was he supposed to know if he knew her."

She punched her thigh, "Damn it! I was hoping he'd seen her. Now I'm still no further ahead than I was yesterday."

"Actually, that's not true. Tompkins did see something. Firstly, he saw the grey car itself, proving that it does exist." He lowered himself to his knees, relieving the pressure on his lower back. "No offence Miss, but we do get faults reports. It's a waste of time and money for my boys to chase down ghosts." She nodded her understanding. "Secondly, he did remember seeing a long scratch along the front fender of the driver's side. It ain't much, but it something." He tilted back his hat, "But remember Nitra, we've just started working on this. It could take days before something shows up."

A car came over the crest of the hill. It slowed down to gawk at the officer kneeling beside the sports car. Wallace waved at her, "Hi ya nosey Bitch!" he said it low enough for Harry and Nitra to hear, but not the passing car. They all grinned at his honesty and waved as well. Their waving unnerved the woman, prompting her to turn her head away and speed off.

"Well, that's all I have for you so far. If anything else turns up, I'll call right away. But in the meantime, you two stick together. Where you off to now?"

Nitra peered around Wallace's head, "Patrick Spencer's place."

A wide smile spread across the officer's face, "Why are you going out to see him? His crop ain't off yet, if that's what you're aim for."

Wallace took personal offence to his accusation. He answered with an abrasive Irish tone, "No. We're not going there for business. We're going there to get back two of Nitra's pages."

Harry realized that his joke didn't go over the way he thought it would and tried to remedy the awkward moment, "Look folks, I was only kidding. I knew you don't smoke that stuff. It's just a local joke."

Nitra tilted her head at him, "I don't get it. If you know he grows it, to the point that you know he hasn't harvested yet, why don't you arrest him?" She managed to ask in a manner that underscored his authority, not question it.

"Oh Miss, you know I can't answer that. Police business. You understand I can't discuss it?"

She nodded her understanding again, "Your right. Stupid question."

From the other side of the road, they heard the cruiser's radio crackle and hiss. He turned his head to listen, but nothing came over it. "Well like I said, so far we've found out nothing about your mysterious lady." The radio cracked louder, distracting him again.

"No problem." Wallace slipped the car in gear, gesturing that the conversation was over. "Anyway, we've got to go. Give us a call if ya find out anything."

"Can do." The radio in the cruiser blared inaudible words that only Harry's ears could understand. Whatever the message was, it sent Harry on the run. He jumped into the cruiser, pulled a U-turn and launched it down the road with the lights flashing.

Nitra giggled out, "Holy shit! I didn't know Harry could move that fast."

"He was moving faster than that at Christmas time." She narrowed her eyes at him in curiosity. He answered her, "Oh that's right, ya weren't outside when he was chasing down Larson. He almost caught him with his bloody bare hands. It was the deep snow slowed him down."

Her forehead furrowed, "Wait a minute? Where was I? I don't remember any foot chase."

"Ya were where ya were supposed to be, locked in the pantry where I put ya." He shifted the gears hard, "Why didn't ya stay where I put ya? Ya were safe in there."

She cleared her throat, "I thought it was over. I didn't hear any sounds, so I thought it was all right to come out." Her words went hushed, "I thought I was safe." She turned her head toward the window and blankly stared at the passing scenery. She wasn't looking at anything in particular; she was trying to stop that troubled night from replaying in her head.

Wallace said nothing. He waited until she was ready to talk again. But when she didn't turn around to face the front, he knew something wasn't right. "Nitra how ya holdin' up? Ya know we don't have to go today if you're not up to it."

She swallowed down the lump in her throat, "No, I'm fine. Besides, I want those pages." She clasped her praying hands together and pointed them to the heavens, "Please God make page one be there. I need page one. Without it, I'm sunk."

"Oh, a fine Christian ya are. Only praying to God when ya need His help. Shame on ya Girl." He shifted the car with a jerking motion.

Never having driven a standard transmission, she questioned if he really needed to shift that often or if it was his way of making a point. Religion was a hot topic between them, one she tried to avoid as much as possible. To her relief, Patrick Spencer's lane way was directly ahead, allowing her to changed the subject, "There's Pat's place. I hope he remembered that we were coming."

He glimpsed at her sideways. She had managed to skirt the issue once again. He'd have to come back to that later. "Wouldn't that be a treat? Us here and him still asleep. Or worse, him high with some other drug addicts."

The word addict reminded her of Tom sister. Her pulse raced. Her guts told her that this might be an unnerving visit. The car came to a gentle stop.

Patrick Spencer's house consisted of old grey wood. It had been left to ruin by weather and time. By the looks of the large front veranda and tall tapered pillars, it had once been a grand home. It was a disgrace what Patrick's neglect had done to the fine old estate.

In the window Patrick stuck his head out to yell, "Come on in. Doors always open." Then he vanished inside.

Nitra let Wallace lead the way inside. His tall frame made a protective shield for her to hide behind. The air was heavy with the strong stench of what had been smoked earlier in the morning. The dim light from the dirty windows

86

cast an unnatural eerie glow on the sparse furnishings in the room. In the center was a large coffee table covered with all sorts of drug paraphernalia — weigh scales, rolling papers, pipes, little vials of seeds, ashtrays, and whimsical lighters of various shapes. The colourful covering of one in particular caught her eye. She took a second peek at that one. It depicted a naked woman having sex with a large smouldering joint. She stood a lot closer to Wallace after seeing that. The hairs on her arm prickled, telling her this was not a safe place to be.

"So … um … grab a seat." Patrick pointed to his dirty broken down couch, "and I'll get you the pages." He turned around and scurried up the stairs. His body was gaunt and skinny, showing his own long time abuse of drugs.

Nitra reached in her tote bag, then tapped him on the shoulder, "Wallace, here, take these." She hand him the forty dollars, "I'm leaving. I don't like it in here. I'll wait for you in the car."

He grabbed her arm, "You'll do no such thing Lass. Just stay put. We have to stay together. This'll only take two minutes. And don't use our names." Before he could explain why, he pushed the bills back at her and pointed behind her with his nose.

Patrick came down the stairs with her pages in one hand and a lit joint in the other. He offered it to Wallace first, who firmly shook his head *No*. Even before he could ask Nitra, she put her hand up to halt the offer. "Okay, but you don't know what you're missing. It's really good shit, man. Best of last year's crop." It was hard to understand his words. He talked through his clinched teeth with a heavy nasal tone; probably from a pot induced sinus infection. Most times if a person had a heavy accent Nitra would take the time to read their lips in order to understand them better. But not this time, she tried not to look at his face. His brownish sunken eyes made him appear as though he was tired and somewhat ill. He sucked in another deep toke and choked on it. Nitra wondered why anyone would do such a disgusting thing to themselves.

When Patrick had finally finished choking, Wallace spoke up. He wanted to make it perfectly clear that they weren't there to purchase his wares. "The papers? We only came for her pages and nothing else."

He cleared his hoarse throat, "Okay, relax. No need for hostility, man." He handed her the pages.

"Yes, they're mine." She was happy yet deeply disappointed. Page one wasn't there. In her hands were pages twenty and twenty-one.

After a hard deep lung clearing cough, Patrick remembered something else. He snapped his fingers in the air, "Oh yah, and I found these too." He shuffled his flip-flop's over to the mantel piece. He scooped up a stack of small crumpled dirty papers, "They had the same handwriting on them so I figured they might be part of your stuff too." He handed them to Nitra, being careful not to drop any on the filthy floor.

She quickly recognised them immediately, "My writer's notes. You found them. Oh, thank you." She was thrilled to have her friends back. She waved the stack at him. "You deserve an extra twenty bucks for rescuing these." In her excitement she spun in a small circle, crashing into Wallace, "Look he found them. He found them."

From outside Wallace could hear car doors faintly closing. Patrick had visitors. A situation he thought might happen. "That's great. So pay the man so we can get goin' to the doctors." He was trying to get her out of Patrick's without raising any suspicions.

She scrunched up her face with confusion; "Doctor's?" He widened his eyes to clue her into the ploy. "Oh yah, we don't want to be late for that." She turned her head towards the sound of footsteps on the wooden veranda, then back to Wallace. Panicking she froze in place.

He said it to her coolly, "Just pay the man so we can leave. Okay?"

She nodded, "Okay." She reached inside her tote, pulled out three twenty dollar bills and handed them to Patrick.

The door opened. Instantly Patrick grabbed the bills and jammed them down the front of his jeans. He quickly did his best to cover up what the three of them had been doing by backing up three steps, "Oh hey boys, I'll be with you in a sec. Just need to finish some business here."

She glimpsed slightly sideways and was surprised by what she saw. Although Nitra couldn't see their faces in the dim light, she noticed by their silhouettes that they were full grown men, not young boys as she suspected they would be. They said nothing, but waited in the shadows.

"Thanks," was all that Wallace said before grasping Nitra by the elbow and guiding her out the door. Even outside, he still guided her to the car and placed her inside, locking her door before he shut it. He hurried around the back of the car, slipped into the driver's seat and locked his door. Jamming the keys in the ignition, he started it in one turnover.

She recognized the licence plate on the limo parked alongside the house. It was the same limo from outside Hadley's Gas and Grill, the exact one Tina climbed inside. That sent a knot straight to her gut. Strip clubs meant organized crime and drug trafficking. "Go damn it! Just go." She was yelling it at him, "Get me out of here."

Ignoring her yelling, he shift into gear and floored it. The car's rear end fishtailed before straightening out at top speed. By the time they hit the main road, Wallace was white knuckling the wheel, his forehead covered in sweat.

Nitra kept her vigil out the back window, but to her relief, there was no one following them. After a couple of miles she finally turned around in her seat, "That was absolutely terrifying. I think I'm going to throw up."

"Oh for Christ sake, stop bein' so God damned dramatic. Why does everythin' have to be such a big damn deal with ya?" He shifted gears to slow down the car. "That was nothin'. God, you've lived such as sheltered life." He set the muscles in his jaw tight, signalling he had nothing more to say.

"But those were men back there?" She shifted in the bucket seat to get at better view of his face, "Do you think they had guns?"

"More than likely. Look, what was going on back there, had nothing to do with us. Nothing ... and I mean nothing." He glanced her way, "And ya need to keep your nose out of it. Are ya hearing me Nitra Ivanka Zupan? Out of it!" He used her entire given name. That meant it was an outright Wallace warning.

"All I meant was that they were men not ..." but she didn't get to finish the sentence. He cut her off, leaving her to sit there with her mouth open.

He glared right at her. His eyes were dark and hostile "I said for ya stay out of 'er and that's final!"

She snapped her mouth shut and sat silent. After a few moments she slinked down in her seat. With her eyes level with the top of the door, she peered over its edge to watch the world go steadily pass. She had a feeling that there was more to this story than Wallace was saying. Was there a connection to his own past? He never talked about his youth back in Ireland. Maybe he was right. Maybe none of it was her business. Maybe it was best she stayed out of it. Nevertheless that didn't stop her from thinking about it the rest of the ride home.

Chapter Six

The strain of silence showed on their faces by the time they returned home. Wallace once again pulled up to the kitchen door to escort her into the house. Neither one was interested in talking to the other. He headed to the refrigerator to make lunch, while she went up stairs to the bathroom. He poured the homemade soup in the pot and put it on the stove to heat. Noticing that he was serving soup for lunch, she automatically put the bowls and spoons on the table along with a sleeve of saltines, his favourite. At the table he dished up the soup into the bowls, returning the pot to the turned off stove. On the way back, he brought her the loaf of bread and the dish of butter. They quietly sat across from each other, not saying a word. They seemed to be ignoring each other, but the truth was, they were both watching the other carefully, looking for signs that the other would start the next conversation. He crunched up his crackers into his soup. She buttered her bread for dunking into her broth. Although they were both calmly eating lunch, the tension between them was building. Nitra felt its strain in her neck, while Wallace's forehead ached again. The *clink* of their metal soup spoons on the ceramic bowls was the only sound shared between them, each *clink* echoing through the exaggerated stillness. To cope with the building pressure, Nitra's fist clinched the napkin on her lap. Wallace curled his toes inside his shoes. Even the sound of the ticking kitchen clock thundered through the air. Each *tick* counting the endless edgy seconds they spent eating their soup. *BRRRINGGG!* The phone rang, scaring Nitra with an automatic jerk reflex, sending her spoon across the kitchen floor. Wallace poked himself in the nose with his.

Understanding that she wasn't to answer the phone, he held his throbbing nose with his fingers. His words turned nasal, "Hello?" Nitra laughed at him. He shot her a death look to quiet her while he listened. "Why yes, ya do have the right number." He watched Nitra butter yet another slice of bread. "Okay, where would ya like to meet?" His face frowned, "I have a better idea. Since you're on the other side of town, why don't I meet you halfway, at Gladys's Diner." Nitra rolled her eyes at him in loathing. "Great, see you then. Bye, bye now." Even before he hung up the phone he pointed at her, "Eat up. We gotta leave in ten minutes, Lass."

She put both of her fists firmly on the table, "Ten minutes! But I ..."

"No buts. Just be ready." With that, he left for the living room, leaving her sitting at the table feeling completely frustrated.

She mocked his words, *'we gotta leave in ten minutes, Lass.'* She laughed at herself. She was getting rather good at imitating his Irish accent.

"I heard that!" he hollered from the other room.

93

She mimicked that too, but this time it was done with a nasty tone.

"You're wastin' time. Get ready Nitra." She heard him run up the stairs.

She bellowed up to him, "Why did you say we'd meet him at Gladys's Diner? Can't we just go to his house?"

"No ..." his feet pounded down the stairs, "We can't."

Putting the bowls in the sink, she demanded an answer, "And why not?"

"Because he is a she, that's why." He was standing at the door pulling on his jacket. "And if ya bothered to notice, I said *I* instead of *we* to throw her off."

She hadn't, but what she had noticed was that the colour of his leather jacket matched his chestnut brown eyes. *Now stop that,* she scolded herself. She then noticed how it made his shoulder seem even stronger than they normally were. Again she disciplined herself, *Stop it, stop it, stop it!* Nitra made herself look away. Finally getting a hold of herself, she realized what he had actually said. "It's a woman?"

He had to correct her grammar, "*She's* a woman. Not, *it's* a woman. Lord, what ya writers do to our English language."

"Me? That's bloody rich coming from someone who butchers it every time he opens his mouth!" She poked him in the belly as she walk by him and out the door. "Get your keys Irishman, before you make us late. Oh yah, you owe me a piece of pie. Cherry would be nice."

She was halfway to the car before he caught up to her. "Hey, not so fast Lass. No more takin' off without me." His expression was serious, "I mean it. Stay close, ya hear." He scanned the yard as he opened her door. For safety, he waited until she got inside and closed the door.

That scared her. If he was that cautious, it meant there was something to be scared about. She locked her door and insisted he do the same when he got in. He thought that was going overboard, but did it anyway to put her mind at ease.

He started the car, shifted gears and roared down the driveway. "When we get there don't be takin' off on me, okay?"

She nodded but protested anyway, "Why? We'll be in public. She wouldn't dare do anything in public." Uneasily she added, "Would she?"

"Now we don't know that for sure Lass. Just stay close so we won't have to worry." He shifted gears again. "Cherry pie? That actually sounds good."

"Oh, à la mode!" She clapped her hands together, "and hot coffee with *real* cream."

"Gee, you'd think ya never been to a diner before." He changed gears, this time he grinded them a wee bit.

"Oooh yah!" She found it, the perfect spot. She was half twisted to the right while her knees pointed to the left.

Wallace scrutinized her from the corner of his eye, "Ya doing okay over there?"

"I'm fine." She pretended to smile as she watched the two boys riding on bicycles along the fence line.

"Ya don't look fine." He took his eyes off the road long enough to lean forward and look her directly in the face. "You're in pain aren't ya?"

"Yah, but it'll ease up in a bit." She turned her head to look out the window and to hide her redden face. It was embarrassing to have her back hurt every time she sat down. And the fact that it was Larson's fault made it hurt even deeper. And if Harry hadn't shot at her, she wouldn't have hurt herself by the back deck. She could still remember the excruciating pain that followed the initial blow. It crippled her. All she could do was to lay in the snow, motionless. Every time she tried to move, the sharp pain left her breathless. She still remembered the ambulance ride to the hospital, the doctors poking at her with needles and the worried looks on everyone's face.

"We'll be there in two minutes." He decided to change the subject. Something that would take her mind off her pain, "What do ya want for supper? Crab or calamari?" He knew his teasing would do the trick.

With that she swatted at him, "Very funny asshole!" She couldn't help it, the pain had put her on edge and it was getting the best of her.

"Oh, that got your goat." He scooted against the door, avoiding yet another swat.

"You know damn well I can't eat either of those." She jammed her arms in a knot.

"But Lass, you're so lovely when you're all green and sweaty." He quickly dodged another quick swipe, making the car swerve a little. "Hey! Don't be hittin' the driver while the car's movin'."

"Jerk!" She turned herself towards the window and winced at the pain in her lower back, "Shit!"

"Hang on! We're only a block away. And I see a parkin' spot right out front." Within a second, he floored it and headed straight for the open space. The speed Wallace was traveling when they got there, they almost slid into it.

After being slammed against the door, Nitra let out a short guttural grunt.

"So crab and calamari are out then?" He waited for another swat ... but none came. Nitra wasn't moving. She stayed curled up against the door. Feeling guilty, Wallace scurried to the other side of the car and slowly opened

Nitra's door. "Are ya all right? Let me help ya out." Slowly she unfurled her body, while he held onto her elbow. She took a step and hunched over again with another loud groan. He bent over to her level, "Nitra, are ya all right Girl? Is there anything I can do for ya?"

She promptly straighten up and grinned in his face, "Yah, you can buy me that piece of cherry pie, you big lummox." As his face went from concern to utter annoyance, she stuck out her tongue and raced to the diner's front door.

Halfway there he caught her by the elbow, "Nitra wait. We should go in together. We need to be careful."

She blew out a huff, "You're right. Time to be serious." She tidied her jacket and fluffed up her hair. "Okay, let's go."

Opening the door to the diner, they heard a squeal come from behind the counter, "Wallace McPhee you old dog you. What are you doing in a place like this?" It was Gladys herself, all 210 pounds of her. She stood stump still with her right hand on her very motherly hip, "I thought you said you'd never set foot in this ... what did you call ... oh yah ... 'grease pot'?"

Nitra watched his face turn bright red. He gathered his boyish charms with a deep breath, "Oh, come on Gladys. Ya know I was just spouting at the mouth. I didn't truly mean it. Ya got my goat. And I was in a mood, that's all, nothing more than that."

By then everyone in the diner was staring at the two of them. Nitra managed to step away from him in hopes that no one would connect her to the pair of bantering lunatics.

Gladys only shifted her weight from one side to the other, "A mood? Holy Christ, if that was a mood, what the hell is he like when his mad?"

97

Nitra suddenly realized that she was no longer scolding him, but instead was asking her about Wallace's daily behaviour. In her head she told herself to keep it light and friendly. A grin slipped across her lips, "Oh, Wallace never gets mad, he's just 'in a mood' most of the time." He turned to face her; his eyes squinted at her to shut up. She merely grinned back. "Knowing him, it was just him being 'in a mood'. You got any of that cherry pie I like so much? Been wanting a piece since *Wally* told me we were coming here." That got him. The name Wally drove him crazy and she was in a position to use it without the fear of instant retaliation. She continued to grin madly at him. His eyes squinted even narrower at her, sending her a death look. To her, that confirmed that she had succeeded in irritating him. "Make mine à la mode please. You want some too … *Wally*?" She couldn't resist the additional jab. "Come on, let's grab a booth?"

He followed right behind her, escaping the wrath of Gladys. When he slipped into the booth, he mumbled under his breath, "Oh, you're so funny. Okay then, we're even. So let's call it a truce. Okay?"

She didn't answer him. Instead she stretched her neck to look over the tops of the booths. "So who's the lady were meeting? Do you know her? Is she here already?"

He rubbed his temples again, "No she's not here yet. Her name is Martina and yes, I know her." At least she kept it down to three questions in a row.

Her eyebrows went high. Petty jealousy seized her, "You do?" Suspicious of the mystery woman, she shifted on the bench seat, "So how well do you know this Martina anyway?" Both pieces of pie arrived along with the coffee and a tiny white pitcher of real cream. But it wasn't Gladys who delivered them; she was busy at the cash register.

Wallace dived in, fork first. He moaned through a tangy sweet mouthful. He carefully flaked the pastry with his fork, "I wish I could get my crust like this."Lowering his head closer to the plate, he examined the layers for some hidden secret sign of what she'd done to accomplish its tiered tenderness.

"Yah, it's terrific." She limply poked at a whole cherry with her fork, pushing it around on the plate.

Finally, he ignored the pie crust and took notice of her change in mood, "Oh Lord, what's wrong now?"

"Nothing. I'm just worried. What if she's the *Lipstick Lady*?" She finally stabbed the cherry and popped it in her mouth.

"I don't think so." He cut off another huge piece and then sliced it in half again.

She stopped chewing, "What makes you say that? How can you be so sure?"

"Oh, I'm very sure. You'll see." He shoved the fork full in his mouth but had to swallow it whole. He pointed with his fork, "There she is. I'll go get her."

She watched him drop his fork on the plate, jumped to his feet and head towards the door. She wondered what kind of woman could make Wallace McPhee hurry that fast. Turning around, she discovered why. Martina was a pretty brunette who just happened to be holding the hand harness of her Seeing Eye dog. Nitra felt ill inside. How on earth could she have felt so malicious towards someone like Martina? She was helpless and harmless. Not at all the enemy she had worried about. Wallace gave her a gentle hug and held onto her while he spied outside the restaurant over her shoulder. She finally pushed him back and said something to him that made him laugh out loud.

"Here we are. Martina, this is Nitra, my boss." He guided her into his half of the booth. With a wave, he signalled Nitra to scoot in deeper into her bench.

"So you're Nitra. It's nice to finally meet you. Wally's told me so much about you, I feel as though I already know you." She patted her dog Ben on the head after he settled down beside the booth.

"Oh, he has, has he? So what has *Wally* been telling you?" She smacked him on the shoulder when she said *Wally*.

"Nothing bad, mind you. He generally tells me about the new books you're working on." Again, Martina heard a slapping sound along with a muffled *Ouch*. "Wait a minute, he only tells me because he knows I'm a fan of yours. There's no need to hit him. I've read every one of your books and I can't wait for the next one to come out."

"You've read all of my books?" her voice sounded cynical.

"Yes. All of them." Ben shifted his snout out of the way.

The waitress slid a cup and small tea pot in front of her, "Here's your tea. The cup's at ten and the pot is at three. Do you want a piece of cherry pie too?"

Martina shook her head, "No thanks Betty. I can't stay long. I've got a class in thirty minutes."

"Wow, you go to school?" Again Nitra's tone was an astonished filled put-down.

Being used to the attitude of the uneducated sighted world, Martina ignored the insult. Instead, she answered her question in the most pleasant manner possible, "No silly." She slowly poured her tea until it touched the fingertip she had lowered inside the cup, "I'm the teacher. I've just the one late class today. Is there sugar? I like my tea rather sweet."

Wallace stopped Nitra from reaching for it, he calmly guided, "Three o'clock, two paces."

"Thanks." She reached to the spot Wallace had directed her to. Her fingers gingerly probed for the glass sugar dispenser. Once Martina identified the shape, she casually picked it up and felt for its nozzle. She poured the sugar in a thin stream and at the same time, counted with a tapping finger, stopping at five. "So when is your next book coming out. I can't wait to read it."

Nitra was dumbfounded. She couldn't believe the things Martina was doing even though she was blind. Or at least she assumed she was blind, she had to know. As Nitra was known to do, she blurted out the words, "Are you really totally blind?"

Wallace smacked his coffee cup down, scolding her for asking such an insensitive question, "Nitra!"

"No Wallace, it's okay. It's a legitimate question." Martina sharply snapped her wet spoon a long side her saucer. Her tone of voice changed to indignant, "Yes. I am completely blind and I've been blind since the age of four. I contracted meningitis which ultimately took my eyesight. So, now I'll answer all your questions." She let out a light sigh, "They're always the same. Yes, I know all the colours and shapes. I have seen tons of sunsets. And I *do* know what a double rainbow looks like. And unlike many normal people, I've actually seen the autumn leaves change colour. There that should take care of it or do you have any other annoying questions?"

Nitra took offense to her attitude, so she fired right back, "Well, actually I do. How in the hell do you read my books when you're friggin' blind?"

Wallace jumped all over her, "Nitra that's enough. I knew this was a bad idea. What was I thinking?" He shook his head at himself, "Two powerful women in one booth – never a good idea."

She waved a stopping hand in his direction, "Wallace for just once, will you just shut up so I can answer my own question." She looked straight into Nitra face, "Don't be stupid. I don't read them; I listen to them."

She didn't like being called stupid, so she shot back, "How? I know for a fact that my publisher doesn't offer my books on tape." She was pointing her finger at her when she realized Martina couldn't even see it, so she jammed it onto her lap. "We never have."

That was exactly what Martina was hoping she'd say, "Oh, and don't I know it! And isn't it a shame that your editor doesn't provide that service for your visually challenged fans." She hammered her finger on the table top directly in front of Wallace. "Thank goodness for people like Wally here. People who take the time out of their busy lives to read books onto tapes so people like me can enjoy what your editor can't be bothered to do."

Nitra first looked at Martina, and then she turned to look at Wallace. Her housekeeper, Wallace McPhee, read her books to tape for the blind. It was a mind boggling revelation. She was speechless. What's more Martina was absolutely right. It was something that her editor refused to do, saying it was an expensive endeavour that wouldn't recoup it costs.

Not really caring what the results of her words were on Nitra, she repeated the question one more time, "So when are you going to release your next book? I hope it's soon because it takes Wallace almost five weeks to read it to tape."

Nitra started to laugh, softly at first then harder. "Well, that kinda depends on you."

Martina forehead frowned inquisitively, "On me? Why on me?"

"Are you going to give me the pages you have? 'Cause the faster I get them, the faster I can be done." She chuckled some more, "Ironic isn't it? Essentially, you're the one holding up the next book."

She pulled the neatly creased white square out of her pocket. "You mean these pages are part of your new book?" She unfolded the quarters to smooth them out.

"And that brings me to one more *annoying* question, how did you find them? I mean … you're blind. It's not like you could see them." She gave Wallace a death look, stopping him from chastising her again.

"Actually, it was one of my students who found them. He was too busy with his medical studies to meet with you, so I said I do it for him. Sherman is a great kid and I know he needs the extra money." Her face showed her disapproval, "It's bad enough he's working a part-time job on top of his coursework because his text books were so high-priced this semester." She slid the pages over to her, "Here you go, three pages. I hope you don't mind but I had Sherman read them to me. Nice bit about the 'Sisters of the Nine Moons' … well played out."

Nitra checked the corners of each page, "Let's see."

Martina joked at her particular choice of words, "That's funny, really funny."

It took Nitra a second to realize what she had said, and let out a soft chuckle too. Nitra knew she was only kidding, so there was no need to apologize, "We have pages 6, 7, and 8." Her tone of voice slowly sunk to dismal before she let out a heavy hopeless sigh.

"What is it? Aren't they yours? Sherman said he was sure they were." She twisted her head to hear her better, "What's wrong?"

"Oh, they are mine. It's just that the one sheet I was hoping to find, isn't here."

"Which one is that?" Martina took another sip of tea.

Nitra's voice mirrored the disappointment she felt inside, "Page one."

She bobbed an insightful nod, "Oh … the hook."

She was surprised by her use of the writer's term, "You know about the hook?"

Again she was annoyed with Nitra's naive pity towards the blind, "Yes, I know about the hook." She mocked her, "Not only I'm an avid reader, but I've penned a few articles myself."

"You have?" As before, the questions all tumbled out at once. "What were the articles about? What were you published in? Did it pay well?"

Martina faced Wallace, "Lord. I thought you were kidding when you said she did that, but she actually does do it." She took a deep breath, "I wrote three articles for a small upstate college that was conducting a symposium aptly named *The Blind Individual Interacting with Society as a Whole*. It focused on attitudes of sighted individuals towards those who are not."

"You folks need more coffee?" Betty poked the coffee pot at them. Betty had perfect timing since Nitra was suddenly feeling rather foolish about her own attitude towards the blind.

Wallace put his hand over the mouth of his cup, "No thanks. Three cups a day is limit."

Nitra shook her head as well, "No more for me either. If I have another coffee, I'll have to float out of here."

"Martina, you need to get going. You'll be late if you don't." Nitra noted that the waitress knew her by name and her routine, which meant she was a regular at this restaurant.

She checked her wristwatch with her fingertips feeling the Braille dots on its surface, "Holy crap! I gotta go."

Wallace poked Nitra in the arm with his elbow, "Don't forget to pay her?"

"Oh, sorry." She dug out six twenty dollar bills and offered them to Martina, "Here's Sherman's money."

Martina held out her hand waiting for Nitra to place them in her palm. She automatically began to fold each bill into fourth so she'd know they were twenties. She quickly discovered there were six bills instead of three. "Um … you made a mistake. There are three extra bills in here." She tried to hand them back.

Nitra lovingly pushed her hand back, "No, those three extras are for Sherman. It's not much, but I'm sure he'll put it to good use. I remember how hard it was being in college and as I recall sixty dollars can go along way when you're broke. Tell him thanks for returning my pages and best of luck in the future."

"Shall do. Look, I have to go before I'm late." Ben immediately stood up to shift into position. When Martina picked up the handle of his harness, his whole demeanour changed to guardian of Martina. He was no longer just a dog, he was now on duty. She offered her hand, "It was nice to finally meet you Nitra."

She took her hand and was quite surprised at the strength it had, "It was nice to meet you as well. Please don't take this the wrong way, but I have to say, you've opened my eyes to a portion of the population I had never considered before. On Monday, I'll tell my editor to have all my books recorded to tape. William won't like it, but I don't care. You're absolutely right. There is no real reason why I haven't done it before this. And somehow, I don't think you're my only blind fan."

"Visually challenged," Martina corrected. There was a long pause between them. Satisfied she'd made her point, she broke the silence, "Well, I must be going. Wallace where's my hug. I can't leave without my hug." She called him closer with her wiggling hands.

She didn't have to ask him twice, he scurried into her arms. "You take care and I'll see you on Wednesday night." To Nitra surprise he even gave her a peck on the cheek.

As she walked away, she quipped over her shoulder, "I'll be dressed in green and carrying something made of mutton. Ta-ta laddie boy." When she had reached the door, it was being held open by one of the restaurant's male patrons. She smiled and curtsied her thankfulness for his assistance in the direction of his voice. As she walked down the steps towards the side walk, Nitra was amazed at the site of the elderly man ogling after her.

"Isn't she the greatest?" Wallace stood, watching after her too.

"Oh yah, she's bloody grand. Makes me want to grow testicles just so I can enjoy her even more." She snapped up her tote bag and grimaced at the site of it with a grunt.

That's when Wallace realized what she had said, "Oh good Lord Girl! You can't be jealous of that sweet thing? I mean, she is beautiful, not to mention the fact that she as smart as the heaven's themselves, but she's nothing compar..." and that's when he stopped himself. It had almost slipped out. That would have been disastrous. He quickly changed the subject, "So short stuff, who's paying for the coffee and pie?" He ruffled her hair with his fingers. He knew *that* would distract her for sure.

She jerked her head away from him, "You are, you big lummox!" She poked him in the stomach and raced for the door in a hell of a hurry. And that suited Wallace just fine. For the mere price of two cups of coffee and pie à la mode, he escaped having to tell her what he really wanted to say about her.

Out at the car Nitra waited for him. She knew damned well what he was going to say and was relieved he'd changed the subject. She was in no frame of mind to deal with that situation right then. Today, she simply wanted to get her pages back. Especially page number one. Without it, she couldn't go any further with the book. It was the one thing blocking her from going forward with the book. Oh, the other pages were important too, but without the first page, they nearly meant nothing.

The sound of rattling keys got there before he did, "So where to now?"

"Nowhere in particular. Do you need to run any errands while we're in town? I mean, we're already here and everything." Essentially, she was trying to persuade him to stay in town so she could go to the stationary store to place an order for her customized writing paper. The truth was, she preferred to order it in person rather than over the phone, so the order didn't get messed up like last year.

"Well, I do need to get some spices and such from the health food store." He knew what she wanted, "I guess I could pick them up today instead of the 'morrow." He bounced his finger on his chin, "Um ... this works a wee better for us. This way I can get my cookin' stuffs and ya can place your order for that paper ya like so much." He smirked as he tilted his head to tease her.

107

Within a heartbeat, his whole demeanour changed when he saw that it was still there. He said nothing to her of what he saw, but decided that it was urgent that they get out of there immediately.

Stunned and slightly insulted, she snapped shut her gaping mouth before mentally cursing him out inside her head. In a counter defiance, she tapped on the car door and barked at him, "Well then, let's get going then, time's a wasting."

Instead of unlocking her door as he usually did, he went to his side of the car, unlocked his door and reached across the front seat to let her in. He turned the key and slipped the car into gear even before she had a chance to buckle herself up. He shifted again, "Hang on to your knickers sunshine – time's a wastin'." With that he floored it.

Her neck whipped back, "Holy crap! Take it easy!"

When he reached the corner, he shift the gears to slow the sports car down, "Don't be worrin', we'll be there soon." Wallace glanced over his shoulder. It was as he feared, it was still there. His instincts pushed into high gear. He slowed down even further to merge into the heavier traffic flow then accelerated to match it. Seconds later, he began to weave through the cars from lane to lane, narrowly missing the bumper of a pickup truck. His hands white on the steering wheel, with the strength of his grip.

"Okay, that's enough! Slow down right now!" she commanded by hammering her thigh with her fist. "You're going to kill us!"

His words were half joking, half warning, "Not if she catches us first." He shifted again, jolting the car to a higher speed yet.

Pulling herself forward in the seat, she asked, "What are you talking about?" She studied his face closely, what she observed frightened her. His eyes held panic, an emotion Wallace never allowed himself to feel. Straight away she saw that Wallace was concentrating more on the mirror than he was on the highway ahead. She calmed her nerves, "Wallace, what is it? What's wrong?" Her guts tightened even before he responded to her question.

"Three cars back. It's a grey sedan." Saying the words invoke the need for urgency. Pressing heavily on the accelerator, he raced the car toward the front wheels of a transport truck. It one quick crank on the steering wheel, he slipped the sports car between it and the tiny car ahead of it, then quickly slowed the car down to hide behind massive trucks body. He knew it was time to tell her, "It's been followin' us since Gladys's. Hold on Lass, it's time to do a brake away."

In her tightening gut, she had to know. She twisted in her seat to peer through the tiny back window. "Do you think it's her?" He didn't answer; he was concentrating on the spacing of the vehicles surrounding them. From where they were situated, she couldn't see the car Wallace was referring to. Suddenly a gap opened in the traffic, the space was narrow, but Wallace was confident that he could squeeze the car into it. Without warning, Wallace swerved out from behind the transport, slipping into it. She gasped at what she had seen. She twisted her body in the opposite direction, jamming her face in the upper outer corner of the window. There, no more than three cars back, was the same grey sedan that she had seen the day before. With eyes narrowed, Nitra focussed on the driver, but her line of vision was severed when Wallace steered the car in another slot just ahead of a delivery van. Instantly angered by the lane change, she screamed at him, "God damn it, pull back out, I need to see her face." Banging on the window with

109

her opened hand, "I mean it Wallace! Pull out where I can see her! I want to see her!"

Even though she was hysterically yelling and beating on the little rear window, he stayed right where he was, the car hidden out of sight. He had to ignore her demands. His main focus was on the next highway exit. Understanding that they had to speed across two lanes of heavy traffic in less than a half mile, he yelled his warning over her persistent screams, "Grab onto somethin' Lass, we're gonna move fast."

Before she could turn around in the seat to grab the door handle, he shifted hard and swerved into the next lane, hammering her body against the hard steel door. "Holy fuck! Are you trying to kill me?"

"No, I'm tryin' to save ya. Now latch on steady Girly. We're not done yet." He floored it, pushing the car even harder, forcing it pass the next car, putting his car next to an open space in that lane. With one sharp crank on the steering wheel, the car jolted into the narrow space. But he didn't stop there; he stomped on the gas, thrusting it through to the other side of it, ending up in the outside lane. With the exit no more than 200 yards away, Wallace did the unthinkable; he slammed on the brakes creating havoc with the vehicles around him. Through her own shocked reaction, Nitra heard the split second sound of squealing tires. Turning around in her seat, she witnessed cars veering around each other while others spun out in the ditch, clouds of dust blasted into the air as they halted. She ignored the chaotic mayhem, instead focussed her attention on the one thing she wanted to see — the face driving of the grey sedan. As Wallace sped down the off ramp, Nitra caught a brief yet blurry glimpse of its driver. Nitra noted one thing she could see; the driver was wearing

110

the most ghastly shade of red lipstick. Then within a blink, it was retreating as Wallace raced up the side road as fast as the little car would fly. She watched the sedan turn into a grey speck as the sped away.

At first her heart sank with disappointment, but was quickly replace with anger. "God damn it! I missed her! I didn't get to see her! All I wanted was to see her face so I'd know who the hell she was!" She punched his arm with a knotted fist, "And it's all your fault. You … you …" In frustration she let out a deafening primeval grunt, *"RRRRR! AAAAH!"* She sat in the seat angrily huffing out lungs full of air and bitterly chastised him through clinched teeth. "I had one chance," she jammed a single finger towards his face, nearly piercing his cheek, "One fuckin' chance to see who the fuck she was and you blew it." She punched him hard in the chest. "I fuckin' hate you!"

Wallace scrunched up tight against the door trying to avoid another hard hammering fist, "Hey, don't be hittin' me while I'm drivin'." Knowing Nitra's temperament; he gradually applied the brakes, slowing down the car until he pulled it over to a dead stop on the shoulder. He shifted the car into park, but left the motor running in case the sedan returned.

That's when Nitra exploded. She swung at him again, both her fists pummelled him over and over. Her voice shrieked at full volume, "Why did you do that? You fuckin' Irish idiot. I wanted to see her face." She took one more swing at his head.

This time he didn't hold up his arms as a shield, but instead grabbed her wrist and gingerly bent it down. "That's enough. Ya stop hittin' me now." He gentle guided her hand back towards her lap, "Now, ya be gettin' a hold of yourself Girl."

111

That's when she lost it. Her adrenaline rush took hold of her. She flung her arms wildly over her head while her feet stomped on the floor making the car jostle in spot. She screamed at him even louder, "Get a hold of myself! Fuck, you drive me crazy! How am I to get a hold of myself with that lunatic out there?" She went to swing at him again, but he stopped her with a *'don't you dare'* look. "She's out there and because of you, I don't know what she looks like. I don't know who she is!" She jabbed her thigh, "Now I have no idea if she's just a curious fan or another raving lunatic like Larson. What if she's dangerous, like him? What if she's got a fuckin' gun? What if she's …" Her loud out of control fit abruptly turned inward. Her hands trembled as she knotted them together in a tight ball on her lap. Her shoulders slumped forward while she lowered her head. Wallace watched her switch from irrational, to a mere lump of trembling fear. She said nothing. She was concentrating on not crying.

Wallace waited, unsure of what to expect next. When he saw her shoulders quiver, he knew what was happening. Carefully he reached across to her, placing his hand softly on her shoulder, "Nitra, she's gone. And that's all we need to worry about right now." He rubbed her back up and down to comfort her. With his hand touching her, she knew she was safe at that moment and released her tears. All of her fears came rushing out in one huge tidal wave. Her body shook hard with each sob. He pulled her into his body, surrounding her with his strong arms, "Oh Girl, let it out. Wally's got ya. There's no one else here. It's time to stop being brave and let it go." She buried her face into his chest and clung onto him tight. The earthy erotic scent of leather instantly filled her nostrils. She closed her eyes and listened to Wallace's heart throbbing in his chest.

112

It throbbed for her. It was all he could do to not pull her face upward, look into her green eyes and kiss her hard on her soft lips. He fought the urge to take their embrace further, to caress every inch of her sensual body. His finger tips ached to touch her soft feminine skin. He reprimanded himself. To take advantage of her in her weakened state was unthinkable. Instead, he awkwardly held her loosely so there was no misunderstanding of his intensions. There they sat, waiting for her to stopped crying. For him, it took an eternity.

Relief came in the form of a police car. It was Harry Palmer who pulled in behind Wallace's car. He jumped out of the cruiser and rushed to Wallace's door. All in time to witness Nitra pulling herself out of Wallace's arms and straighten up. She turned her face away to wipe her tears. Harry thought otherwise, "Oh, sorry folks, I didn't mean to disturb your … um …well, you know."

"No, I don't know. What are ya sayin' there Harry?" he frowned at him, "Nitra's shook up over what just happened and I was simply consoling her. Nothin' else is happenin' here. Ya got that officer."

Harry took notice that Wallace was protesting a little too much, which to a cops mind, it meant the exact opposite. That theory was squashed when Nitra loudly blew her nose and pulled out another tissue to wipe her eyes again. "Yah, I heard about that. I knew it was you when they mentioned a foreign sports car. Quite the little mess you left back there. Legally, I should charge you with hit and run."

"Now just a minute, I didn't hit a damned thing. I just applied my breaks rather quickly." He turned off the motor and shot a *'don't say a word'* look at Nitra.

Harry chuckled at him, "Relax, I'm not pressing charges … yet. But do you want to tell me what the hell that was all about?"

"Did anyone get hurt?" Nitra finally spoke, "Please tell me everyone's all right?" She pulled out another tissue, "It's all my fault. The *Lipstick Lady* was following me again and Wallace was trying to get me away from her." Nitra started to cry again, this time quietly to herself.

As a cop, Harry had become familiar with weeping women and simply continued with his questions, "Lipstick Lady? Who's that?" He was looking to Wallace for the answer.

"She's the driver of the grey sedan. We've nicknamed her the Lipstick Lady because she wears bright red lipstick."

"Yah, really ugly red lipstick." Nitra interjected through a muffled tissue. "It's that orange red that was popular in the early 80's." She blew her nose again before she added her theory, "That might mean she's in her forties."

Harry nodded his agreement, "Sounds right."

"Now how in the hell do ya know that?" Wallace's face showed his disbelief at their skills of deduction.

"Simple. Most women will continue to wear the same style and colour of makeup that they wore in high school or their early twenties. An unfortunate age confessing blunder, but yet a fact." She poked her head around Wallace, inviting Harry to finish the explanation.

"So if she's wearing the same lipstick that she wore back then, twenty year ago, and it's the colour of the early 80's that might put her in her forties." Wallace's face revealed that he grasped the logic of the theory making Harry smirk at his own brilliance, "So, did you get to see her? Do you recognise her Nitra?"

Wallace rolled his eyes at him. That was the wrong question to ask. In fact Wallace squished against the door just in case she exploded again.

"No." was all she said. She shifted in her seat, but nothing else. "Did you? She must have been in with the rest of the vehicles."

"Negative on that Miss." Then a grin lit up his eyes, "You mean you went through all of that and neither of you saw her." Harry started to laugh, "Well ain't that a hoot! Wait 'til the boys hear about this. Two rear ended cars, along with a transport ditched and you didn't see a damned thing. Christ that's funny." The radio in his cruiser crackled out a long sentence of inaudible words. "Oh Christ, gotta go. Wallace, I'll expect you to come down to the station and fill out a report. Mostly to keep the insurance companies happy. I'll help you with the details so you don't hang yourself." He turned to leave, but bend over with a firm smile, "And Wallace, no more car chases or I *will* press charges, for this one and any others you're involved in."

Wallace nodded that he understood the warning.

From the far side of the car Harry heard Nitra's timid voice, "It's my fault Harry and I promise I won't let him do that again. I swear." She actually lifted her hand in oath as she said it. "And we're going home right now so we won't cause any more trouble. Right Wallace?"

Again, he nodded in agreement, "Home it is. I'll be in tomorrow around noon. Would it be okay if I bring some cinnamon buns?" He avoided looking Harry in the eyes; it would have been too obvious that he was bribing him with fresh baked sweets.

He smacked his mouth in anticipation of the sticky icing, "Noon. Yah ... that'll work for me." Harry knocked twice on the side of Wallace's door before leaving for the cruiser, a thing cops did to signal all was clear.

They both watched in their mirrors until Harry was in his cruiser and pulling away. That's when Nitra chuckled at Wallace, "Cinnamon buns? Why you cheap hussy you ... toying with that man's deepest desires. Shame on you."

"That's the smile I like to see." He turned the ignition on and shifted into gear, "Feeling better are ya?"

"Yah, I'm better." She cleared her throat, "And I'm sorry for hitting you. It's just that I'm so damned ..."

He broke in, "Scared out of your bloody mind." He watched her woefully nod as he turned a corner, "Here's a clue for ya Miss Detective, I weren't runnin' from the Lipstick Lady 'cause I was feelin' all safe and secure myself. I'm scared witless too. Witless enough to put other people's lives in jeopardy just so we could get away from that woman."

"Wait, you're scared too?" Her eyes focused on his face.

"I am now." He flicked on the signal to turn down the road to the house. "Well to be truly honest, I weren't too worried until today. But when I saw her car outside the restaurant, it finally sunk into my thick scull that the lady meant business. She scared the hell out of me, right there and then."

She squirmed in her seat, "Why now and not before?"

"Before, you happened to run across her path, but this time she was waiting for you." He shift gears to get up the hill without slowing down, "Nitra, she wasn't there when we arrived. She showed up right after we got there."

She crossed her arms in judgement, "Now how in the hell do you know that? You were sitting with me the whole time."

116

"Not true. Remember when I got up to greet Martina at the door? That's when I saw the grey sedan parked across the street. Meaning, she followed us there."

"Ah ha! So she *is* following me. I knew it! I knew it!" She wiggled victoriously in her seat.

"Well, don't sound so pleased with yourself Lass, she's still bloody following you." He pulled the car up to the kitchen door, "Wait in here while I look around a wee bit." He reached across and locked her door. "And stay put." He locked his door before he closed it behind him.

She watched him visually scan the yard, paying close attention to the bushes adjacent to the house itself. Then he rummage through the garage and garden shed, leaving a light on in each building. Next, he searched through the house. She fidgeted in her seat, but kept an eye on her surroundings. Her head was turned around to look out the back of the car when Wallace tapped on her window, scaring her half to death. He motioned with his fingers to unlock the door and follow him into the house. He walked directly alongside her, prepared for anything the *Lipstick Lady* might throw their way. Once inside the house, he flicked the upper lock and slid the latch tight. That sound brought back memories for Nitra. It was a reminder of the night Larson tried to attack her.

"Well, here we are all safe and sound. Now don't leave my sight." He pointed his index finger at her, "That's an order."

She was in no mood to argue, "Try and shake me tough guy." She hooked her finger with his, interlocking them together, "I'm sticking to you like glue."

"Great, first things first. I need to get the chicken in the oven for supper. Follow me." He headed up the staircase and got to the fourth step before she stopped him.

117

"Um … where are you going? The oven's that way," her body was half twisted towards the stove. "Why are you going upstairs?"

"Because I need to get out of these street clothes so I can change into some working clothes. So come on then." He continued up the stairs fully expecting her to follow him.

She stood at the base of the stairs, watching his body as it ascended each step. At that moment she realized that she was going to have to be in the same room as him while he changed. "Now, wait just a damned minute. There's no way I'm watching you change your clothes. I have my limits, you know?"

"Don't care. Close your eyes if my body offends you that much. But you're coming in the room with me and that would be now." He opened the door to his bedroom.

She slowly climbed the steps. "Okay, I'm here. Where do you want me to sit?" She stopped dead in her tracks. Before her stood Wallace, his shirt unbuttoned exposing his muscular chest. She swallowed hard at the site.

"On the bed." He watched her eyes grow the size of walnuts and quickly added, "'cause everythin' else is loaded down. I've been clearin' out my old stuff for the rummage sale." He slipped his shirt off his square shoulders and hung it over the back of a crowded chair, "Next week at that Irish hall." Suddenly he became very aware of her eyes on his body. His face flushed pink with the thoughts of her craving him the way he hungered for her.

She pulled her eyes off him and scurried across the room. She carefully sat on the very edge of his mattress. Climbing fully onto its top would create a temptation that simply must be avoided. She shut her eyes, "Okay, my eyes are closed."

It made him turn around. There she was, sitting on his bed with her eyes closed. She looked like she was waiting to be kissed — kissed hard and long. He quietly inhaled a deep breath to control the urge to do so.

What he didn't know was that she was peeking through her left eye. She saw him watching her. She saw him clinch his hands in sexual frustration. She watched him collect himself together and continue to undress. He unzipped his jeans and let them drop down to the floor. Her blood thundered at the sight of his thick muscular thighs and hard taught shoulders. It was all she could do to stay sitting on the bed's edge without sliding off due to her weakened knees. Thinking it was best; she shut both her eyes tight to disconnect the visual temptation. Then she struggled to say something – anything – intelligent to ease the silent tension between them, "So um ... what's for dinner?"

"Chicken." Equally as nervous, he answered her immediately, but was too anxious to add anything to the conversation. He left the talking to her, so he could cover his naked body as fast as possible.

Secretly, she was taking in the essence of Wallace through the surrounding bedroom. She deeply, yet quietly, inhaled the scent of him. It made the core of her body ache. She clinched the edge of the mattress, trying to control the urge to jump into his arms and devour every inch of his naked flesh. Releasing her hands, she lightly stroked the cottony texture of his duvet with her fingertips. It felt sensual, soft and inviting. An image of them tangled together on its top, flashed through her mind. She let it linger, taking pleasure in the fantasy. Indulging herself more than she should have, she nearly let out a low moan. Catching herself in time, she instead cleared her throat, "Chicken, huh? What else are we having?" Inaudibly she

119

blew out the tension she was holding in her fluttering stomach.

"Green beans and maybe roasted potatoes." He slipped his other foot into his older faded jeans.

She heard his zipper go up. It was a relief and a disappointment to hear that sound. Relieved that she was safe from his tempting naked body, yet saddened that she could no longer peek at its well built profile. He was fumbling with a deep blue t-shirt, trying to find the neck opening. Again, she diverted the situation back to dinner, "Do mean the kind with fresh rosemary and hunks of garlic. Mmm, I love you." She popped her eyes open with shock and motioned a halt with her hands, "No, no. I mean, I love *those* ... *those* potatoes. The ones made with the olive oil, garlic and herbs." Again her eyes were confronted with his half clad body. But it was his expression that turned her face deep ruby red. It was the *'deer caught in the headlights'* expression — frozen and bewildered by a horrible encounter. Then his eyes changed. Tenderness gleamed within his brown eyes, he was love struck.

Inside her head, frantic questions swirled wildly. What if he was to follow through on what his face was conveying? How should she react? Could she avoid this situation without hurting his feelings? Better yet, did she actually want to escape from him? She still hadn't decided precisely how she felt about Wallace. She stood up from his mattress.

He took two hesitant steps forward, but stopped, unsure of what to do next.

Her heart pound hard beneath her breasts. She wanted to say something insightful to halt him from advancing, but no words came to her mind.

Without warning the phone rang downstairs in the kitchen. One ring, second ring, third ring, then the machine cut in. Wallace's monotone voice bellowed through the house, "Thank ya for callin' but we're not on hand right now. Please leave a message and we'll get back to ya in a wee bit."

"Hello? Um … this is Tom … Tom Harper. Oh … ah … this message is for Nitra. I was kinda hoping to hear from you by now. I guess you're busy and all. Anyway, you've got my business card so you know how to get a hold of me. And like I said the other day, I wouldn't mind us getting together and searching for those pages of yours … or … ah … maybe dinner. I mean, if you can find the time, that is. Anyway, I hope to hear from you soon." There was a brief silent pause, "Bye." The machine clicked, declaring the recording had ended.

The t-shirt in his hand dropped limply to the floor. He lowered his head in despair. For a moment, he didn't move, standing stone cold solid with the pain.

Her face showed her anguish at his pain as she sat back down on his mattress. She managed to form a few words, "Wallace, I don't …"

He didn't let her finish, instead he snatched up his t-shirt and bolted down the stairs.

"No! Wait! You didn't let me finish. I was trying to say …" But by then he was gone. Exasperated by his leaving in a huff, she flung her arms up into the air and flopped backwards onto his bed, "God damned idiot!" She lay there for a few minutes, numb with all the emotions she held inside. "Yep, that's what I am, a God damned idiot." She heard the sound of him beginning supper preparations. He was hammering at something with a knife, making it *thwack* hard against the wooden cutting board. She sat upright, ringing her hands in her lap, "How am I going to smooth this one over?" She let out an enormous sigh, "Just like I always

121

do … avoidance." Normally, she'd lock herself away in her writing room and soon all would be forgotten, but she knew that wouldn't work this time. She had to stay in the same room as him for protection. "Well, here we go." She pushed herself to her feet and wrenched with the pain in her lower back, "Oh shit!" She was caught between halfway down and halfway up. She braced her knees and waited for the spike of pain to subside. In the minutes it took, she mentally cursed both Harry and Larson to hell with all its fiery glory. Finally, the pain eased up enough that she could straighten up and walking with a limp, she slowly made her way down the stairs, step by step. With each step she took, she wondered what mood Wallace would be in, when she got there. What she needed, was a double dose of painkillers. What she hoped for was placid harmony.

Chapter Seven

There he was, standing at the counter, cutting up a whole chicken into pieces. He swung the knife with such force that Nitra wondered if she should turn around and go back up the stairs. Her back told her otherwise. Climbing the stairs would be painful and pointless, she'd have to come down and face him eventually anyway, so why not now. She stood at the bottom of the steps, waiting for an opportune moment to connect with Wallace. She watched as he added the chicken pieces to a flat roasting pan. That was the moment, and she knew just what to say. "Can I help?"

He didn't answer right away. He was still hurting inside. Then he changed his mind. He too, knew that they'd have to make peace again. "Yah, ya can help with the chicken and the potatoes." He stepped aside to make room for her at the counter. "Wash your hands first. Then I'll show ya what to do." She did as she was told and stood beside him waiting for further instructions. "First, ya take that bowl and put in a big gob of butter." She plunked in about a tablespoon of soft butter. "No Lass, a big gob, like this." He added enough butter that it tripled in size. "There, that's better." With his well-developed forearm, he swept four large spice jars her way. "Now put a teaspoon of each one into the bowl." She reached for the drawer that the measuring spoons usually sat in, but was stopped as soon as her fingers touched the handle. "What are ya doin'? I mean, besides makin' more dishes for me to wash." Gemma meowed at his feet, hoping for a nibble of human food, but Wallace nudged her away with a gentle push of his foot.

She shook the oregano at him, "I'm measuring out the spices, like you said I should."

"No Girl, not like that." He quickly washed his hands before he loosened the lid of the parsley jar. "Ya pour it into your palm 'til it gets this big. That's a teaspoon. Three times that size gives ya a tablespoon. For a girl, ya don't know much about cookin'." He rubbed the herbs in his palm. "That releases their oils for a richer flavour." He tossed the green flakes on top of the butter.

That could have been insulting to Nitra, yet in a way it was the truth, so she decided to let it go and tease him ruthlessly instead. "So teach me, oh Kitchen Wizard." She mockingly bowed to him with a smirk that lit up her eyes. "So I may become as wise as you, oh Kitchen Wizard." Again she bowed sardonically.

He harrumphed at her, "Lord, that'd take a life time and a half."

"So we should get started right away then." She batted her eyes at him, but abruptly stopped herself. She instantly began to ponder how many times she had performed the same flirtatious act without realizing the consequences of it. No wonder the poor boy was confused. In its place, she substituted the eye fluttering with a drawn out childish whine, "Pleeeeease?"

He pushed the jars closer, signalling to get on with it and went back to scrubbing the potatoes. She added the remaining garlic powder and marjoram. "Okay, now salt and pepper." He watched for the right amounts, "Not too much salt. It's no good for my blood pressure."

She peered at him sideways, "Are you having blood pressure problems?"

"I work for ya, don't I?" She chuckled along with him, he dried his hands and rolled a lemon across the counter, "Now take that spoon and whip the daylights out of it while I add the juice of this lemon." First, he tossed in the freshly grated zest and then poured in its juice.

She couldn't believe her eyes, "But this is butter. You can't mix a liquid with a fat. They won't blend."

"Oh hush up and keep mixin' it" He went back to drying his potatoes with a towel while she continued to take out her aggression on the butter.

"While I'll be damned. It *did* work." She didn't know whether to be pleased with him or with herself, but she was pleased just the same. "Okay, what's next?"

"Oh, now comes the fun part. Ya rub the butter all over those chicken pieces." He quartered the potatoes and let them fall into a large casserole dish.

Nitra daintily picked up a thigh and smoothed on a small amount of butter with the back of the spoon. Wallace laughed at her. She stopped what she was doing, "What so damned hilarious?"

"Ya are Pet!" He washed his hands was liquid soap and water, then wiped his hands on a towel, "No Girly, like this." He reached into the bowl and scooped out a large glob of the butter mixture with his fingers. Next he picked

125

up a breast and slathered every inch of it. "Ya know ya can jump right in anytime ya like."

By the expression on her face, she was in no hurry. After a sarcastic look her way, she pushed up her sleeves. With reservations, she scooped up her own mound of butter and proceeded to massage it into a thigh. At first she was gentle, but as she became more comfortable with the greasy texture, she rubbed the aromatic butter into every nook and cranny using up every last bit of butter. "All done. Now what?"

"Well, you've been touchin' raw poultry, so go wash your hands with hot water and plenty of soap like I did." Next, he set up the ingredients for the potatoes.

She wiped her hands on a fresh towel, "Okay. What's now?"

"Well, for starters ya can stop using up my last two clean towels. I still got the dishes to do later, ya know." He slid the potato filled casserole dish in front of her. "Okay, time to make those potatoes ya love so much." He lowered his eyes as he said it, trying to hide his lingering feelings of what had been said. "Add about three tablespoons of olive oil, all over the top." He watched in absolute amazement as she held out her palm to measure the oil, "Oh Christ. No child, like this." He took the bottle from her and poured as he counted, "One, two, three. There that's a tablespoon. Now you add the rest." She mimicked his moves exactly, drizzling oil directly over the potato chunks, returning the cap to the bottle.

"Fine job Lass. Now ya be adding one teaspoon of each of those herbs." He pointed with the tip of his knife. He was chopping garlic ... a lot of garlic.

She read them out loud as she did it, "Rosemary." She inhaled its earthy evergreen scent. "Yum. Oregano." She smelt it right from the jar before adding onto the oil. "Basil. Why am I suddenly craving pasta with pesto sauce?" It wasn't a question, just an observation. "And parsley. It seems like you put parsley in everything."

"Almost, but I draw the line at me cup of tea. Now make way." He scooped up the garlic and tossed it in. "Now churn it up with your hands. And take care to coat every one of them completely. If ya don't, they won't crisp up."

Again, she shoved up her sleeves and dived right in. She tossed and mixed while he slid the chicken into the oven. He pulled the pan right out from under her hands and pushed it in beside the first one.

"There, that's that." He slammed the oven door tight. "It'll be ready in one hour. Time for a wee lie-down." He headed for the living room.

"Um … aren't you forgetting something?" She stood at the sink washing the oil from her hands. The scent of the heated herbs filled her nostril, which in turn, made her mouth water and her stomach grumble.

"What now?" He turned on his heels, "Look it's been a tryin' day and I need a wee nap if I'm goin' to make it through the night." He clinched his hands in a pleading knot and shook them at her. "Just thirty bloody minutes. Do ya think ya can stay out of trouble for thirty minutes?"

That hit a sore spot, "Me? Stay out of trouble?" She poked her chest with her finger, "Oh, brother that does it." Then she turned the dreaded pointing finger on him and shook it like a nun in the school yard. "Now just a God damned minute! This is not my fault. I didn't ask the *Lipstick Lady* to hound me. She did that on her own. And I still don't know why the hell she is chasing me. Or who the hell she is." She stamped her foot to emphasize her annoyance, "This is not my fault." She watched as his face cracked a

127

slight smile. "Oh, screw you." She stomped pass him and headed for her writing room, where she slammed the door with a picture rattling THWACK.

He stood in the doorway and watched the performance with a grin. "Well, that worked out just the way I wanted." He stretched his arms above his head. With her out of the way and safely locked in her writing room, he strolled to the sofa. He leisurely spread the woven throw over his long legs and fluffed the cushion under his head. Within minutes he was wheezing with deep sleep.

She could hear him from inside her room. It was exactly what she was hoping for. Then she cursed herself, her tote was hanging by the kitchen door. In her anger, she hadn't brought it with her. While she searched through the phone book for the number, she once again reminded herself to exchange her tote for another purse. Her finger ran down the list of names, stopping at Tom Harper – *Antique Restorations*. After scribbling the number on the front cover, she cracked the door open and listened to make sure he was truly asleep. Gemma slipped in the thin opening and purred by her desk. When Nitra sat down, the cat jumped up into her lap, as she nervously dialled the numbers on her old rotary phone. It rang. One ring, two rings, three rings. His answering machine kicked in, *"Hi you've reached Tom Harper's Restorations. I'm probably up to my elbows in lacquer right now, so please leave a message and I'll call you back when my hands aren't sticky or dirty."* It was followed by the usual beep.

At first she panicked a little, but she pushed herself through it, "Hi Tom, this is Nitra. I got your message and yes I would like to go hunting for pages with you. But I'll have to make it next week when things settle down around here. I'll give you a call later in the week to make plans. Sorry I

128

missed you. Bye." She quickly hung up the phone and blew out the tension in her thumping chest. Suddenly, a loud thud boomed from the living room, followed by a low guttural moan. Gemma jumped down off her warm cozy perch and waited by the door for her to open it. Nitra raced into the room, stopped short, erupting into laughter. Wallace had apparently fallen off the sofa. When she got there, his butt was stuck up in the air and his face was pressed into the hand woven area rug.

He slowly pushed himself up to his knees and scoffed at her, "What are ya laughin' about? It's all your bloody fault."

She stopped laughing long enough to question his statement, "My fault? How can it be my fault? You're the one on your face."

"I was dreamin' of you bein' chased by the bloody Lipstick Lady, that's how." He struggled to get to his feet. "I was pullin' her off ya when I fell off the ..." His words trailed off as the phone rang. Instinctively they both waited for the answering machine to kick in. The message as before echoed through the house. Mentally, Nitra prayed it wasn't Tom returning her call. That was the last thing she wanted Wallace to hear.

After the beep, a heavy accent blurted out, "Hi my name is Gina and I have some of your pages. You can reach me here where I work, *The Wharf*. We're open from five to five everyday of the week. I've got four pages here. If you want them, come and get them." There was a buzzing sound in the background, "See ya, bye."

Then there was another buzzer. This time it was the oven announcing that the chicken was done to perfection. Not that they needed to be told. The fragrance of roasted chicken mingled with the lemon and herbs, wafted through the entire house. He rubbed his forehead, the pain was back. "Okay Girly, are ya ready for more lessons?"

"But I thought we already cooked supper? There's more to this meal? What else could we possibly need? How about the green beans you said we were having? No wait, it's a salad, right?" She kept it down to only five short questions this time.

"Well yes, a salad would be grand, but I was speaking more about the fine art of presentation." He held the kitchen door open for her, "It's more important than ya can imagine." He headed straight for the china cabinet and took out four platters, one bright yellow, one deep red, one a pale green and the last one, a brilliant blue. "Now, I'm goin' to show ya how colours influence your desire to eat." He pulled both dishes from the oven and began the lesson. He placed two pieces of chicken on each platter. "So which plate looks the most appealing to ya?"

Nitra examined them closely. To her, the pale green made the skin appear pasty and under roasted. The Mediterranean blue enhanced the brownness of each piece. And to her surprise the bright yellow evoked a sense of summertime barbeque, yet it didn't match the flavours of the chicken. Her mouth and her eyes confused each other. It was the deep red that brought out the best of everything. The roasted skin seemed browner, while the golden undertones shone through. Even the flecks of green herbs appeared more vibrant. "The red is the best. It looks fiery, almost festive, like I should join the party and eat it at once." She tried to pick at its skin with her finger tips, but motherly Wallace swatted her hand away.

"Very good choice Lass. Now to 'present' this fine feast." He carefully arranged the chicken pieces so that they formed a crescent shape around the outside. On the other half, he poured the potatoes into a circular mound. Then he carefully turned several of the potato chunks so that they showed their best roasted side. Even the chicken pieces got a final adjustment. Lastly, he sprinkled a palm full of fresh chopped parsley over the top, adding that bright touch of herbal green. "There. Do ya see what a wee time and effort can produce? Fit for a king … or in this case, a queen." He bowed a sweeping hand towards the table, "Your majesty."

She curtsied in return, "Why thank you, Sir Kitchen Wizard."

"Oh, I've been raised to knighthood, have I? I'm honoured."

"Don't flatter yourself. It's merely the pungency of the chicken that's going to my head." She laid the back of her hand across her forehead, "That's why I'm fading from hunger."

He stacked the dishes for the table and handed them to her, "Here. Ya set the table and I'll find us a good bottle of wine." He was gone down the stairs before she could protest at being left by herself again.

Placing the last fork in place, she headed for the china cabinet. There in the corner were two fine cut crystal white wine glasses. She had bought them in Germany during her whirl wind European tour. Sixteen signings in seven days was exhausting. She selected those two, carefully placing them above and to the right of each plate.

He stopped dead at the table, "Um … ya can't use those glasses. It's not right to use those glasses."

"But I thought they'd be nice. I know there a little extravagant, but why not? We only live once and tonight I'd like to live a little." She stopped her foot from stomping on the floor in objection.

131

It was obvious that she had her heart set on using those particular glasses yet he persisted on, "No, it's not right."

"Why not? They're my glasses and my choice." She plunked down hard in her chair as a form of protest at his stubbornness.

"No dear, you don't understand what I'm tellin' ya. They won't work 'cause this is a red wine, not white." He held the bottle up higher while pointing to the label. "We're out of white, so red it'll have to be."

"Oh," was all she said at first. Then she added, "So who cares if we serve red wine in white wine glasses? Who's going to know? And if they did, would you give a damn? Are the 'wine glass police' coming to take us away? I mean, won't it taste the same? Are you that particular about what you drink what out of? Have you always been this way?"

"Okay, okay. We'll use these glasses. Red in white it is" She came close to breaking her record of consecutive questions so he thought it best to give in now instead of having her continuing on and on.

While he uncorked the bottle, she made a quick salad of hand torn lettuce topped with chunks of cucumber and tomatoes. He poured the wine while she tossed in the vinaigrette. They were working together in such unison that she wondered if it could be like that all the time. Could Wallace McPhee be the man she'd been looking for all these years? Once again, she disciplined herself in her head, *Stop it, stop it, stop it*. She sat herself down in her chair and forced herself to concentrate on the meal.

Wallace poured the wine and sat down himself. He served them both and watched as Nitra immediately dove into the crispy yet moist chicken. Through a mouthful she moaned her approval, "Mmm … Wallace this is fabulous. I can't believe something so simple to make, is so damned delicious." She sliced a potato quarter into smaller chunks. "You know, you should write a cookbook. I know people who'd love to make this type of food, but have no idea it's so damned easy to prepare." She stuffed another chunk of potato in her mouth and grinned with delight at its tastiness.

"Ya mean ... people like you?" He sipped from his glass as a sign of smugness.

She ignored the jab. "No, I mean it. You'd sell hundreds of copies. And I do have a few connections that could help you with the publishing and distributions. All you need to do is to write them all down in a book." Another chunk popped in her mouth, shutting her up long enough for him to finally answer.

"Ya mean like the one that's on that shelf over there." He pointed to it with his fork, "It's loads beat up, but that's because it's been around for a lifetime or two."

"The brown leather one? How long have you been adding recipes in it? Are they all yours or do some of them belong to other people? Are they all Irish cuisine or are there different ethnic dishes in it too? How many do you have?" In went a fork full of salad.

He wasn't sure which question to answer first, but started with the silliest one. "Oh yah love, roasted lemon chicken with herbs is definitely a traditional Irish meal." He gave her a *'are you totally goofy?'* look. "I've been addin' recipes for over twenty-five years. That's when I started cookin' for a livin'. Most of them I've created on my own, but many are me Mums." A smile of pride slid across his face. This was no surprise to Nitra; Wallace had always been his mother's son. "Other recipes are ones that I ate at someone's home and I wanted to have for my collection. Oh and there must be over three hundred recipes in there

133

by now? More, if I wrote down all the ones roaming around in me head."

"A collection? I never thought of a cookbook in that manner ... but that's a good way to describe it." Again, the cat tried her luck with Nitra. Gemma rubbed her fur against her leg hoping for one tiny bit of food, but after being completely ignored, she padded off upstairs to sulk.

He noticed that she'd eaten all of her potatoes and offered her the red platter, when they heard the phone ring. They waited for the machine to kick in. The usual message annoyed them again, but this time the caller left no message and loudly hung up. Nitra was sure it wasn't Tom, she was sure he wouldn't have hung up so rudely. He was too much of a gentleman for that. But that left the remaining question ... who did call and hang up? By the look on Wallace's face, he was asking himself the same question. She was afraid of what he was thinking to himself, mostly because she was thinking it as well. She cleared her throat before asking it, "Do you think it was her? I mean, it's a possibility, right?" She took an extra big gulp of her wine.

"Now Lass, let's not be jumpin' to any conclusions. Might have been a wrong number?" He poured her another glass of wine, emptying the bottle. "We don't know for sure."

"But I know how we can find out. Do you still have that separate phone line in your bedroom?" She watched his mouth drop open. "Oh don't be like that, I've known about it for a long time now. Just answer the question. Do you still have a separate line?"

"What's that got to do with anything?" He was astonished that she figured that out. His room was off limits, as was hers to him, and he had it installed while she was on tour in New York.

"Because I can call Harry and have him trace it." He shrugged his shoulders at her, signaling that he didn't understand what she was going to say. "If we call Harry with my phone line, it will break the connection and he won't be able to trace it. Come on, I need to use your phone." As she rose from the table she saw the disappointed expression on Wallace's face. "What's wrong?"

He sheepishly revealed the dilemma, "I got rid of it last month."

"Damn it!" She threw her napkin on top of her plate.

Suddenly, he felt he had to defend himself. His voice went higher, "I wasn't using it. I'm always in this damned kitchen or about the yard, so I got rid of it. Why should I spend me hard earned money for something I never used?" He truly was Irish, frugal to the bone.

She blew out a heavy breath. "Okay, that's out of the question then." She began to pace around the kitchen with her glass in her hand. She stopped and took the last gulp of her wine. Seeing the empty bottom, she hoisting it into the air, "Is there any more?"

"I can get another bottle, if ya want." He was hoping she'd say yes. It had been a long day for him as well and the thoughts of a slightly numbing brain buzz seemed very inviting. He scurried down the stairs when she nodded a definite yes.

When he returned, he produced a much larger bottle than before. "1988 ... that was a good year for Canadian wine. This one's from the Niagara region in Ontario. Been wantin' to try it for awhile now." He stabbed the cork with the silver screw and twisted, "To bad ya can't see her number, then we'd know who the bloody blazes she is."

135

"That's it! Lord, I'm stupid sometimes." She ran to the phone and hit the call display button. Her heart sank when she saw it blink *blocked number.* "Damn it!" she slammed down the receiver.

He offered her another refill which she enthusiastically accepted. He slugged back the remaining bit of his first wine and poured another for himself. "So how is it?"

"Miserable." She hadn't been paying attention to his words. "What? Sorry, what did you say?"

"I was asking ya how ya liked the wine." He was trying to be patient, but she was making it very difficult. He watched her take another huge gulp from her glass. "Ya know you should slow down a wee bit before ya go getting' yourself crocked. Bein' bagged and belligerent ain't a good brew." His words started to echo his Irish accent. "Besides, as I recall, ya do tend have nightmares when ya drink a wee too much. And this evenin' is getting' long in the tooth."

That's when it hit her — bedtime. But that thought vanished from her mind the instant the phone rang again. It scared Nitra so much she jerked her wine glass, spilling most of it down the front of her white blouse. "Shit!" She pinched the wet clinging fabric away from her bosom.

He hurried to her side, "Quick, take it off." Her mouth gaped at him while her eyes grew wide with shock. "No, I don't mean that. Take it off before it stains. So I can rinse it out right away. Now shut up and listen." His message had finished and they waited for the caller's voice to cut in. But there was nothing, not a sound, only the clattering clack of someone hanging up.

"It's a regular phone not a cell phone. Do you know what that means? " She spun around and pointed into the darkness outside, "It means she's not out there, but somewhere else. She's in a building someplace else on a

136

regular phone." She exhaled a huge sigh. "And that means I'm safe."

"Yah, yah. Now get out of that shirt so I can wash it." He took the glass out of her hand and placed it on the counter, "Go. Go on. Do it now." He nagged at her like an Irish Mum on Sunday morning.

"Isn't it great? I can finally stop worrying. She's not outside watching me." She was half-way up the stairs when it dawned on her, "But what if you're right, what if it's not her calling. What if it is only a wrong number?" She stooped down to look pass the ceiling and out the kitchen window.

Two wrong numbers in one night? Wallace knew better, but he wasn't about to burst her relief by informing her of that fact. "No. Ya heard it clatterin'. She's somewhere else. Now go change that top." He shushed her further up the stairs with both hands.

While she was upstairs, he peeked outside the kitchen window, searching for any signs of her. There was nothing but long dark shadows from the outbuildings stretching across the driveway. He closed the curtains tightly. As he cleared the table and rinsed the dishes, an uneasy feeling settled in his gut. The two calls set off an alarm inside him. Something wasn't right. For the first time, Wallace was truly concerned for their safety. He knew he had to protect her and the best way to do that was by isolating her within his reach, something he'd learned in Ireland. He absentmindedly took out the big box of table salt from the cupboard, placed it on the counter. If the woman did attack, he'd be ready to kill her as he'd been train to do in his youth. He studied his strong clinched hands, reconfirming that he could, and would, kill for her. The difficulty was getting her to cooperate without Nitra actually knowing she was cooperating.

137

She came bouncing down the stairs, "You should call it, *My Cookbook for You – A Collection of My Life*."

"What?" He wasn't fully listening, but heard the words anyway. "Oh yah, that sounds great." He took the blouse from her, "I think we should get your pages first thing in the morning. I'll throw this into soak, and then I think its best we head up to bed. It's been one hell of a day and I'm tuckered right out. We both could use a good night's sleep." He didn't wait for a reply, he quickly snatched up the salt and disappeared into the next room.

And there it was, the one thing she was dreading, night time and the sleeping arrangements they hadn't made yet. Although she was terrified by the perplexing Lipstick Lady, in secret she was as equally terrified by the very man that lived under her roof. Earlier in the evening she was quite comfortable with the idea of sleeping alone safely locked in her room, him just across the hall in his bedroom. Or to even keep sleeping on the sofas like they had the night before. However, it was the second call that impressed upon her that she needed to have him closer than that. But wouldn't having Wallace so close, simply create more problems? She wasn't sure if it was worth having the added tension. When the eerie sound of the wind whipping through a tiny crack in the old kitchen window, giving a ghostly moan, she hastily made up her mind. The image of Larson's face flashed in her mind. Her heart began to thump as her chest tightened. She couldn't breathe, the air wouldn't come. The room narrowed in on her and slowly began to spin.

She was having an anxiety attack.

"Nitra Breathe!" Wallace was shaking her arm, "Come on Girl, breathe."

Instantly, she gulped a mouthful of air, then she choked on it. He rubbed her back while she inhaled short shallow amounts. Finally, she slowed it down to a regular rhythm.

"Oh, that be better. For a moment there Love, I thought you were goin' to kiss the floor." He gently shoved her towards a chair, "Here, sit down. I'll get ya some water." Through a mental fog, she watched as he slouched down to hand her a glass. "Wee sips now, like ya did before." He straightened up, "Lordy, ya were paler than white when I come down the stairs. What happened this time?" This was not the first attack she had suffered. In fact Wallace had lost count over the last year. Each one triggered by some unrelated insignificant event, but the result was always the same, Nitra turning white, sweaty and not breathing.

"Nothing." She watched the patch of floor in front of her, avoiding eye contact with him and confessed, "Wind blowing through the window. It made that *Ooooo* sound. It scared me." She lowered her head into her hands, "This is ridiculous. Now I'm scared of moving air."

"Cut yourself a break Lass. You're tired. You're stressed, not to mention that you've belted back almost a bottle of wine by yourself! It's completely understandable. What ya need is a good night sleep, that's all." He held out his hand, offering to help her up, "So, come on, upstairs we go."

Feeling she had no choice, she took his hand and allowed him to pull her to her feet. Timidly she asked the one question she'd been dreading, "Wallace, where are we sleeping tonight?"

He cleared his throat, "Your room of course. You in your bed and I'll take the settee by the window."

"No, that won't work. The lock on my door doesn't lock." She cleared her throat, "And I won't sleep a wink if the door's not locked."

139

He squinted with embarrassment, "Oh ya, I meant to mend that." He inhaled a deep breath, "Then that leaves my room." A lusting lump formed in his throat. "You'll take the bed and I'll sleep on the floor."

"That's crazy, we'll sleep together." The words streamed out of her mouth before she could stop them. She hurried to correct herself, "I meant, we'll share the bed. You sleep on one side and I'll sleep on the other."

Relieved that she corrected her phrasing, he nodded in agreement, "That sounds grand. We're all set then." He tried to act as normal as possible for her sake. "I don't know about you, but I'm pure tucker out." He slightly clapped and rubbed his hands together, "Well, time for us to settle in then."

She reluctantly nodded in agreement. "Yah, let's get on with this." She headed up the stairs slowly, taking each step at a time, hoping to prolong what was coming. In her head she scolded herself for insisting that he sleep in the same bed as her. Had she lost her mind? What was she thinking? This was a recipe for temptation — and trouble.

He quickly raced up ahead of her, "Um ... could ya give me a minute to tidy up?" His face turned a slight shade of pink. "Me first. Like I said, I need to straighten up." He stopped her half-way up the stairs, "Just give me a wee extra time."

"Well, I do have to change into my pyjamas. Is that enough time?" she grinned up at him. She wasn't sure why he was so concerned about the state of his room; she had already been there earlier.

Whatever the reason was, he was determined about it. "Yah, that should do it. See ya then." And with that he scrambled up the stairs as though his pants were on fire.

She chuckled to herself, "This is going to be one interesting night. Let's see who's the stronger sex … person." The Freudian slip made her face flush, "Who knows, who'll the winner will be."

Chapter Eight

She knocked lightly on the door, "Can I come in? Is it safe yet? Are you decent? Do you want me to wait out here? What are you doing in there anyway? Do you need help?" The questions spilled out as always. She waited patiently for some kind of reply, but none came. "Wallace?"

"Can ya just give me a bloody minute? Lord! Ya got the patience of a two year old."

"Oh fine. You don't have to be so nasty about it." She heard shuffling and a brief grunt. "Are you sure you don't need help?"

"Okay, come on in Lass. It be good now."

She quickly flung the door open while scolding him for wasting her time, "I don't know what the problem was. It was just fine before ..." she stopped in mid-sentence. Somehow, in that short period of time, he had managed to completely re-organize the room. The surfaces were all cleared off and shone as though they had been newly polished. She slowly spied around, examining every corner of the room. There, in the north corner, was a tall stack of boxes covered with a white sheet. "Wallace, you didn't

142

have to do all this. It was just me and I've already been in here." Gemma slipped passed her ankle and bounded up in the chair by the window.

"Good God Girl! Are ya balling me out for cleanin' up me room?" He crossed his arms at her. "Lord Nitra, you're a hard woman."

"That's not what I meant. I meant you're making a big deal over nothing." She crossed her arms too. It was a standoff — or at least the first one of the night.

"Look Nitra, I've never had another person sleep in here before and I wanted it to be a cheery time. It's not always about Nitra Zupan, ya know." He witnessed her dropping her arms down to her side as an apology. "Now which side do ya sleep on? The right side or the left?"

"The left generally, but if you prefer that side, I can switch." It was peace offering for insulting his kindness. "After all it *is* your room, so it's your choice." She also noted that he admitted to not having company in his bedroom prior to this. She had always assumed that when she was away on tour, he was doing whatever he wanted in the house — and that included his bedroom.

He laughed at her, "It's okay Lass, I sleep on the right. Lordy, loosen up a wee bit, would ya." He went to his bedside table and turned on the lamp. The light shone upon a small silver framed picture of an elderly woman sitting on the front steps of a porch. "Now if ya don't mind, I like to read before I get to sleep. It's a habit that Mum started in me when I was a little lad. Do you mind?"

It was her turn to laugh. She pulled out a folded up square of red lined writing paper from her pyjama pocket, "Funny, that's when I do my editing. This is perfect." With the gusto of a two year old at story time, she climbed across the top of the bed and shoved her feet under the thick duvet, pulling the covers up under her arms. What she wasn't counting on was the deep pile under the bottom sheet. That's when she caught the scent of fresh clean linen — he had also changed the sheets! She thought to herself, *Wow, he has been a busy boy.*

"It's sheep's hide. It's normal winter bedding back in me motherland. Keep's a body warm. That and it will form to your back, helping to support it while ya sleep." He gently sat down on the edge of his mattress. But instead of getting in right away, he thumbed through his book and read a page or two before he slipped under the covers beside her. He pulled his t-shirt out of his jersey shorts and slipped his feet under the covers. Once in, he squashed down the duvet with his arm, creating a barrier between him and her. She took it as a sign of his chivalry. Next, he stood his book on his chest and focussed on the words. She noticed it was a hard covered instructional textbook on learning the *Gaelic* dialect.

In contrast, she turned her back to him and smoothed out the pages flat on the mattress, creating crackling sounds with each sweep. In her head she began to read the words, one by one, to herself. She quickly scribbled down the writers symbols within the text. Sometimes she would completely stroke out an entire sentence. But to the annoyance of Wallace, she eventually read the words aloud to herself, one word at a time, checking for unseen errors. *"It-was-Uncle-Thaddeus-who-introduced-him-to-ancient-books.-By-the-age-of-twelve,-he-had-taught-George-to-read-well-over-twenty-different-types-of-ancient-script-and-the-details-of-the-civilizations-they-had-come-from."*

He let it go for awhile, but after twenty minutes he decided he'd had enough of that nonsense, "Um … are ya goin' to do that all night?"

"Do what?" She honestly didn't know what he was referring to.

"Mumbling the words out loud like that." He closed his book with his thumb holding the page like a bookmark.

"Was I doing that? Sorry, didn't know that I was doing it. I'll stop, I swear." She stuck her hand above the bed in oath, "And if I do, just poke me and I'll stop. Okay?"

He only smiled his agreement and went back to reading his book.

Within a half a page, she was back at it again. *"Three-sprays-of-lavender-for-cleansing-and-healing;-three-star-anise-to-increase-clairvoyance;-and-ten-drops-of-desert-rain-for-cleansing-and-revitalization,"* pronouncing each word separately within the sentence. She was trying to concentrate on each word – how it was spelt, its grammatical use, and then the flow the sentence itself.

He lifted an eyebrow at her, "What are ya reading out there? Might that be a spell or the like?" He didn't abide by magic in general, let alone it being read in his own bed. Real or not, the words of charms disturbed his religious upbringing.

"It's from my new book, *MARKED*. It's page 14, one of 'Sid the Kid's pages." She half turn to look at him. At that angle the light caught his eyes just so, reflecting the specks of gold in them. A strong tingle began to erupt inside her, slowly flowing down toward the middle of her legs. She turned back quickly before she acted on the heated impulse she shouldn't.

He didn't hesitate, "That wouldn't be a magic spell that you're workin' on, now is it?"

"Yes ... kind of, but not really." She didn't bother to lie, he'd only see right through her.

He slammed his book shut, "I'll have none of that in here. You know how I feel about those types of goings on." He sharply tossed the textbook on the nightstand, almost knocking over the framed picture. "Time for lights out."

"Are you kidding? I just got started." She protested at being dismissed so rudely, "Look, I'll stop reading out loud."

"No. It's time to go to sleep and that's that. Now let me know when you're all set so I can turn out the light." He folded his arms over his chest to stress that he was serious and there would be no more arguing about it.

"Oh, fine." She tossed her pages onto the floor and pulled the duvet back up to her chin again. "All bloody set then." She mocked him with his own Irish accent. "Now don't be like that, I'm entitled to my rights."

He had made her angry. It wasn't what he had intended to do. What he wanted was to hold her close and protect her from the world. To share his bed and his dreams with her. But to his disappointment, it wasn't turning out the way he wanted. The stubbornness between them wouldn't allow it.

She didn't say a word, but instead showed her angry response by hot-headedly flipping over on her side to face the wall and away from him. But her stunt became a painful blunder, in the act of being childish, she strained her lower back. She held in the scream of pain. There was no way she was going to let him know that she was in agony. He'd probably want to give her a back rub. Again the hot tingle returned. This time she suppressed it by concentrating on her back pain as a form of distraction. Knowing she would not be able to fall asleep in the position she was, she slowly shifted on her back again, adjusting her hips so her back didn't hurt so intensely.

146

He took the time to alter the tone of his voice. As soft and caring as he could without blurting out the words he shouldn't say, "Good night Nitra. Get some sleep. We've got that meeting in the morning with the lady from *The Wharf*." He turned off the light and pushed up the pillow under his head to make it a larger lump.

"Night." She exhaled a slow shallow breath in hopes of relieving the pain. "Sleep tight." She tried not to move, making her even tenser than she already was. Her private nightly ritual was to roll over at least four times before her back and body found the right comfortable position. To do so then would have helped ease the pain, but with him beside her, she couldn't do just whatever she wanted — she'd have to be considerate. She noted that he was obviously having no problem with this arrangement, he was already wheezing in his sleep, a fact that made it even harder for her to get comfortable.

Wallace McPhee was in an awful state — a pure self-imposed torturous misery. He was lying next to her, the naked muscles of his leg touching the fleshy softness of hers; her skin felt silky and warm. He moved his leg a mere fraction just to feeling the sensation of it again. It felt just as luxurious as he'd remembered it, with the heat and electricity that flowed from its gentle glowing beauty, igniting every nerve in his body. He forced his hands to stay bound in place, daring to not let them move, for fear of what they might do. He wanted — no needed to — touch more of her flesh, to devour it inch by lavish inch using his lips and tongue. To indulge in her fiery power, drown in her very soul. Ecstasy is where he longed to bring her. His heart ached for more, each of its hammering pulses laced with the suffering agony he held inside for her. But he knew he

147

couldn't release those ravenous yearnings, it was forbidden — she was the forbidden fruit he must never taste. The only defence against his own heat driven impulses was to act as though he was asleep. An illusion he created by the faint sound of deep breathing during sleep. He lay on his back with his arms tightly knotted across his chest, holding in his tortured passion and emotion, he longed to share with her. Agony, pure suffering agony.

She carefully moved her back this way, then that way, hoping to find just the right spot to relieve the pain. It took her several tries before she finally managed to get comfortable. She lay quietly, waiting for sleep to come, but the sound of Wallace's wheezing kept her from doing just that. Carefully and gently, she slipped her hand under his shoulder and shoved at him, encouraging him to stop. But he didn't budge. She nudged him over and over again until he finally submitted to her by giving a snort and jolted to move his body slightly.

He almost felt relieved when she shifted her leg and his calf no longer touched her skin. But at the same time it intensified the ache to touch her again. He felt her hand sweep soothingly across his shoulder setting him on fire. His groin ached with her scent, the heat of her touch. He had to make the torture stop or he'd lose control. The urge to take her, just take her, was becoming impossible to resist. *Stop it!* he screamed in his head. He had to break away, to end her electric euphoria. He blew out a great 'harrumph' in hopes it would scare her away, ending her caresses of his flesh. To his misery, he succeeded. She withdrew her soft, warm hand from the taught muscles of his shoulder. Feeling the cooler air rush into the same searing spot, he knew she was no longer connected to him. A different ache tightened in his heavy heart. Torment.

She gently wiggled her back into the thick sheep skin. Its rich pile snuggled around her, like a mother's arms hugging her sick child. The warmth of the duvet and tiredness of the day, took its toll. Finally, Nitra surrendered to deep sleep and its own thoughts.

In her sleepy subconscious the handwritten words floated across her memory as vividly as the first day she had read them in his fan letter. But this time the words that she missed stood out thick and black amongst the other normal rational words. If she had identified them when she originally read the letter, she would have never responded to it. His closure *'Your beloved admirer'* was rather creepy, but it was the phrase *'our time spend together'* that evoked another image in her mind — the image of Marty Larson standing before her at the signing table. She remembered his overly eager smile and dark needy eyes gleaming down at her. His hands trembled as he gave her his copy of her book to autograph. That image of him quickly swirled, shifting into the recollection of the man standing in her kitchen doorway last Christmas ...

... the memory of those events came back in a flood so real, it was as though it had just happened ...

... she had been mixing yet another drink for her and Wallace when she heard a knock at the kitchen door. With it being Christmas Eve and a gut full of double-rum eggnogs, she ignored her usual precautions by simply opening the door without first checking through the gingham curtains.

149

Even in her deep state of sleep the same intense feelings overtook her as it had that night; the harsh rush of surprise and fear still paralysed her where she lay. She could no more physically move now, than she could that night. From her memory she felt the snow swirl around his head and hit her in the face like a hard cold slap. Then Wallace's voice asking her 'Why are you taking so long?' echoed slowly through her dream as it did through the kitchen that night.

She inhaled the same deep breath to scream as she had that night, but even in her dream, the scream wouldn't come out, it froze in her throat. Her heart pounded violently in her chest. The terror of Marty Larson's daunting image pressed hard upon her, weighing down every muscle, recreating that same captured fear, as on that night. She once more experienced Wallace's hand grab her shoulder from behind, pulling her away from Larson. Next came the reoccurring voice of Wallace's words, warning her she needed to run. In her groggy sleep, the words were thick and muffled, but she knew exactly what they meant. Again, in her head, she witnessed Wallace shove Larson back into the snow swirling darkness. His red jacket disappeared into the blackness of the night.

Fear cemented her feet to the floor. The slamming door made her body jump, but her feet remained where they were. It was the scraping sound of the door latch being locked that made her legs go weak, her knees almost buckling beneath her. The recollection of her body being pushed towards the kitchen pantry door blurred in her dream. Instantly the darkness surrounded her, fuelling her fears even further. Solely out of fright, she did exactly what Wallace told her to do. She trusted him and his Irish judgement. She jammed the ironing board under the knob and wedged it against the floor with a stomp of her foot.

Finally feeling safe, she gave over to her fear and crouched down on the floor, curling into a tight frightened ball next to the door. All she could do was concentrate on the sounds beyond the blocked door. She heard the wooden floor squeak as Wallace made his way to the drawer by the refrigerator. She knew what he was getting — his favourite knife. She had no doubt that he was skilled with a knife and would protect her at all costs. Wallace's words were muffled by the pantry door, "Stay inside that closet 'til I came back for ya. Don't be openin' the door to no one but me self. Ya hearin' me Girl." In the darkness of the pantry she silently nodded *yes* in response. She heard the kitchen door latch scrape open and the door slam behind Wallace. Then there was nothing except the muffled sound of soft Christmas carols mixed with dead silence.

She waited, listening intently for some type of sign that it was safe. The silence was crushing to her ears. Not a footstep or floor creak could be heard. Blood pounded through her ears and the thunderous noise of each breath drowned out the Christmas music coming from the living room. The seconds turned into what seemed to be hours of anxious waiting. Finally, she heard the faint sound of a siren coming from the far off distance. As the siren came closer and grew louder, Nitra identified it as a police car, not an ambulance. She was relieved — help was on its way.

She heard shouting, yet couldn't make out the exact words over the siren blaring. Her head began to spin. She realized she hadn't been breathing, so the lack of oxygen was affecting her mind. On the verge of passing out, she inhaled deeply several times before scolding herself to breathe slowly and steadily. This was not the time to be out cold on the floor, helpless and unprotected.

151

The siren ceased and was quickly replaced by yelling. It was Harry and Wallace shouting back and forth. With new hope, she uncurled her terrified body, shifting to her knees. She stretched her head higher to hear more clearly. Even though she still couldn't make out exactly what they were saying, it was comforting to know they were there together. They would work together to rid her of the unwanted intruder. The tightness in her chest loosened slightly, while her shoulders slowly slipped back down into place. In the distance she heard another siren calling out its urgency. More help was coming. Nitra inhaled deep, filling her lungs with additional well needed oxygen. The blood in her ears calmed to a soft rush, allowing her to finally notice that the Christmas music had stopped playing in the living room. In fact, she listened hard for any type of sound from within the house. She heard none. She focussed her breathing back to a regular rhythm. As her heart rate slowed, the loud siren in the driveway died away and was followed by more silence. Holding her breath she strained to hear any sounds that indicated what was happening outside in the darkness, beyond her closet darkness.

Suddenly a shout broke the silence. Although it was muffled by the thick wooden door, the words registered in Nitra's head, "He's got a gun!" She quickly curled up again, cowering with the ominous words. Images of a bloody Wallace flashed through her mind. Controlling her breathing, she stopped her heart to a slow thump so she could listen closer. In minutes she not only heard voices, but felt the vibrations of footsteps running past what she thought should be just outside the kitchen.

"STOP! HAMLIN POLICE DEPARTMENT! PUT DOWN THE GUN!" She heard Harry yell it again, "STOP! HAMLIN POLICE DEPARTMENT! PUT DOWN THE GUN!" The sound of footsteps doubled — then tripled as all four men ran by. Then she heard the one sound she feared hearing — a gunshot. The loud sharp sound cracked through the crisp night air. It bounced off the garage, garden shed, and the surrounding trees, bursting into a barrage of quieter echoed shots. Nitra sprung to her feet and gasped in a breath, then held it. Fearing the worst, she couldn't control her emotions any longer, she let herself go. Tears filled her dark eyes. Her body shook with the intensity of her unleashed sobs. All she could envision was Wallace injured, or worse, his body lying dead in the snow with dark red blood seeping into the white snow. Over her crying, she heard the one thing that made her stop — Wallace yelling at Harry. "He's gone behind the shed! I'm going that way!" To her that meant he was alive and the chase was still on. She wiped away her tears and rose to her feet. Nitra pressed her ear against the door. The vibration of feet running by rattled the jars of preserves on the shelf that were level with her head. She watched them tremble and immediately placed her hands on them to quiet the tinkling sound.

Within seconds the outside world fell silent again. She waited and waited, still nothing happened. There was neither sound nor movement. To her, time seemed to stretch on without end. She remembered the words that Wallace had told her, "Stay inside that closet 'til I come back for ya." And that's exactly what she did. She waited for him to return. Again the vibration of chasing footsteps pounded passed the house.

Joey's voice called through the air, "Is he gone? I can't see him anymore."

Harry answered his deputy, "I don't see him either." But his tone was more of a question than a reassurance. "Wallace where are you? Do you see him?"

153

Wallace hollered back, "No. But how do I see anythin' in this God damned blowing snow."

The sound of footsteps stopped. No one yelled, they stood and listened.

What Nitra couldn't see or hear was that the three men were grouped together just outside the shed. The trio watched for any signs of the intruder. Still holding their weapons high, they scanned through the swirling snow. Harry nodded that he was going around the north side of the house, while Joey signalled that he was heading southward. Wallace pointed his knife toward the shed and calmly stated, "I'll check the out buildings."

Inside, Nitra began to relax slightly. There was no more shooting or shouting. In her head, she came to the conclusion that Larson must be gone. It was finally safe. Now she could leave the safety of her protective pantry. But why wasn't Wallace coming to get her? It must be safe, there wasn't any shouting or running — or gun fire. And she had heard Joey say he couldn't see Larson anymore. The other two men did agree that they couldn't see him either, so logically Larson must be gone then. She turned in spot and began to pace in the darkness. Five paces one way, five paces back. She couldn't understand why Wallace wasn't coming to get her out of the pantry? Didn't he understand she was scared? Didn't he know that she hated being locked up in there like some kind of weak captive? Where was he? She paced some more, back and forth. For the first time she realized how tiny the pantry was. Suddenly the walls seemed to be too close to her, almost squeezing in on her. Her heart raced. What if they were all dead? Each body spilling red blood onto the pure white snow — leaving her alone, imprisoned inside the dark pantry forever — never to see her Wallace again? She stopped pacing to giggle at herself. She truly was a writer, one that was letting her imagination completely runaway with itself. After all, she was the one that jammed the ironing board under the door knob. She was the one who had the power to free herself at any given time. But it still didn't answer the question as to why Wallace hadn't come to get her.

In her mind she imagined Wallace, Harry, and Joey swapping hero stories while totally forgetting about her locked in the closet. Well, she won't put up with it. She was going to release herself from her self-imposed prison. Wait for Wallace McPhee, be damned! She planted her feet solidly on the floor. With one hard sweeping side kick, she knocked the ironing board from beneath the door knob. It clattered on the floor, announcing she was free. But Nitra was no fool; she slowly opened the door to a thin slit. She peeked through it, twisting one way, then the other, allowing her to take in the entire kitchen. It was empty. For courage she exhaled a held breath. Opening the door wider, she looked once more to be sure. Again, there was no one in site. She called out, "Hey what's going on? Is he gone? Wallace?" But there was no answer from inside the house. "They must be outside?" she told herself. She slipped on her heavy red coat, pale yellow tuque, and black gloves before heading out into the cold snowy darkness.

Outside, she shielded her face from the blowing snow. She squinted against the streaking streams of white, trying to identify one blurry shape from another. She managed to make out the two police cars and her truck in the driveway. And that meant she needed to walk in that direction to get to the garden shed. In her imagination, she had decided that was where the men were standing around boasting about their acts of bravery. Again, she covered her eyes against the thrashing snow. She placed each step carefully through the deep drift, cursing a boot full of chilly snow. When she reached the garden shed the door was wide open. To her surprise, it was empty except for the usual garden paraphernalia. And by the amount of snow that drifted across the floor, it had been open for some time. But if the men weren't there, where were they? They must be back in the house, looking for her. She turned about almost, slipping on an icy spot, but managed to grab the doorframe to stabilize herself.

Back outside, it was hard to decide which was worse to fight with, the whipping snow or the empty darkness. Nitra barely made out the light that was above the side door just off the sundeck. She overlapped her collar, pulling it over her mouth to block out the cold wind. With her face protected by her coat, she once more shielded her eyes and headed for the faint pinpoint of light. She counted her paces in her head. She guesstimated that it was probably twenty paces from the shed to the decks eastern set of steps. When she reached the twentieth pace, she swept her foot to find the first bottom step. She inched several smaller steps forward, sweeping with her foot before she found the edge. Grasping the railing, she hoisted herself up the set of five snow filled steps, until her feet were flat on the deck's floor. The cold wooden deck boards snapped with the four steps she took towards the living room sliding door.

Unbeknownst to Nitra, on the other side of the deck, Harry saw a red form through the swirling snow. He pointed his gun and ordered, "STOP, HAMLIN POLICE DEPARTMENT! STOP OR I'LL SHOOT!"

Not thinking, Nitra naturally held up her hand to wave at Harry, signalling that it was her who was standing in front of him, and not Larson.

Harry saw the upward motion of a red arm, its end black, and automatically believed it was Larson pointing his gun. His police training instinctively kicked in. Harry aimed for the shoulder and fired at the assailant.

Nitra felt the sting of the bullet pierce her flesh long before she heard the muffled sound from Harry's gun. She felt her upper body twist in the direction of the bullet's force, knocking her off balance, turning her completely around. Her whole body toppled forward, pulling her over the railing of the deck, hurtling her face first onto the hard frozen ground with a brutal blunt thud. Blackness penetrated her mind.

Even in her unconscious state, she could still hear the heavy footsteps and shouts.

Harry yelled out, "I got him!"

"Where are ya?" Wallace yelled back.

"He fell over the deck." Harry had reached the edge of the steps and was lowering himself to the snowdrift at its base. "Got him right in the shoulder! Joey, you radio in for an ambulance." He pointed his gun directly at the head poking out of the red coat sprawled on the ground. "Hamlin Police! Don't move!"

Wallace ran up behind him, "Where's the gun?" Realizing that the body wasn't moving, he dropped to his knees and began searching through the snow for it with his bare hands. It was best that one of them had the gun, eliminating the chances of Larson getting the gun back.

Detached from her body and its pain, she heard the distorted words of Joey talking on the police radio, "Yah, you'd better hurry, there's a lot of blood."

That's when she felt a sweeping nudge against her body and she grunted with agony.

157

Hearing the female voice, Wallace looked closer, "Holy shit! It's Nitra!" Wallace was kneeling beside her. "Harry, you shot Nitra!" He turned her body over slowly, trying not to pull at her gunshot wound. He removed his coat and rolled it into a pillow to raise her head off the cold snowy ground. "Nitra, wake up! Come on Nitra, wake up!" He slapped her face lightly, trying to bring her around. Her eyes fluttered, signalling that she was alive.

Harry knelt down on the other side of her, "Christ all mighty! I thought it was him. I saw him raise his gun, so I at fired at him." He shook out his folded white handkerchief. He formed a small knot in the middle which he carefully packed it into the gunshot whole. Its center slowly turned deep red. He pushed Wallace's hand on top of it, "Keep putting pressure on that." He hung down his head beside her ear, "I thought you were the guy. Sorry Nitra. Forgive me?"

Joey got back on the radio, "Emma, hurry that ambulance up. It's Nitra that's shot. Tell them to bust a gut on this one." He didn't wait for an answer; he only pulled out his gun, grasped it at arm's length and scanned the surrounding area. "Bastards still out there, ain't he?"

"Yep!" Harry did the same with his gun. He yelled out into the darkness, more as warning than a threat, "And this time I ain't shooting for the shoulder!"

Wallace ignored them both. All he could think about was Nitra. He was still trying to get her to come around, "Nitra wake up. Come on Lass, wake up." Panic rushed his heart. His Nitra was hurt and there was nothing he could do about it. For the first time he realized how much he truly cared for her. Not as his boss, but as the woman he'd come to know — and to love. If she died that night, he would be lost. His whole reason for living would no longer exist. His heart would die along with her. He brushed the snow from her cheek, "She so cold. Maybe we should move her into the house where we can keep her warm. Joey you grab her feet, I'll take her upper body."

Before either officer could say a word, Wallace moved her body, shifting her into a lifting position.

The pain tore through Nitra, pulling her out of her shock. Her scream pierced the frigid air. Realizing what he'd done, Wallace gently lowered her body back onto the ground. She wasn't sure which hurt more, the bullet wound in her shoulder or her lower back. Huge tears spilled from her dark eyes and rolled down her cheeks. Through clinched teeth, she grunted one short sentence, "Move me again and you're fired."

Through the tears, she watched a smile sweep across Wallace's face. If she was telling him off, she was going to be fine. "Ya got it boss."

Harry put his hand on Wallace's shoulder, "Son, I know you mean well, but it's best she stay right where she is. The cold will slow down the bleeding and we don't know if her back is injured or not."

Nitra answered that question, "God damn right my back hurts. Like I said, move me again and I'll … I'll …" Abruptly, she stopped threaten him and began listening instead. "I hear it. The ambulance is coming." In her excitement of knowing that medical help was coming, she tried to sit up, the pain shot through her again …

… Nitra sat straight up in her bed, her mental pain jolted her out of the nightmarish hell. Beads of sweat had formed on her face and body. Her heart thundered in her chest. It was the same nightmare she'd had a hundred times since that night. She had relived it over and over again. But this time, Wallace was laying there with her. Somehow, that fact made her feel less frightened than she had in the past. Instead of panicking, she was able to remind herself that Harry had shot Larson dead, there was no way he was ever bothering her again. She looked down at Wallace, lying on his back beside her; he made her feel a little safer. Even from the threat of the Lipstick Lady. She lay back down on her other side for comfort. She closed her eyes and calmed her breathing, trying to sleep again. But sleep didn't come as easily as the last time. Her fears about her new nemesis spun through her mind a million miles an hour.

Without notice, Wallace rolled over and draped his arm over her waist. She was about to say something when she realized he was sound asleep. It was a human reflex and nothing more. But in an odd way, it was exactly what she needed at that moment. The strength of his arm felt like a shield against the dangerous world. He then pulled her into him and shifted his legs in behind hers. She froze, unsure of what to do. Then that familiar tingling came flooding back. This time she decided to let it happen. Before long she convinced herself that her back wasn't hurting anymore. She indulged in his masculine hold by wiggling further into him. She let his heat penetrate into her body. She slowly released the tension in her back, letting herself relax, allowing his warmth to comfort her soul. A dreamy smile slipped across her lips as she drifted off to sleep, this time without a care on her mind. For now she was protected from the world.

Chapter Nine

Gemma pawed at Nitra's face that it was time to wake up. She puffed out a heavy sleepy sigh before shooing the cat away with gentle sweep of her hand, "Oh leave me alone, you crazy ass cat." Gemma exited the room through the slightly open door. She knew when she wasn't wanted. After a huge yawn, Nitra remembered the night before and reached for Wallace. But he wasn't there. The clock read 6:18 am, a time Nitra was not used to seeing. She closed her eyes and dreamily indulged in the thoughts of Wallace's arms — then the robust aroma of coffee and salty bacon filled her nostrils. "Breakfast!" She jumped out of the bed and bounded down the stairs.

In the kitchen Wallace was standing at the counter, breaking eggs into a bowl with Gemma begging at his feet. He had heard the thump of her heavy steps, "Do ya want scrambled eggs?" His voice was quiet, yet stern.

His mood took the 'happy' right out of her. "Yah, scrambled is fine." She sat at the table waiting for him to bring over her plate. He placed it in front of her and headed for the stairs. "Hey, where are you going? Aren't you going to eat with me? Are you mad or something?"

He stopped at the bottom step but didn't turn around to face her. "I've got to get dressed. We have to go to *The Wharf* to get your pages. And before we go, I need to check over me car. After that wee road race yesterday, it's best I look her over. It'll do us no good at the side of the road, broken down or the like." He took two more steps and answered her last question, "And no, I'm not mad." Yet he didn't give her any additional information either. That was a huge hint for Nitra to keep her distance for awhile.

The car ride to town was quiet. Neither spoke until they reached Mead Avenue. The street was lined with a few small shops. It held an old fashioned bakery, a hardware store, and a tiny café with tables for sitting in the open air. Wallace carefully scanned the streets, looking for any signs of trouble.

"I don't see the car either." Nitra confessed, "And she's not following us. I've been watching since we left the house."

"Not to worry Lass, I've got your back. I even brought an old friend with me, just in case." He pulled open his jacket front to show her. Tucked into a leather harness was the blade of a long knife, its handle was made out of a dark wood. To Nitra, its intricate carvings implied a sense of religious valour and motherland rivalry.

Her eyes grew the size of bottle caps. "You brought a knife? Are you crazy? Do you think you'll need it? Better yet, do you know how to use it?"

He smirked reassuringly at her, "I grew up in Ireland, didn't I? Yah Lass, I know how to use a knife. Used it to save me life many a time back in Ballyclare. It was a hard land to live in." He closed his jacket, caressing the leather over top of it, "I can also throw this beauty almost thirty feet and hit my mark dead on. Better than a handgun, they kill. Knives will maim the bugger 'til the coppers come. And they're nice and legal."

More fragments of Wallace's past life that Nitra knew nothing about. She knew he was from somewhere near Belfast, but until then he had never admitted the actual location. The whole conversation left her feeling more fearful than she had felt before. "Why bring it this time?"

She had only asked one solitary question. To Wallace, this was a sign that she was on edge and needed to be reassured she was safe. "Oh Lordy, it's only a precaution. Pay no attention to it. Just forget I've got it and act normal. Whatever that is, when it comes to you?" He purposely sent her a jab, hoping she take the bait and forget about the knife. It didn't work.

She basically ignored him. She stooped her head down to look below the roof of the car, at the sign above the door. It was painted in an old scribe style with large fluid letters done in the blues and greens of the sea. "I wonder what she looks like."

Convinced that the streets were secure, he finally turned off the ignition, "What a question?"

"Not really. It's a question that, as a writer, I ask myself constantly." She opened up her tote and checked for her money. She still hadn't switched it over to a nicer handbag. *Tonight!* she scolded herself in her head. "Each time I create a character, I have to ask myself the same questions. What is the characters name? A name can break or make the readers visualization of a character. What do they look like? Old, young, fat, skinny, happy, or mean. What nationality are they? European, American, or a person of visual ethnicity? What is their position in life? Are they born rich, a careless drifter, nasty lawyer, or a stupid criminal? Then I have to decide what part do they play within the book – main character, secondary character, sidekick, or a fleeting cameo? So no, it's not that unusual of a question if you happen to be me."

"Okay, I'll take that as to be the truth." He checked in the rear view mirror again.

"I bet you that she's a sweet little Italian babe. You know the kind? No brains and they stand by the front counter to make the place look good." She had her tote bag clinched with her hand so tight, her knuckles were turning white. "Shall we go?"

"To meet an Italian beauty just standin' there. You bet Love! Let's hurry then." He gave her a smile while opening his door. He waited at the front of the car for her.

"Asshole," she muttered to him as they walked across the street together.

"Yah, yah. When we get inside, let me do the talking." He wasn't asking her, he was directing her.

He insisted on opening the door and going in first. Nervous, she stuck to him like glue and dogged his heels every step of the way. At the back of the shop was a person reaching up to the top shelf, for what looked like a roll of butcher paper. The t-shirt road part way up the back, revealing a heavy black leather belt holding up a pair of loose faded jeans. When the person turned around, both Nitra and Wallace was surprised to see it was a woman and not a man, as she appeared to be in the first place. As they agreed upon earlier in the car, Wallace spoke first. "We're

164

looking for Gina." He looked past her towards the plastic curtain behind her, "Is she here?"

"I'm Gina." She saw the look of doubt on Wallace's face and popped her hand on her hip, indicating she caught the implied, yet unspoken insult. Her blunt rough words reflected the insult as well, "So what'a want?" As well as her physical features being Italian, she spoke with a slight broken accent.

Nitra thought she better save Wallace from himself. She stepped in front of him and turned to give him a disgusted look before talking to Gina, without his male induced judgement. She smiled sweetly at Gina, "You called us about the pages you found."

"Oh yah. Found them while I was on a delivery. That no-good brother of mine stuck me with the deliveries, while he went out drinking and whoring." She walked to the front of the shop with a profound swagger, making her butch like appearance even more masculine. "Are those pages from a book or something?"

"Why, yes they are." As Gina got closer, so did her smell. Nitra politely rubbed the end of her nose in attempts to conceal the fact that she was actually covering her mouth and nostrils to stop the stench. She took a step back as Gina passed directly in front of her.

"So ... like ... you're a writer?" She put the large roll of paper on the front counter as though it weighed next to nothing.

Wallace got a snout full too. He cleared his throat, "Ma'am ... Gina ... no offense to ya, but we're in a wee bit of a hurry this mornin'. So could we please get the pages so we can go?"

Gina saw Nitra's hand near her nose and quickly guessed the real reason he was in such a rush. "Oh sure, follow me." She headed to the back of the shop and held open a clear plastic curtain so they could go through to another smaller room with lockers and more shelves. The odour of decaying fish was over powering. It was all Nitra could do to stay inside the tiny store room, while holding down her breakfast.

Gina witness Nitra's face turn pale and offered her kindness, "Smell bothering you? Breathe through your mouth, not your nose." She reached into her locker for the pages, pulling out a beautiful tote bag that caught Nitra eye. It was the style that Nitra longed for. It was surprising that a manly woman such as Gina would own such a feminine purse. Nitra regarded her differently after that. From inside it, she pulled out a tiny square wrapped in heavy white plastic. Gina explained the reasoning for the strange packet, "I thought that if I sealed it inside the plastic, it wouldn't end up stinking like this place. God knows once the scent of fish gets into things, it's impossible to get it out." She examined her hands, "Not even lemon or bleach helps."

Nitra carefully peeled off the flap to peek inside. It was her writing. She slipped them out and quickly checked the upper right hand corners. She read pages 3, 23, 24 and 29. Again her heart sank. Her first page wasn't there. The page she wanted — no, needed the most — was still out there. She thought to her herself, *Poor thing is probably somewhere out there in a cold wet ditch all alone and frightened, wondering if anyone would ever come to rescue it.* She shook her head, reminding herself to stop being a writer and think like a normal person. Wallace grinned at her as though he knew exactly what she was doing — and that made her blush.

"So, um … look, I don't mean to be rude, but can we go out back so I can at least have a smoke?"

"Oh, sure. By all means, show us the way." Wallace rolled his eyes at Gina, disapproving of the time being wasted, not to mention that the smell was finally getting to him.

As they walked through the tiny kitchen in the back, a small man with a large knife yelled out, "Hey! No one's allowed back here, so you turn yourself around." He pointed at the door with the lengthy blade.

Gina scolded him, "Oh, shut the hell up. They're with me jerkface. Speakin' of jerks, did the idiot show up yet?" Her angry voice pierced the air, along with Wallace's ear drums.

"No." He tossed his knife at the countertop. It stuck into a pile of white fleshed fillets. "And I've got a shit load of work to get done for that catering job tonight."

"Well, when he comes in, tell him he's fired." She opened the back door and shuffled both visitors outside. "I'll call in Mama. She can run the front while I help you get caught up back here." Once out in the fresh air Nitra breathed again. Wallace did the same while scanning the back alleyway just in case.

"Sorry about that. Reliable help is hard to get these days. Idiot brother. No one wants to go into the fish business. Not even my family. God damned computers have ruined the work force." She lit up the cigarette she held in between her fingers. "I got three," she jabbed three fingers in the air, "count 'em, three catering jobs tonight and no one to help us out. God damned little jerk."

Wallace had suffered enough. The stench from the adjacent garbage can, plus the grating of Gina's voice was too much to endure with his throbbing headache. With a pleasant as possible voice he encouraged, "Nitra please pay the woman so she can get back to work." But his eyes really

167

said, '*pay the ruddy nagging wench so we can bloody escape this stinking hell hole.*'

Feeling the same way, Nitra didn't hesitate. She immediately dove into her tote and pulled out the money. The four twenty dollar bills were carefully handed to Gina, so that she didn't touch her skin or her clothing in anyway.

"Eighty bucks, that's good." She shoved them down the front of her top. The delicate lace trim of a pale pink bra poked out from under the stained navy t-shirt. Inside Nitra cheered for Gina. Gina was truly a woman. Under her rough manly exterior, she was still a hot-blooded Italian goddess dressed in soft pink lace. "Maybe my brother's an idiot, but it was good he was an idiot that day."

Nitra's eyes beamed at Gina, "Thank you for wrapping them up. That was a very thoughtful gesture." She smiled a '*girlfriend secret grin*' at her, "Just one more question. Where did you get your purse? It's beautiful."

Within a split second, '*Gina the fish gutter*' switched into '*Gina the giggler*'. "I found it in that fancy shop over on Maple Street. You know the one? Right next to Sammy's Seafood Shack. It was in the window and I knew it was the one for me. Took me two weeks to save up the money, and when I went back to get it, it was on sale too." She was a proud bargain hunter.

It brought to mind a favourite saying of hers. '*Men hunt wild beasts and bring them home to their women proving they are men, while women hunt wild wears to bring home to their men, proving they are not men.*'

"Thanks. I'll go there next week to see what else they have in purses." Wallace cleared his throat loudly, signaling to Nitra to speed it up. "Well, we should be going. Again, thank you for returning my pages." Wallace had already placed his hand on her shoulder, guiding her down the alleyway towards the street. She waved and yelled, "Bye. Thanks again."

On the far side of the street Wallace finally had to ask, "What the hell was that all about?" He mockingly squeaked out her words, "*Where did you get your purse?* Did ya pull it out of your arse?" Unlocking her door, he ordered with his finger, "And ya be wipin' the bottom of your feet hard on the cement before ya get into me car."

Which she dutifully did. "No, she was sweet. Underneath all that brawn, she's a woman. And whether you recognized it or not, she wanted to, just for once, be treated like a woman. One of the girls. When this is all over, I'm coming back here and inviting her out for coffee."

He knew her all too well, to let it go at that. Wallace scoffed at her with a snort, "Oh, so she's a character study then?"

Nitra blushed at his comment, mostly because it was true. She couldn't imagine being her friend in the least, but she was still fascinated by Gina's persona. She needed to know more about the woman hidden in the man.

Wallace turned on the ignition and shifted the car into gear, but held the car in place, "We've got company." He pointed with his chin. Nitra gasped at what she saw. Standing on the corner was a large woman wearing the orange-red shade of lipstick Nitra had described to Harry. "I'll drive by slow so you can get a good long look at her. Take a writers look at her Nitra. Paint her in your head. Harry will want to have her sketched out for the boys to pick her up." He scanned the street for the grey sedan in hopes of getting the licence plate number. "She must have hid her car out of sight." An amateur would have left it in view by mistake. This forewarned Wallace that she might be a pro after all.

169

There she stood, in her faux leopard print coat. Its bell shaped ampleness stopped at mid-thigh, making her appearance seem shorter and heavier than she already was. Her bleach blonde hair was teased beyond any recognizable shape or style, making the wrinkles in her face deeper than her youthful blue eyes reflected. Nitra guesstimated she was in her fifties, but it was hard to judge her age from her ravaged exterior. It was her attempt to present herself as a woman of class, yet she had done it to the extreme, resulting in a harsh trashy demeanor.

In return, the Lipstick Lady inspected Nitra just as intently. Her eyes never left the car as it rolled past her. Nitra examined her meticulously and memorized every detail. The coat, the scar — even the ring on her finger didn't go unnoticed. The initial 'R' was set in tiny black stones. A list of names ran through Nitra's head. However none of them seemed to fit her accurately. She needed to hear her voice to determine more about her — her name, her inner character, or whether she even meant Nitra any real harm.

Wallace had slowed the car practically to a halt, "Did ya get a good look? Or should I go around the block again?" Wallace was getting bolder. He had learned that the easiest way to defend himself was to not be intimidated by the fear that others created. Then he changed his mind and floored it. The Lipstick Lady had taken several steps towards the car and that was close enough for him. "No? Good. Home we go then." But he was basically talking to himself. Nitra was already deep into her writer's process. He watched the Lipstick Lady disappear into a tiny dot in the rear view mirror.

Nitra had pulled out a pile of red lined sheets and began to record everything she could remember. The first page consisted of short descriptive term scribbled down wildly in no particular order, while the second was organized with more details, fashioned in full legible sentences. Even as the car raced down the road, she still managed to write it all out in tidy, readable handwriting. By the time they pulled into the driveway, she had a complete itemized portrait of the Lipstick Lady from head to toe.

The second Wallace got inside the door, he locked it behind them. All the bolts were slid into place and the house once again, checked thoroughly.

"I don't understand why you are doing that? She's back in town." She'd been so busy writing that she hadn't thought of watching for the grey sedan. She swallowed down her uneasiness before asking the question, "Isn't she?"

"I didn't see her follow us here, if that's what you're asking. But Ni, ya have to keep something else in mind, we still aren't sure if she's working alone. She could have an accomplice. Hell, we don't even know what the damned woman wants from ya." He was froze there, his hands flung high in the air when the phone rang. This time Wallace ran to pick it up, instead of letting the answering machine get it. He had enough of the foolishness and wanted some answers to his questions.

Nitra held her breath. What if it was Tom calling her back? She prayed in her head to the Good Lord above, to wait another week before allowing Wallace to discover that she had, in effect, accepted Tom's invitation for a paper hunt and dinner.

"Hello?" Wallace winced with pain at the loud voice on the other end. "Hold on a minute, I need to turn down the volume on my phone." He rolled his eyes at her as he adjusted the buttons. "Okay, that's better. Go ahead then."

He nodded while he listened. At one point his face lit up and he gave her the thumbs up. Nitra could hear the voice on the phone ramble on and on, yet couldn't make out the words themselves. Finally Wallace wedged in a word, "How about noon today? Perfect! See you then?" He hung up the phone and smiled widely at her, "He has four of your pages. Isn't that great news Girl?"

Nitra counted on her fingers, "Let's see, that's one page from Tom, two from Sid, and one from Katie. And that reminds me. Ask me about Irish immigration laws later." He frowned at her. It annoyed him when she did that — putting him in charge of her memory. "So that makes four. Next came Martina's three pages. Three from Patrick ... no wait, it was actually two pages and my writer's notes wasn't it? So that's nine. Oh yah and Mrs. Hollander return my Marion notes but that one doesn't count because it was just an extra. Who am I leaving out? Oh duh, Gina's four. So that makes a total of thirteen. And now another four from that caller, that makes seventeen." She thought quietly for a couple of seconds, subtracting the total returned against the total missing. "That means that I'm still one page short." Her stomach plummeted. The notion that page one might not be in the next batch of pages turned her gut to tight knot.

Wallace read her face and tried to encourage her. "Oh now, don't be doin' that Love. Ya don't know for sure what page the fella has. Be patient. Ya should wait to see which ones they are before ya go getting all down and out." She didn't reply to his bolstering, she simply stared at him. Feeling the strain of her stare, he changed the subject to a happier note. "Well, we should get a bit of food in us before we go to meet that fella."

She broke her stare, "And which fella would that be?"

172

"He said his name was Teddy of 'Teddy's Timeless Attire'. I said we'd meet him at noon at his shop. He says he sells vintage clothing. Ya know — old gowns, hats, purses and such. Sounds like a bloody pouf to me."

That made Nitra laugh, "Why is it that every time a man does anything that involves clothing apparel, you automatically assume he's gay." As she pointed at him she chuckled, "Quite frankly, it's a case of the pot calling the kettle black. I mean, here you are a housekeeper and according to most men, you'd be the one labelled the pouf." She covered her mouth while she laughed at the absurdity of it all.

He had managed to cheer her up, purely at his own expense, but it did the job. "Well then it's a chilled chicken sandwich and off we go to meet Teddy boy, the fancy frock peddler."

"Not until you call Harry with this information." She waved her page at him, "And you read it word for word and don't leave anything out or there will be hell to pay."

"Nope." He snatched the paper out of her fingers, "If this gets done first, you'll have to do some sufferin' by makin the lunch."

"But, but I don't know how. I could never make those sandwiches the way you do." Her face pleaded with him, "Please don't make me? I'll mess them up."

"No, you won't Ni. All you have to do is de-bone the cold chicken from the carcass and chop it up in a bowl. Then you add ..." He stopped himself. "Oh for Christ sakes. We don't have time for this, just look it up in the book." He pointed to the brown bound cookbook on the shelf, "It's all in there. Just do what the steps tell you to do and it'll be fine." She gave him a grin of gratitude, which he easily erased with one sentence, "That, and anyone with half a

173

brain can make a chicken salad sandwich." He ducked a swat and scurried into the other room, leaving her fuming where she stood.

"You rotten shit! You better run." She added one last bit just as the door closed, "Ya bloody pouf ya."

He closed Nitra's writing room door tightly behind him. This was call he needed to make without her hearing his words. He stood with his arms crossed while he scanned the contents of the entire room. It was a total disaster. The wreckage of stacked books covered every flat surface and the waste basket spilled over with crumbled up pages. And there on the second shelf, was the tea cup that had been missing for over a month. "God save us all from writers," he muttered. Many times he suggested that he could tidy the room up for her and was promptly chastised. He could still hear her yelling at him, 'You stay the hell out of my space. I know exactly where everything is and if you move things around, I'll never find them. Stay out!" He chuckled about it as he lowered himself into her chair. It held her scent. For a moment, he allowed himself to get lost in her essence that lingered in the room. He stroked her papers with his fingertips and rolled her pencils, both red and regular, through his fingers.

From the kitchen he heard a streak of curses from Nitra. It rapidly brought Wallace back to reality. He pulled himself out of his daydreaming and got down to business. He mumbled under his breath, "A rotary phone? Lord the girl's batty." His fingers dialled the number on the card Harry had given him. A crash came from the kitchen. "What is she ... Yes, hello? This Wallace McPhee and I'd like to speak Chief Palmer." Another curse erupted. "Yes, I'll wait." He noticed the phone number scribbled on the front of the phone book and wondered whose it was. "Yah, hello Harry, I've got good news. We saw her up close." He waited for Harry to stop asking a hundred questions. "Well, Nitra wrote it all down. The list is out-and-out painstakingly descriptive. Ya better get a pen if ya want me to read it to ya." Wallace laughed at his answer. "Oh ya, adjectives are her best mate on this one. I got a better idea. Ya got a fax machine? It best I just fax the sheet to ya." He scribbled down the fax number beside the other number on the phone book. "Okay, I'll do it straight away." He pushed the chair towards the fax machine, "Hold on to your pants, I'm doin' it right now. Then what do you want us to do, Harry?" He punched in the numbers and slid the upside down page into it. "Uh-huh ... yep, I can do that." He watched as the page reappeared out the bottom. "Yah. I'll talk to ya tomorrow. Bye." Wallace turned off the machine before rolling the chair back into place. In the background, he heard another inventory of foul language and decided he better get in there before she destroyed the kitchen.

By the time he reached the kitchen, she had the table set for lunch. She sheepishly pulled out his chair, "Um ... you know that blue bowl with the thin white stripes on it? Well, if you tell me where you bought it, I'll replace it."

He was sure she was going to cry, so he took pity on her and lied, "That old thing? I got that a penny sale at the Irish Hall. Don't worry about it. It was chipped anyhow." It wasn't. It was one of the dishes he had brought with him from Ireland when he left, a memento of hard times past. He took a bite of his sandwich. "This is good." Again, he lied. In reality, it was revolting. The onion wasn't minced small enough and there was a bitter aftertaste he couldn't quite identify. He held it up and inspected the cut edge, "What did you put in it?"

Feeling relieved that it wasn't his favourite bowl or that it didn't belong to his grandmother, she poked fun back at him. "Not telling. It's my secret ingredient."

He took another mouthful and immediately realized what it was by the crunch of course crystals between his teeth. She had added his French sea salt. He didn't have the heart to tell her it was only used in oven cooking so the granite like granules had time to breakdown. But he said nothing, instead he moaned loudly to mollify her further.

While Nitra wasn't looking he dropped a tiny piece of his sandwich onto the floor for the forever begging feline. He watched from the corner of this eye as Gemma sniffed it. Next, she batted it with her paw and bit at it. The cat drew her body back, her head shuddering in disgust. Wallace chuckled to himself, not even the greedy cat would eat it.

"What's so funny?" Attempting to take the first bite of her sandwich, a large glob dropped on her shirt front. "Oh Christ, the diced tomato will stain. I better go change." She carefully picked the clump off her pale peach blouse and flicked it back on her plate beside the sandwich. "I'll be back in a jiffy."

Wallace listened for her to squeak the top step, signalling that the coast was clear. He immediately sprung to his feet and jammed the remains of his sandwich into the cookie jar in the corner. Gemma meowed at him. "Oh shut up, she'll never find it there anyway." The cat simply flipped her tail at him as though chastising him with a finger.

By the time Nitra had returned to the kitchen, he was standing at the door waiting for her. "Come on then. We'll be late."

176

"But … my sandwich?" She was surprised to see that Wallace had cleared the table and tidied the kitchen completely. The truth of it was, he saved her from the grittiest, saltiest chicken sandwich he'd ever eaten.

"No time Lass, we got to go. We'll get something when we get back."

Nitra squinted at him, "You're sure in a hurry. What gives?" She pulled her tote from the hook and cursed herself for not switching it again.

"Nothing. Now get yourself together and let's go." He gently pushed her on the back and swept her out the door. "This time I'm takin' the back way into town. She'll not be followin' us that way." He locked the door behind them and they headed out to meet Teddy of *Teddy's Timeless Attire*.

Chapter Ten

Driving into town, he brought Nitra a way she'd never gone before. Speeding up and down back roads she didn't know existed. As he came over a hill top, he slowed down the car and pointed out the window, "Look at that. Ain't that a sight for sore eyes?" Pulling into a niche on the side of the road, he let out a long sigh.

For some reason she identified with the scene immediately, "It's like an Irish moor isn't it?" He only nodded. "You miss home don't you?" He shrugged his shoulders, dismissing what he was feeling deep in his heart. "Why don't you go home for a visit? You should go at Christmas time. You could see your Mum."

"And me brother." He shifted back into gear, pulling out onto the roadway.

"You have a brother? I never knew that. Do you have any other family?" She knew she was prying into his personal life, something he didn't care for.

At first he stayed quiet, letting memories roll around in his mind. Then he decided she needed to know more of his

178

life before her. A time he'd rather forget, but wasn't allowed to, by both the authorities and himself. Letting go of his reluctance, he let the words flow from him without restraining them as he always had before. "Well, I did. I had a sister and a nephew. But there gone now. Died in the streets, they did." He swallowed down the lump that was forming in his throat. "Ya see, they were comin' home from the grocery store and gunfire broke out. They were no more than a half a block from the house. Brigit pulled Collin into a doorway to take cover 'til the firin' stopped." He inhaled slow and deep, trying to control his voice so it didn't tremble. "Brigit was holding onto two paper bags of groceries when an orange broke through the bottom and rolled out into the street." He lowered his voice, trying to control the despair he held in his heart, "Collin ran out after it. In those days, that orange was a treat for him, like chocolate sweets for ya American kids. Me sister ran out after him just as the shooting started again. They got caught in the open." He swallowed down another lump, "He caught a bullet in the back, piercing through his heart. Thank the good Lord he died instantly. Brigit took three bullets in the back before she reached him, then she got another bullet to the belly. She bled to death holding onto her boy." He stopped talking. He had to, if he kept going he'd start crying and he wouldn't allow that in front of Nitra. Wallace McPhee was neither weak nor emotional, he was an Irishman. "We watched her die through the front window. Mum wouldn't let me go help them. She held onto my belt with all her might. Said, she wasn't loosin' another child to the God damned war." He blew out the emotional strain in his guts, "When the bullets stopped and the streets were clear, I got their bodies and carried them back to our house. I was nineteen and that was the day that changed me

179

forever." He shook his opened hand in the air, "Blood of your kin on your hands makes ya change." He shift the car hard. "As for going home, I can't. If I do, I'll be automatically arrested for murder."

Nitra was stunned by the confessions of his previous violent life. It revealed a world she couldn't fathom living in. But one question needed to be answered. "So you killed someone?" Her stomach churned at the thought of her Wallace committing a murderous act. It seemed an unnatural thought.

"For revengin' my sister and her boy's death. It's not somethin' I'm proud of Nitra. But ya have to understand, that in Ireland, that was the way we lived. Eye for an eye — life for a life — kin for kin." He pulled into the parking space across the street from Teddy's shop. Wallace turned to Nitra, his eyes filled with sorrow, "I do miss me Mum. I miss me homeland. But this is where I live now. For me, home is somethin' I read in me Mum's letters and see in the pictures she sends me."

She broke in, "Is that your mother in the picture beside your bed?" She studied him with sympathetic eyes, "Did you grow up in that house? How old is she now?"

"Yah, that be her. She sitting on the front step of the house I grew up in. Funny how somethin' never change. The old house, me Mum, and the way you drive me crazy with your bloody questions." He sat waiting for her to react to the last bit.

It took her a second or two before Nitra finally slugged him. "You God damned idiot. It's not funny." She slugged him in the arm again.

"Oh hold on there, Girl. It's noon, and I know ya don't like bein' late. So out the door with ya."He gave her a light shove towards her side of the car and quickly exited his. He scanned the area for the grey sedan; it was nowhere in sight. He yelled over the top of the car, "Last one there is a rotten little beggar." He had to lighten the mood or he'd never get through the day without falling apart. To boost the stakes, he stuck out his tongue at her, a childish move generally reserved for her.

It worked. She yelled back at him, "That's not fair! You cheated! You got a head start! You cheater!" But just the same, she chased after him.

He slowed his pace down so she could catch up, reaching the door at the same time as him. To beat her, he slammed into the door. "I win! I win!" He jumped in a tiny circle, giving her a victory whoop, accompanied with a single finger salute. Miffed and not thinking clearly, she went to heave open the door, when he grabbed the edge of it. "Hold on 'til I check out the shop for you know who." He pushed her aside with the back of his hand. "Stay right behind me, okay?"

And so she did. Nitra fell into place, mirroring each of his steps in slapstick style mockery. When he turned, she turned right behind him. When he stopped and looked around, she did the same, only she added a little gesturing to it. She placed the side of her hand over her eyebrow and bent her left knee, lifting her foot behind her. The effect was apparently hilarious because Teddy gave her a light handed round of applause from the back of the shop. "That's so cute. Listen Honey's, I'll be there in just a sec. You start without me, okay?" He said something to the person inside the change room before heading to the front of the store. As he approached, he offered his hand to Wallace first. But Wallace only shoved his hands in his pockets and nodded at him, refusing to shake it back, just in case he was a frock selling fairy.

181

Nitra stunned, couldn't believe what she saw before her. The shop was filled to the brim with every type of clothing she had ever imagined. Full length gowns, purses, shoes, and opulent jewellery. All of it displayed cleverly to enhance the beauty of each piece as well as the adjacent items. But what really caught her eye, was a tiny sign over the cash register. The words were neatly hand written and to the point.

NO GARMENT ON THESE PREMISES
HAS EVER BEEN WORN BY A CORPSE.

To any other person that might have been shocking or misunderstood, but to Nitra, it made perfect sense. Teddy's was simply reassuring his customers that none of the item in his shop were ever exposed to formaldehyde, which if came in contact with a live human's skin, would poison them within hours.

"So, how can I help you today?" He eyed Wallace for a long moment, making Wallace very nervous. So nervous, that he stood behind a rack of clothing so Teddy would stop admiring his physique. "A gown for the lady perhaps?" His fingers touched his lips in apology, "Oh wait. Oh, I'm so sorry, I didn't recognize you. It is you, isn't it?" He rushed at her like a lonely Aunt at Christmas time. Before she could back away, he had her confined in an eager embrace. "I love your work. The last book was fab. When is the next one coming out?" He switched from the hug to holding her hands in his. She noted that they felt rather soft for a man.

From the back of the shop, a set of dressing room curtains flopped open, "I don't know Teddy, it seems awfully tight to me. Are you sure …" her words trailed off when she realized she wasn't alone. "Oh sorry, I didn't mean to interrupt." Wallace straightened up erect at the sight of her statuesque figure. "Please continue."

Teddy simply called her to his side, "Come here darling, I'd like you to meet someone." Walking to where they were, Teddy introduced them, "Tina, this is Nitra Zupan and her housekeeper, Wallace McPhee." Instantly both women acknowledged each other and the connection between their lives with a pleasant grin. Nitra risked glancing at her forearms. To her relief there were no track marks, meaning that her drug of choice wasn't heroin.

Although Wallace was taken back at how Teddy knew his name, and the position he held for Nitra, he was quickly distracted by the charisma and figure of Tina Harper.

"So you're Nitra? My brother talks about you a lot." That bit of news brought a warm smile to Nitra's lips. "He's slightly smitten actually, but I'm sure you know that by now." Wallace didn't understand who her brother was, so he listened closer to their conversation, trying to piece it together. Tina examined herself in the nearby mirror. She was draped in a full length strapless satin gown. "Hell, he even bought one of your books to read. I think it was the one about the two cops. You'll be good for him."

"Oh, Tommy's a dreamboat. Why her brother fixed my chair back to its proper state. You see it's Irish, but crafted in the Queen Ann style. He restored one of the support brackets with a tiny wooden block, like the others originally had. He's also an intellectual. He also informed me it's worth $3,000.00." Teddy was out and out bragging at his wealth. "And I've got four of them."

As per usual, Tina ignored Teddy's boasting and made herself the focal point once again, "So, what do you think? Is it me?" She twirled in front of the mirror to make the bottom flare and its silver satin shimmer in the light. By the smile on his face, it was a dance Wallace apparently enjoyed. "No really, is it me?"

Teddy answered first, "No. No. It's much too pale for your hair and skin colour … it washes you out."

After Wallace's attentive reaction to her, Nitra added her somewhat tainted opinion, "In a way, it's too similar to a regular slip. I'd find another style. Maybe something a little less … revealing?"

Wallace took a step forward and with a tone Nitra had never heard before, voiced his amorous thoughts, "They're right, but I think you'd look lovely in anything you wear." His cheeks flushed slightly pink when she giggled at his not so subtle flirtation.

Teddy saw the jealousy erupting in Nitra's eyes and decided that a well placed interruption was needed. "No, I told you that the blue gown is the one. It's going to show off your best features."

"Oh and there are a lot of those." Wallace's eyes scanned the entire length of her slender, scantily clad body. The clingy gown left nothing to his male imagination. A sinful curve slipped into his smile.

Again Tina giggled back, using that flirty shy tactic that women used to drive men crazy. She covered her grin with her finger tips and batted her eyes at him, pretending his attentions weren't wanted. She followed it up with an equally nauseating, "Oh, stop it. You're embarrassing me."

Teddy watched Nitra silently fume again, and decided to turn the tables on Wallace, making him feel like a hunted piece of sexual flesh. He tossed a turquoise sweater at Wallace. It clung to where it landed on Wallace's chest. "Try it on. It's your colour Hon. It'll play up those gorgeous eyes of yours. Not that they need any help. You got some glorious peeps." He scanned down the rest of his body, but decided that Wallace couldn't handle his next comment, keeping it to himself. Wallace quickly peeled the sweater off his torso and tossed it on the table in front of him. It was his way of saying 'not a chance'. Teddy had met Wallace's kind before and knew exactly how to manipulate his own beloved masculinity against himself. "What's the matter Wallace? Are you some kinda sissy that you can't try on a sweater in front of everyone?" He swept his hand passed the on lookers, pulling them into the situation.

He watched Tina's smile wilt. Teddy had finally got Wallace's goat. "Never mind that. How did you know my name?" Wallace dropped his voice lower proving that he was tough and masculine, trying to dispel any notion that because he was housekeeper, he was therefore gay.

Teddy laughed at his display of manliness, "Oh, don't be silly. Everyone knows you work for Nitra." With wiggling fingers, he shooed Tina toward the back dressing room . "And you are a friend of Martina's, who's a friend of my kid sister." He handed Tina another gown and pushed her through the curtains. "It's a small town and you live with a celebrity. Need I say more?"

Nitra remembered the Irish adage that Wallace had mumbled many times, *Fame is a magnifying glass.* It was his way of reminding her that if you ask for fame it will find you, no matter what the time of day or your emotional state. A paid price that is demanded, never offered. "Speaking of being a writer ... do you have my pages here at the shop?" The whole situation was getting on her nerves and an early escape was needed.

"Of course dear. That's why I called you here, wasn't it?" He promptly headed for the front of the shop. Nitra couldn't decide whether Teddy was gay or just an eccentric. She thought to herself, *No, he's just an odd fella.* Nitra followed him to the front counter while rummaging inside her tote bag for the money, when a squeal pierced the air.

"Oh ... My ... God! Where did you get that bag?" He almost ran right into her, trying to get a look at it. "Can I see it up close?" His eyes were glued to every movement it made. She slipped it from her hand and reluctantly gave it to him. He held it high in the air to examine the underside of it. "Oh my God, it is. It *is* a Hamner." He stroked the fabric with his fingertips, "What fabulous beading work. Handmade glass I suspect. How absolutely divine? And it's in excellent condition. How much do you want for it?"

His question caught Nitra off guard, "I'm sorry. I ... I don't understand. You want to buy my tote bag?" Teddy nodded wildly. "You actually want this ugly old tote?" Wallace rolled his eyes at her. She was simply useless at that sort of thing. Anyone else would have shut up and inquired 'how much do you want to pay for it?' But not Nitra, she just babbled on and hung herself.

"That my dear child, it's a Hamner original." He drew the handles through his hands. "And by the look of these, it's one of his earlier pieces. Where on earth did you get it?"

"Um ... let me think? Somewhere in New York, I don't really remember exactly." She looked at her tote and tried her hardest to admire it more then she had before the revelation. It didn't matter; it was still ugly in her eyes. "I was at a book signing and during a break William whisked me to a boutique next door to escape the overcrowded bookshop." She frowned at trying to remember the details of that day. "I remember that it was in the window. I needed something to put my schedule and pages in, so I bought it. I think I only paid ..."

Before she could reveal how little she paid for it Wallace spoke up, "Oh, I remember that trip. That was last spring."

Teddy shot him a look. Wallace had interrupted at the most inopportune moment. He inhaled deeply, smiled sweetly and inquired again, "How much do you want for it?"

Nitra's eyes opened wide, "You're serious aren't you?" She looked at the tote then back at his face. Then she did the one thing Wallace thought she'd never do. "To me it sounds like you're a collector of her work. How much do you think it's worth?" Nitra Zupan had turned the tables on him, putting him in the hot seat. Wallace nodded his silent approval at her taking control of the situation.

He held it up to examine it again. He was about to say something when Tina budded in, "Ted don't you dare offer her anything but a fair price. You know she'll find out the true value eventually and tell everyone how much of a cheapskate you really are." Oddly enough any woman could appear motherly as long as she parked a hand on a hip just the right way — even in a full length cerulean blue sequined gown.

"Or better yet, she could recommend your shop to all of her friends," Wallace added his part. "Not to mention her friends from the city. Friends found in high places."

"And there are lots of men in the publishing business." Tina winked at Nitra. "Are any of those men tall and good looking?" Nitra simply nodded with a sinful grin. She changed her mind again; maybe he was gay after all.

Teddy looked at the tote one more time. He bounced his index finger on his lips before handing it back to her. "Fifteen hundred dollars."

187

Nitra's stomach lurched. She couldn't believe her ears and by the expression on Wallace's face, he couldn't believe it either. She took a deep breath and went with her gut instincts. "Now I thought you were going to offer me a fair price?" She tilted her head adding an innocent touch to the question.

Tina grunted, "That's a man for ya. Always giving you less but telling you it's worth more."

Teddy took that as a direct insult, "Oh fine, two thousand." Then as an extra bargaining chip he added "And an autographed photo for my wall." His thumb pointed to the back of the shop, to the wall covered in framed pictures.

Inside she laughed. Even in the act of bargaining, he was still eccentric to the core. "And you'll throw in that brown briefcase. Deal?" She had been admiring it since she came in the door.

He rolled his eyes at her, "Lord you're tyrant. Just let me think for sec." He began to pace in a small oval while he tapped his bottom lip. Then he stopped short, "Fine ... but one more thing."

"What's that?" She was expecting him to demand something outlandish, like her shoes or a dinner prepared at her house.

But he didn't. In fact, he didn't demand it, he bashfully asked for it, "Could you write me into one of your novels?" He pressed his spread open hand against his chest, "Not me exactly, but a character like me."

Nitra smiled at him. She understood where he was coming from now. Although he put up a strong front, he was like everyone else in the world ... he wanted to be recognized, and loved. "You're already a character in yourself Teddy, but I'll do my best." She motioned for a hug and he obliged. With the sight of the phony coddling, Wallace thought he was going to be sick.

He broke away from the hug and headed for the register, "Cheque or cash?"

Wallace answered in true Irish style, "Cash is best, don't ya think?" It was just like Wallace to not trust a man that owned a store filled with glittery gowns and high heels.

With pursed lips and a glaring look, Nitra corrected him, "No, a cheque is fine. I can't imagine that you'd have that kinda of money just kicking around the shop."

Tina laughed out loud, "You'd be surprised, Sugar. You see this dress? It's nine hundred dollars." She did a tiny twirl to show it off, "And a bargain at that. Most of these gowns are over fifteen hundred. There top quality, the majority being vintage." She swept her hands down the front of her body. She pushed her breasts up with both hands so that they nearly burst over the top, "This one's straight from Hollywood." She cupped them slightly while flashing her eyes at Wallace. At being caught seeking an eager peek, he quickly averted his eyes back to Nitra.

"And fits like a glove too. You should really get it Honey. It's so you." Teddy started to write out the cheque, "So, should I deduct the payment for the pages?"

"No. Please keep them separate. Business expense, you understand." She was busy transferring the contents of her tote bag into the briefcase.

"I hear you Honey. My accountant keeps telling me that receipts are a must. But most of the stylists I purchase originals from don't want a paper trail." He ripped off the cheque and exchanged it for Nitra's tote.

As Tina returned to the dressing room, she pointed out the reason for their reluctance, "That's cause they're hot. And thieves don't like to be found out. One of the girls I work with has a friend in the business. He sells off stuff all the time. If his boss questions where it is, he simply tells them that one of the actors took it home." Unconsciously she had started to unzip the gown she was wearing. "Let's face it, they'll never ask a star if they stole a piece of clothing."

Teddy waggled his finger in the air, "Honey, you can't do that in here. You ain't at work. You have to be *inside* the room to do that sort of thing."

Tina glanced at Wallace's face to see his reaction to Teddy's comment. She was hoping that he didn't already know where she worked. To her surprise, his facial response was to have no response at all. But Teddy's statement still left an awkward tension hanging in the air. It was Nitra who veered the subject away from Tina. "So tell me Teddy, where did you find these pages." She flipped through the corners. Pages 26, 28, 30 and 31 were placed in order. It was what she had feared, her first page was missing. She was about to swear out loud when Teddy shocked her out of her anger.

"Ha! Don't be so stupid. Me pick up dirty papers? Never." He carefully hung the tote on a hook, displaying it within the largest showcase. "I didn't find them, I bartered for them. Norma Jean wanted one of my fur wraps and I wanted to meet you. So I traded him the fur for your pages. By the way, it was a three hundred dollar stole ... and worth every penny."

"Him? Norma Jean is a guy?" Wallace shivered at the thought.

That's when Teddy tapped on the wall. It was a sign that was posted over a case of jewellery.

We sell gear to the queer.
If it makes you fear, don't be here.

190

"Wallace! Honestly, you have to let people be people. Besides, he might be a transvestite and nothing more." She handed Teddy the bills. "But do you know where Norma Jean found them?"

"I think he said, near the Memorial Park. It's hard to tell with Norma Jean. He was pretty wired that day. He's got a little problem with …"

Tina cut in, "He's trying to get clean, but it's hard. Really hard." She had changed into her street clothes, a skin tight red t-shirt and dark blue jeans. "Give him the time and support he needs, and he'll make it." She laid the blue gown on the counter. "If I can do it, so can he." She proudly smiled at Nitra, letting her know that she was clean and free of the beast that had once controlled her. "Teddy can you find it in your heart to put this one on my account as well?"

He sighed dramatically. He said it with a sidelong glare, "Oh Honey, you're gonna have to pay me soon. You're at almost nine thousand again."

"Really? No? It can't be that much?"

"Oh yes it can, and it is." He placed his hand squarely on his hip. Nitra decided that the bossy stance wasn't as effective on a man. A mother had to be a woman to pull it off properly.

"I get my bonus on Saturday night." Her oath hand popped up into the air, "I'll pay you Monday, I swear."

"Oh fine." He waved a small black ledger at her, "But no more charges until you pay this off." His face flushed, "And make it Tuesday. I'm closed this Monday. Remember?"

"Oh yah, right, I forgot." She jerked in a deep breath, "Tuesday. I promise."

"Box or bag, Sweety?" He gently folded the gown into a tidy rectangle.

191

"A bag. I've got to get it altered for a new show I'm working on. Me and Dixie are going to do a two girl show. A classy act, not like the other acts I've been doing at the club ..." She stopped herself short, but knew it was too late and added "... in the past." She had openly admitted that she worked in a strip club and Wallace heard it all. She watched from the corner of her eye as his body language changed. The gleam in his brown eyes faded away, leaving them dark and judgemental. He refused to look at her and started staring out the window instead.

The air was charged with an ugly tension, something Teddy didn't care for at all. An attitude adjustment was in order. "I envy you. Up there in the lights, singing your heart out." He carefully wrapped the gown in tissue, "You should hear her. The voice of an angel, she has." He slipped the gown into one of the shops rich burgundy bag, "It's nice that your boss lets you just sing. You never did any dancing, did you?"

"No. Charlie wanted me to, but I refused. I told him there wasn't enough money in the world to make me do that sort of thing."

"So you don't actually strip then? You just sing there? How can that be, men only go to those places to see naked women and for ...well ... the sex acts?" She stopped at the last statement. She saw Tina's nostrils flare and knew she had gone too far with her questioning.

"Some of the girls do those sorts of things ... *I'm not* one of them. Never have, never will." Teddy came around to the front of the counter to hand her the weighty bag by its handles. "Thank you Teddy. I think it's time I for me to leave." She held her head high with dignity, "It was nice to meet you both. Teddy, I will see you on Tuesday."

Teddy gave her a double cheeked kiss goodbye. "See ya Honey. Take care." He held the door open while she left. The door closed with a soft thump. In no time flat Teddy turned on the others, his voice condemning, "Well, that was mighty gracious of you two. She's a singer, not a stripper. People are so cruel sometimes. Just because she works in that club, doesn't mean she's one of the girls there. Charlie runs a classy place ... well sort of ... he tries to anyway. And he pays her top dollar for her talent. It's well known that he treats her proper too. In fact, I heard through the grapevine that he, and a couple of his boys, went out to that creep Patrick Spencer's place and warned him to stay away from her. If he continued to torment Tina with any of his drugs, Charlie was going to come after him." He nodded his head hard, adding a stubborn defiance to the declaration, "She's finally clean and is determined to stay that way."

"I didn't know. I had heard that she worked there and naturally assumed she was a dancer. Now I feel awful." She stood silent for a minute, thinking back to what Sarah said and what she saw outside of *Hadley's Gas and Grill*. "So why are she and Tom always arguing? I saw them fighting earlier this week. Why?"

"Probably over money. You see, Tommy think she should invest her money. And in a manner, Tina is. But not the way big brother wants her to. And well, I'll be truthful, Tom doesn't believe that any female can manage their own financial future." He frowned as he confirmed it, "Unfortunately, he's that breed of 'old fashioned' guy. But Tina's strong, she invests almost every penny she has back into her singing career, trying to get it back to where it was."

"Where *it* was? What do you mean? Did she have a singing career before? What happened to it?" She was going to ask another question, but Teddy stopped her with a halting hand. Wallace had a feeling this was going to take awhile, so he slouched down on the rack in front of him, making himself comfortable. What Teddy had mentioned about Tom's attitude toward women was tucked away in the back of her mind. Chauvinistic behaviour was not acceptable to her way of life. The subject, one Tom Harper, required more research.

"This is not the first time she's got herself clean. Back, oh almost ten years ago now, she stopped doing drugs all together and was working her way up in the music business. A new rising star, they called her. Then the one thing happened that kills many careers, her fiancé screwed her over. You see, Donald was also her accountant. The greedy bastard positioned himself to be in charge of her finances and then took her for everything she had. Shame she was too in love to see it. He secretly sold off all her stocks and cashed in her life insurance policy, cleaning her right out. Then to make it worse, the rotten shit took out a credit card in her name. He forged her signature and coerced his mother to say she was Tina on the phone when the credit card people called to confirm the authorization. Told his own mother he'd toss her in the streets if she didn't do what he said. " He let out a heavy sigh, "When it all came down, and the police stepped in, she was left with nothing. But what burns my butt is that the bastard got away with it all." He shook his head in disbelief, "And when the people started to blame her for all *his* crimes ... well, that's when she started on the drugs again."

Suddenly, very happy with her own accountant, Nitra asked one more question. "So how'd she end up working at the club? Sorry, *singing* at the club."

"Charlie. He had heard singing in a little bar three towns over. Fell head over heels in love with her voice and offered her a job at his club. He had one condition though … she had to leave the drugs behind. And she did it. It damned near killed her, but she got through it. She did it for one thing … to sing again." The door opened and a rather tall woman came in. "You should go see her perform. She's top notch. Right, Norma Jean?" Wallace immediately straightened up. He nervously shuffled back and forth on his feet while hiding behind the rack. There was no way he was letting Norma Jean ogle him over as Teddy had.

"Who? Tina?" Norma Jean's voice was out of sync with his appearance. He truly was a woman on the outside, but his tone was deep and manly. Nitra had to look hard to see the masculine features in his face. They were there, but very subtle, a light five o'clock shadow and a mannish chin. "A voice like velvet." He examined them both over before holding out his hand to Nitra, "Hello. My name is Norman, Norman Jean. And you are?"

She went to answer, but Teddy did it for her, "Oh Norma, it is my true pleasure to introduce you to the famous Nitra Zupan."

"Nitra who?"

"Nitra Zupan." Teddy's voice squealed while he tried to impress upon Norma that she was indeed someone he should know automatically. He widened his eyes for emphasis, "You know? The famous writer."

Norma shrugged his shoulders, "Sorry, I'm not a big reader. But it's nice to meet you anyway." Teddy rolled his eyes in his head.

She felt half insulted, half amused. Deciding to have a little fun, she let it go and daintily pointed in his direction, "And that's my housekeeper, Wallace." She grinned wildly as Wallace instantly panicked. He wasn't sure what he was supposed to do, so he stepped deeper into the rack, concealing him completely. His head was starting to throb again.

Norma simply nodded at him and huskily grunted out a, "Hey." Although one of them was dressed in a lavender pants suit, this situation was no different than two men saying 'hey' at the hardware store.

Wallace's shoulders relaxed by an inch, while Nitra chuckled to herself. "Wallace we need to be going. Time is a wasting." She bowed slightly to Norma Jean, "It was nice to meet you. Maybe someday, us three could go out for coffee?"

Teddy's face lit up, "Coffee ... with me? Oh, that would be lovely."

"Again, Teddy, thank you for my pages and this fabulous briefcase. I will send you that photo, I promised you." She gave Teddy a light peck on the cheek and noticed over his shoulder that Norma had crossed his arms at hearing about the pages. "I'll call you in a couple of weeks, so we can set up the time with Norma here." She sent a smile towards Norma, which included an apology that should have come from Teddy.

"Sounds great." He walked her to the door. Wallace was already halfway out and holding it open for her. "I'm looking forward to it. Bye bye now."

Nitra exited the door first with Wallace close behind her. They weren't at the car before Wallace let out an enormous sigh, "Oh Christ, I thought we'd never leave. That's a freak show in there?"

"Oh for Christ sake, stop bein' so God damned dramatic. Why does everythin' have to be such a big damn deal with ya?" She mocked him with his own accent and the exact words he used to scold her with, as they left Spencer's drug house. "Hell, that was nothin'. God, you've lived such as sheltered life."

It took him a few steps before he recognized the phrases. He turned to face her, "Oh that's nice, really nice. Pick on a man with his own words."

"Well, what did you expect from a rotten little beggar?" she swatted him in the butt and ran for her side of the car.

He stopped long enough to scan the street again. On her side of the car, he unlocked her door and whispered in her ear, "Get in the car quick." She slipped in the opened door and locked it after he closed it.

When he climbed in his side, she started her list of questions. "Why? What's wrong? Is she here? Where is she? Are we in danger? Should I hide down in the seat?"

That's where he broke in, "Yah. Get down." He shoved her down by the top of her head. "And don't come up 'til I tell ya." He started the car and sped off at a high roar. She couldn't see the wicked grin on his face from bellow the dash.

They were almost halfway home when Nitra finally spoke up, "Is she gone yet? Are we out of danger? Can I come up now?"

Wallace grinned down at her and flippantly motioned with his chin, "Oh yah, ya can come up now."

She finally caught on to what he'd been doing, "You bastard! She wasn't there at all, was she? You've had me bent over for no good reason? You idiot!" She swatted at him only once before clenching at her lower back. Her eyes winced as she straightened completely up right. He opened his mouth to apologize for aggravating her back condition, but she held up her hand, terminating his words. She snapped out, "Don't talk to me. Just get me home." Then she closed her eyes and turned her face towards her window.

He meant it to be a joke. He chastised himself for not thinking it out thoroughly. After a mile or two, he tried to put things straight. His words were soft and remorseful, "It was only a wind-up. I was poking back at ya for mimicking me." He watched closely for her face to reappear, but she didn't turn around. That's when he knew he'd gone too far. "Nitra, I'm sorry. I really didn't mean to hurt you. Honest Lass."

Nitra said nothing, not a word. Instead she stared out her side of the car, staying as still as a stone statue. She didn't dare speak; inside she was too angry to talk calmly. If she did start talking, all of what she'd been feeling would rush out in one long nasty scolding. How she felt about him, the way he acted towards Tina, and the victimizing fears that were building up inside her. This time it was best she stayed hard and cold like granite. And that's the way she stayed for the remainder of the trip home.

Chapter Eleven

Wallace walked her to the door, "You go and lay down on the sofa and I'll bring in your pills." He locked it behind them. "And Nitra ... I am sorry it hurts."

She was in no mood for his apology, "Yah, yah, whatever. Just get my pills. And a shot or two of your scotch wouldn't be so bad right about now." Limping pass the answering machine, she noticed that the light was blinking, so she pressed the play button.

"Hi Nitra, it's me William ... your editor. How are you keeping down there? And how's that next book coming. You know I've been waiting for the first draft and maybe chapters one and two. Give me a call when you get back in. We do need to talk at some point Nitra. Time is a wasting. Bye for now ... but call me pronto. Bye."

"Christ, what is it with that saying?" she pushed the erase button.

"What saying?" He handed her two pills and a tulip shaped tumbler of his best single malt scotch.

"Time is a wasting. Christ, I've heard it at least five times in the last ..." A second message kicked in, cutting off her words. Alcohol with pain pills was never a good idea, but with her being mad at him, he wasn't about to point that out to her.

"Now that you've seen me, it's time to talk. I'll call back tonight at six o'clock. Sharp. And if I were you, I'd answer the damn phone by yourself. No cops. If you bring in the cops, I'll walk away from this." The receiver was hung up loud and hard.

"It *was* her who called last night." Wallace raced to the window and peered through the curtains. No one was out there. He turned around in time to witness Nitra pop in the pills and toss down the scotch in one gulp. He walked over, taking the tumbler out of her hand. "Oh, that's just bloody great. Get yourself tanked so I have to take care of ya with all this goin' on."

She stared right into his eyes, "If you hadn't been such a jerk, I wouldn't hurt so much that I need to be impaired." She put her hand on her hip and leaned in further, their noses almost touched. "Now are you calling Harry or shall I?"

"Oh, I'd better do it or I'll never hear the end of it, now will I." He pulled the receiver off the wall and paced to the other side of the kitchen. He yanked on the lengthy cord as he muttered to himself, "Bloody cantankerous woman."

While he waited for the police to answer, Nitra retrieved her mini-tape recorder from her new briefcase. She carefully recorded the Lipstick Lady's message, not once, but twice, on separate mini cassettes. It was something she had seen in a documentary on the problems associated with incriminating evidence used by the courts. If it was missed on the first recording, it would definitely be there on the second taping.

Wallace was now standing behind her, waiting for Nitra to finish and move out of his way, so he could play the message for Harry. "Okay. Here ya are." He held the phone down to the machine and pressed play. As the message prattled on, Wallace turned his attention to Nitra. He boldly went beyond the normal boundaries by stroking her cheek with the back of his hand. "How are ya holdin' up?"

Until then she had been holding it in, but with the stress, and the scotch, she let it all go and buried her face into his shoulder. He held her tight while she started to cry. The message ended. "Well, now what do ya think we need to do Harry?" He pulled her closer and listened intently to Harry's plans. "Okay. I'll have everything ready here. Oh and Harry, no police cars or uniforms. Sounds like a real nutter to me. Hell knows what she wants or what she'll do to get it." He softly stroked Nitra's hair with his thumb while listening to Harry's plan on what they'd do about that. "Good. I'll see you then." He shifted both him and Nitra over three steps, so he could hang up the phone. He said nothing, but held her tightly until she cried herself out.

When she broke away from his arms, she wiped her eyes and then inhaled deeply, "Okay, I'm good now. What did Harry say we should do?" Her face was streaked with red lines from her tears, but her expression had turned stern with determination. "What should we be doing Wallace?"

"I need to open the garage door so they can pull their cars right into it. You stay in here, while I go do that." He headed for the door, "Lock this behind me."

Panic showed instantly in her eyes, "No wait, you can't leave me here alone."

"No, ya have to. I'll be two minutes, at the most. Ya can watch me from the window." He didn't give her a choice; he opened the door and vanished to the other side, "Now lock it Lass."

She ran and did exactly what he said. Next, she sidestepped to the window and watched as he yanked open the huge door. She noted that he scanned the yard as he returned to the door. She slid open the latch to let him back in, slamming it locked again. "Is she out there?"

She was only asking one question at a time, something that didn't surprise Wallace considering the stress she was under. "Not that I could see. Now we need to get the kitchen ready for the boys." He pointed to the small desk under the phone. "Harry wants a bigger table than that one so he can set up the taping equipment. And he'll need that table cleared off. No placemats or such. Ya can do that part, can't ya?"

She nodded and got right to work. Having something to do was a relief. She stripped the kitchen table bare while he got the other table from the living room. Within minutes everything was in place. Feeling helpless, she wondered what to do next, "So now what?"

"We wait." He knew it wasn't what she wanted to hear, but the reality was, that was all they could do. As always his motherly instincts came out in times of despair, "Are ya hungry? I've got some soup in the freezer. I can heat it up for ya."

She stood with her shoulder slumped down and a lost expression in her eyes. "No. I can't eat anything. But if you're hungry, you go ahead." She slowly made her way to where he was in the kitchen. Having him closer made her feel protected. "What do you think she wants? I mean, I've never met her before, so what could she possibly want from me."

Wallace had his own theory. He was sure it was another fan that had finally flipped, thinking that Nitra was more than a normal human being. It had always been there in one way or another. Most fans kindly kept their distance, others didn't. Some felt that Nitra was public domain, therefore they had the right to impose themselves on her, making it unbearable for her to go about her everyday life. "Harry thinks she's a nutter, like Larson." Nitra's head jerked upward, showing her concern. "Look, there's nothing to worry about Love. Harry and the boys will be here in a minute." He put his arm around her shoulder, "They'll find out who she is and have her in cuffs by the end of the night. Hell, chances are that you'll never even have to talk to her." He twisted her around to face her, "And no Lass, ya can't go have coffee with her at the prison."

That made her burst out laughing. She sarcastically snapped her fingers, "Damn it! And I was so looking forward to it." She flung her arms around his neck to give him a huge hug, "Wallace, you know me all too well." There they stood in the kitchen hugging each other because of his silly humour when they both realized that they were actually in each other's embrace. She looked up into his eyes and began to tell him what was in her heart, "Wallace, I think I'm ..." A loud knock at the door interrupted her confession.

"Hey, open up in there." Harry was balancing a nylon bag on top of a large black box.

Wallace looked at Harry through the door's window, then back at Nitra, standing where he left her. Still feeling the warmth of her on his body, he simply couldn't take it any longer. It was now or never. He kissed her passionately on the lips, then immediately pulled her away, "Sorry, but I got to go." He stepped around her to unlock the door for the fumbling cop. Nitra groaned to herself. Had Harry seen them?

"It's about damn time. This stuff's heavy, ya know?" He quickly hurried to the kitchen table to unload it in the center, "Don't lock it, Joey's right behind me."

"Hell Harry, I told you no uniforms or cruisers." He kept a watch on the door.

"Firstly, did you hear a siren?" Both shook their heads *No*. He flopped a coil of cable onto the table, "Don't be stupid. Joey's not in uniform, he's wearing his hunting gear." As if on cue, there was a knock on the door. Wallace pulled it open to find Joey clad head to toe in khaki camouflage. Even his face was blotched with several shades of green paint.

Nitra started to giggle. She couldn't stop herself, the sight was hilarious. Joey had covered every inch of his face leaving a pinkish rim around his eyes. He looked like a pink eyed opossum hiding in the leaves. Joey was the only police officer she knew that had a pony tail. It was a waist long braid and glossy black. She presumed it was because of his Native Indian heritage that he was permitted to wear it on the job.

"What's with you?" Harry spotted the bottle of scotch on the counter and made the connection. "Oh, I get it." Then he wagged his finger directly at her, "But no more boozing. I need you with your head screwed on straight."

Although she cleared her throat in attempts to stop laughing, she finally found relief by turning herself away from Joey's jungle face. "You got it Harry, no more booze." When she turned back to the men, she was surprised to see that everything was set up in place. Her phone had been tapped while still hanging on the wall as it always had. The heavy black wires led to a massive amount of equipment now spread out on the kitchen table.

Harry was plugging in his headphones, "Nitra, some quick instructions. When she calls, delay her as much as you can, without it seeming obvious. Drag out your answers. Leave a couple of seconds in between sentences. And for Christ sake, don't answer the phone 'til I tell you it's okay and clear. We'll probably only get one chance at this, so we can't screw up." He pulled the headphone jack back out and examined the tip. "Wallace, I need your help. I forgot a piece of equipment in the trunk of the car. It's in a small blue box." He tossed him the keys to the cruiser. "Watch your back." Once Wallace was out the door, Harry turned his attention to Nitra, "How you holding up?" She only shrugged her shoulders at him. Looking up at her from the table, he grinned accusingly, "Well, I see Wallace has been supporting you just fine."

Her face flushed hot. Now she was certain he had seen her and Wallace through the window. "He's not all *that* supportive. In fact, that was the first time he's been supportive at all." Joey didn't understand what they were talking about, something that suited Nitra just fine.

"Is that right? Seems to me that with the two of you living under one roof, he might have been supportive long before this." Harry tried to conceal the true meaning behind the statement by adding, "'Cause he'd be the right guy to support you, in my opinion."

"No. Just this once." She busied herself with the lunch dishes in the sink. "Um … and yah, I think your right there. I just have to figure out if I really want him supporting me any further."

Joey opened the door for Wallace, locking it again. Both Harry and Nitra were staring at him, making him very nervous, "Oh what am I being bloody blamed for this time?" Both immediate diverted their eyes.

With a slight twinkle in his eye, Harry took the box from him, then turned away from him and focused back to the taping equipment. Nitra busied her with the dishes again. Wallace watched them both, trying to surmise what they were up to. Not being able to, he finally asked Joey for assistance. He whispered it to him, "What were they talking about before I came in?"

Joey blushed slightly, "Look, I don't like ratting on anybody, but they were talking about how you were supporting her earlier. You know, when we first got here. I think it's great the way you support her. You're only her housekeeper, but sometimes you treat her like she was your woman."

Over hearing Joey's comment, Nitra dropped a plate on the counter which then clattered to the floor. She stood staring at him, but turned her eyes away from Wallace. But it was Harry that broke the awkwardness by grumbling at his deputy, "Don't you have to get in place, like I told you to?"

Joey knew he was in trouble, but had no idea exactly why. "Yah … sure … right away." He slowly stepped back from Wallace, but glanced at Nitra one more time. Then it hit him. With his finger he pointed back and forth between them, "Oh, I get it now. You and h …"

"HEY!" Harry's sharp yell stopped Joey's words cold, "I believe, I ordered you to get to your post Officer Wolf. Now get!" His index finger jabbed towards the kitchen door. "And don't come back in 'til I tell you to. Now get!"

His body went straight as a board, "Yes sir." Joey scurried to the door, whipped open the latch and disappeared pass the window.

"Sometimes that boy can be as stupid as a shit pile." Harry didn't even look up when he said it.

Nitra needed to change the subject, and fast. "So where's he going? Where's his post?" She peered out the window to see Joey sliding into the garage. "Is he leaving in the cruiser?"

"For the last time, we did not bring the God damned cruiser." He slowly blew out a breath, counting to five in his head like his doctor told him to. "We brought our unmarked car. It's old and beat up, but the motor will outrun Wallace's sports car, any day. And no, he's not leaving with it. He's getting his rifle." He watched as Nitra's lips parted and answered her question before she asked it. "He's getting the rifle so he can get on top of the garage." He held up his hand to stop her words. "From up there, he has a clear shot at the kitchen door or right through inside the window if need be. Not to fear, Joey's got your back."

"Oh, like a sniper. Wow, that *is* exciting?" She put the dried plate into the cupboard. Wallace could see her mind arranging the words that described the situation.

"Oh yah, a real thrill." Harry's tone was nothing near excited, more like sarcastic and bored.

"So, what do I do next?" Absent-mindedly she was heading towards the window when Wallace grabbed her by the arm and yanked her back to the far side of the kitchen.

"What the hell do you think you're doin'?" He was yelling at her, "Tryin' to get yourself killed. God damn it Nitra, we don't know if she's out there or not." When he started to shake her arm, that's when Harry broke in.

He threw his pen at them, making them freeze it spot, "Okay, you two idiots knock it off. Christ sake, I'm nervous enough without you two squabbling like a pair of wolves at a rabbit carcass." By then he was on his feet and yelling at them, his face very red, "Now sit down somewhere and shut the fuck up." He glared directly at Nitra with a pointed finger, "And that means away from the windows."

But Nitra wasn't ready to be so cooperative, "And do what? What's next?"

With a calming breath, he composed himself before answering, "You sit on your ass down and wait." He plunked his own butt down on the chair and continued to tinker with the equipment.

She protested loudly again, "That's it. We just sit around and wait? Like sitting ducks?"

"Nitra, you heard the man, sit down and shut the fuck up." Wallace pointed to her chair that sat adjacent to Harry's. "I'll get some paper so you can start writing it all down. It'll keep your mind off things. Now sit."

With the two men ordering her around she did what she was told, but rather reluctantly. She took her time getting to her chair while holding her head high. Harry ignored her; while Wallace brought her the red lined paper and laid it out in front of her. But instead of writing, she just sat in the chair with her arms crossed waiting for it to all start.

To her, the last three hours had been completely hellish. What with Wallace pacing about the kitchen, asking her if she was alright every five minutes; and Harry calling Wallace to ask him the most inane questions — she'd finally reached her limits with the two of them. Now she was truly infuriated with them both. Knowing this, Wallace created space between them, by making himself comfortable near the telephone. All three sat quietly, waiting for something to happen.

Harry checked the clock on the wall. It read ten to six. Harry's chest tightened. Harry wasn't exactly clear as to what the strange woman wanted or if she was working alone. That's what Harry worried about the most, maybe there were others that they weren't aware of, lurking about outside. Harry was grateful that the Lipstick Lady showed herself. To the seasoned police officer, that proved three things – One, she was not as clever as they feared; two, this may not be as serious as it was first thought to be; and lastly, she was an older overweight woman, an easy criminal to capture. He finished the last twist of the stripped wires and pushed the new plug into place.

At the exact moment the plug clicked, the phone erupted, *BRRRRRING*.

Nitra jumped in her chair but caught herself before she fell off it. The Lipstick Lady was early.

Harry pointed at it, "Don't just sit there ... answer the damn thing."

Wallace got out of her way, giving her his chair. She reached up for the receiver ...

Harry yelled, "Wait! Not yet! Wait 'til I say so." He flipped three switches and turned up a knob. He muttered to the station through his head set. "Brian, are we ready? Great." He looked at Nitra and signalled with a stuck up thumb, "Okay ... go."

At Harry's nod, she took a deep breath and lifted the receiver, "Hello?"

The voice was bass and to the point, "I have what you want."

Using a soft-hearted friendly voice, she asked the Lipstick Lady a direct question, not one that would normally be asked right of the bat, "What's your name? I need a name to call you." Nitra hoped she'd panic and slip-up by giving her entire name.

She didn't. "Rosella, but you better call me Rosie. You got that." It was evident that she was trying to maintain her tough veneer, along with her position of control. Rosie repeated the precise words she'd said before, "I have what you want."

Although she made an effort not to, her voice still made the words come out cynical, "What could you possibly have, that I'd want?"

The words were said individually, "Your ... Page ... One." She followed them up by a cold harsh silence. Only her raspy breathing could be heard.

Nitra's gut twisted, "I don't believe you." Her heart pound hard in her chest. If she did have page one they would have to meet. She needed to be certain it wasn't a hoax. "Prove it to me. Read the opening line."

"George Oscar Dack loathed his life." Rosie read further to distress her even more, *"It was dull, predictable and uneventful. And tonight he was going to put an end to that. He had a plan."* Then she stopped reading, "Sound familiar? Should I burn it ... or do you want it back?"

"That's enough." It was as she feared. This woman did indeed have what she wanted — her first page — the last page. "What is it you want?" There was always something Rosie's type wanted.

"Twenty-five thousand dollars." She said it in a manner that made it clear she meant business. "In cash."

Nitra held her hand over the receiver, checking to see if Harry got her extortion demand recorded to tape. He shook his head no and rolled his finger in the air, to keep the conversation going. Nitra had to get her to repeat the demand from Rosie's own mouth using her own words. "You want *what*?"

"You heard me, twenty-five thousand." This time her voice revealed that she was getting irritated.

Harry nodded that he got it recorded that time. Now it was Nitra's job to keep her on the line long enough for a trace to connect at the police station. She counted two in her head, "Why so much?"

"'Cause I heard what you said in Gladys's. You said you *need* this particular page more than the others. That's why so damned much." It came out sarcastic and nasty. "Like I said, I got what you want."

Harry signalled to stretch it out two more minutes. Nitra tried to keep her cool. She reminded herself of what she had to do – to leave gaps of two seconds and mutter a lot, just the way Harry told her to do. "Um …well … that's a lot of money to come up with at such a short notice." She counted to two, "It'll take a bit of time to get it together." She added another one second gap. "And I'm not sure I have that much money."

"Don't give me that crap. You're a fuckin' rich bitch with bucks coming out your ass. And I want some of that money. So are you paying up or what?"

Sitting in the chair, her shoulders went back and her chin pointed high, "Then I think I'll take the *what*." She said it sharp, with a scorch of scorn in it. Nitra's words and tone caught Wallace's attention. She was standing up to Rosie instead of buckling in. It was uncharacteristic of her to behave so recklessly. He was curious as to what Nitra's next move would be.

"What? What are you saying?" She was yelling at that point, making Harry hold his headset away from his ears, with wincing eyes. "I'll burn it bitch. I mean it."

Nitra forced herself to make the words sound nonchalant, as though she didn't care what Rosie did with the page, "So burn it." But once said, she swallowed those three words down hard. It was the last thing she wanted to have happen to her precious page one, but it was the best card she had to gamble with.

"Are you fuckin' nuts?" In the background they heard what sounded like a fist hitting the surface of a window, "Look lady, don't screw with me. I'm fuckin' serious here." There was a trace of panic in her voice, something Nitra was pleased to hear.

Nitra gripped the phone cord and twisted it through her fingers before she asserted herself, "Well, here's a news flash for you sweetheart, without me, all you got is a piece of paper with a bunch of words on it." She added another two and a half second gap. "Ain't worth anything to anyone else but me, now is it?" Two more seconds. "So now it looks like it's *me* who's got what you want." With a straight index finger in the air, Harry signalled one minute to go. "And I believe that the price just dropped down to fifteen thousand." Her stomach churned inside her, almost making her vomit on the spot. She swallowed down hard and reminded herself to continue to breathe.

There was a long pause on the line. Nitra counted the seven seconds in her head. Then the cursing started, "Fuckin' bullshit! Look bitch, I want my fuckin' money and I fuckin' want it now! Stop fuckin' with me."

Her selfish greed angered Nitra, "No, you look *bitch*. It's my money. I earned it, not you, so shut up and listen carefully. The price is now ten thousand. Last fuckin' offer. If you don't like it, burn the damned thing." But this time she didn't give her a chance to think about anything, she added the question immediately, pressuring her to agree right away. "Now, where do you want to meet for the exchange?"

Rosie's answer came immediately, as though she had it planned out ahead of time, "I'll be in the empty warehouse on Quinn Street." She was ordering her, not asking, "And come alone. No cops. You got that."

"Yah, like the cops give a shit about a piece of paper." She tried to sound disgruntled when it came to the police to throw Rosie off guard. "Besides, the cops around here are a joke anyway. They couldn't find the bottom of a paper bag." She shot Harry a look of apology, but he was busy talking to Brian at the station.

"What-ev-er. Just be there at eight o'clock tonight. Don't be late." The phone clicked and the line buzzed.

"No! Wait!" Hearing the silent drone, she dropped her hand into her lap, still clinching onto the receiver.

Harry threw his headset across the kitchen, hitting the hanging plant in the corner. It hung limply in the tangle of leaves. "We didn't get it. God damn it, I hate this fuckin' shit. Sixteen more seconds and we might've had it. A few lousy God damned seconds. If we would have got it, we could have picked her up tonight. And worst of all, now I gotta go and untangle my head phone out of that." He pointed to the ivy with his thumb.

Cherishing his beloved tri-coloured duck-foot ivy, Wallace jumped to his feet, "No, no. Please let me get them for ya." He basically ran to save the plant from Harry's massive clumsy hands.

"That only leaves one question ... now what?" Nitra held her breath until he responded. Although she knew the response, she was hoping for an alternative answer.

Harry said it plain and simple, "Now you go meet with her."

213

Nitra closed her eyes with the terrifying realization that she was now going to meet a crazy woman, in an empty building, in the dark.

He flipped off the tape recorder. "Nothing?" He was still talking to the station. "Shit. Okay then, onto the next phase. I'll be there in twenty minutes. And Brian, no hero bullshit, just do it the way I trained you." Harry hung up the phone, "Well, that's that. Nitra we got two hours to get everyone in place and get you up to speed on the procedure. If you got any questions, ask them now. 'Cause once we get you to Quinn Street, there ain't no turning back."

"Harry, why don't we just let this go? It's only a page. I can write another opening." The thoughts of meeting the Lipstick Lady was making her change her mind. It wasn't worth getting anyone hurt over.

"Too late. You already got us involved and she did make the statement of extortion. We have to find her and charge her with attempting to blackmail you, for trying to obtain money under duress. Nitra, I know you're scared, but you can't let her get away with this. I know you well enough to know you'll never forgive yourself if you do. What I need you to do now is change into some jeans and a pair of comfortable shoes. Ones you can run in. You might not need them, but there damned handy to have when you do." He began to coil up the cable running to the telephone. "I'll set up a tap on your phone 'til we have her locked up. If she calls you again, it will automatically be recorded." He stopped and stared at her, "Well what are you waiting for, go change."

She was still trying to avoid meeting her, "But I don't want to press charges."

"I told you it's too late for that, so go change already. Wallace, you make her do it, I've more important things to do than dealing with a mule headed female."

"Oh, thanks Harry," was all Wallace could say with her in ear shot.

She narrowed her eyes at them, "For Christ sake, are you two idiots just about done bullying me around?"

"We're not bullying ya about. We're tryin' to get you to the station in time to have ya wired up." He saw the glimmer in her eye. It worked, he hoodwinked her with her own curiosity. "Ain't that right Harry?"

"Yah and it takes awhile, so the sooner you get there, the better." He placed the transmitter into the box.

Without any further prodding, Nitra bounded up the stairs to change. Wallace scoffed, "Thanks for jokin' about with me. Lord if ya hadn't, it would have takin' us forever to get her goin'."

Harry grunted, "I wasn't joking. We *are* going to wire her up. I ain't sending her in that building without a wire. That would be downright dangerous."

"Okay, all set, got my fast runners on." Her mood had changed. She was looking forward to the excitement that awaited her at the police station. As a writer, this was an adventure she had only dreamt about. "Now what Harry?"

"Wallace will drive you to Gladys's. When you get there, go to the kitchen and Brian will be waiting for ya. He'll take you two to the station and get you fixed up." He stopped packing to looked directly at Wallace. "Don't let her leave your sight or you'll have to deal with me. You hear me?" His face was dead serious.

"Yes sir." Wallace turned to Nitra, "Well shall we go. To think they're goin' to wire ya up to a buggin' set."

This time Harry chuckled, "Oh hell Wallace, we're wiring you too."

Wallace whipped his head around, "You're gonna do what to me?"

Nitra burst out laughing. She teased him, "What's the matter Wally, you ascared?"

"No it's not that, it's just that … that … that …" his mind went blank for a second or two, then the perfect excuse popped up, "She's expectin' ya to come alone. If I go too, she might run." He put on his best convincing Irish grin, "Ya don't want her to be runnin', now do ya?"

Both Nitra and Harry roared at him. She grabbed him by the hand, like a two year old, "Come on scaredy cat. Let's get you shaved and wired, so you can protect little ol' helpless me from the big bad woman."

"They're gonna shave me?" Now he really was upset, "What are they goin' to shave?" Nitra giggled as she pushed him out the opened door.

"Have fun you two?" Harry waggled his fingers after them. He packed the longest cable into the box and grabbed the hand radio to pack it as well. That's when it hit him, "Oh shit, Joey! I forgot about Joey." He pressed in the side button, "Palmer to Wolf. Are you there? Over." Static shushed through the kitchen.

"Wolf here. Over."

"Palmer. Time to come in Joey. Over."

His voice was sarcastic, "Yah, I kinda figured that out when I saw them leave the premises." The radio garbled static for a bit before Joey radioed Harry again, "What did ya do Harry, forget about me again? Over."

He hung his head then answered Joey back, "Oh no, I couldn't forget about my favourite deputy. Just get yourself down here. Out." He tossed the radio on the table top and muttered to himself, "Ain't it good to know that Wolf the Wacko is on duty."

"I ain't no Wacko." Harry swung around to see Joey standing in the doorway. He'd been standing there the whole time and heard the every word of the last sentence. "Take it back."

Harry's face flushed, "Shit, ya know I didn't mean it Joey. I was just joking to myself. Ah hell, it's this fuckin' job. It's finally driving me batty. Now grab that box and put it in the cruiser." Joey glared at him. "And if ya knock that crap off, I'll let ya drive back. Deal?" He dangled the cruiser keys in mid-air.

He couldn't stay mad at Harry for long; he respected him like a father, "Okay. Deal."

He threw the keys at him, "That a boy."

Joey smiled widely. "I'll meet you out front." Joey picked up the box and headed outside for the garage.

"Yah, I'll be there in just a minute." After Joey left, Harry watched until he was out of sight. Then he did the one thing no one would expect the chief of police to do – he raided Wallace's cookie jar. First, he ate a chocolate chip one, next a few vanilla wafers and he ended with two peanut butter cookies. Left with a dry cookie mouth, he gulped milk directly from the carton and returned it to the top shelf where he found it in the fridge. To finish off his little binge, he let out a sideways burp and wiped his milk moustache on his sleeve. Grabbing the nylon bag and zipping it up, he walked to the door and yelled at Joey to hold his horses, he'd be right there. With that said, he slowly closed the door behind him, shutting down the kitchen and the first crime scene.

Chapter Twelve

Pulling up to Gladys's Diner, Wallace parked Nitra's pick up right in front. As with times before, he assisted Nitra out her door in order to escort her directly to the diner's entrance. Only this time, he was on high end alert. Internally, his aggressive temperament was battling with his equally strong instinct to stand back and wait until it happened. He was aware that either side could ultimately win, but at that moment Nitra needed his powerful confidents and protection. He slipped his arm around her waist, holding her tightly against him until they reach the front door.

To their surprise, Brian was already waiting at the entrance to the kitchen. He signalled them with a summoning wave, having them come directly through the kitchen doors. He looked behind him for any traces of Rosie. Feeling confident that they had eluded her so far, he prodded them into a corner by the walk-in freezer. To Wallace's amazement, the kitchen staff went about their duties as though nothing odd was happening. For them, the three of them huddling in the corner wasn't that unusual, they had seen it all before, a habitual procedure arranged by the police forces of Hamlin. Unknown to Nitra, Gladys's late husband, a police officer, was killed on duty ten years prior. Gladys never forgot the importance of the public assisting the police during certain covert missions.

"Nitra, I'll need your truck keys." He handed Nitra a long navy blue coat in exchange for the ring of keys. Here put this on." The coat was three sizes too big and definitely not her style. The hood had fur trim that tickled her nose when Brian pulled it up over her head. "You'll go out through that door and get in the van waiting outside. Wallace you put on that and follow her." Brian pointed to another deep blue freezer coat, "Whatever happens, just keep walking to the van."

Gladys came in with two huge paper bags and a large silver thermos tucked under her arm. "Here you go. Tell Harry to watch his ass. I ain't in the mood for another wake just yet." She gave him a peck on his bristly cheek. "You need to shave." She soothed her lips with her finger tips. "See ya later."

Wallace zipped up his freezer coat as he glanced in Nitra's direction. She simply shrugged her shoulder slightly, indicating she had no idea why Gladys had kissed him. But it was Brian's cheeks, flushing pink under his five o'clock shadow that really made Nitra speculate their actions. And with an amused grin, she detected how his blue eyes began to sparkle when Gladys walked into the room, a dead giveaway of a smitten heart. The question was — what was really going on between them? Yet Nitra could be completely off base, witnessing clues that weren't there. She filed that question away in her head to be asked at a later date.

219

"Okay, I'm first man out. Nitra you follow straight behind me. Wallace you're next. Ryan here will bring up the rear." He tossed Nitra's keychain to a slim middle aged man leaning against what appeared to be a broken broom handle. "Are you ready?" Everyone nodded in unison. "Grand!" With his meaty hand, he guided Nitra towards the back of the kitchen, everyone else fell into place. From the corner of his eye Wallace witness Ryan assume a martial arts stance, the broom stick gripped with a hand at each end. "Now." He flung open the door and stepped into the fading daylight, with a nervous Nitra glued to his back.

It all happened so fast that it seemed like Wallace hesitated, even though he didn't. "Go! Go! Go!" yelled Ryan, shoving on Wallace's back to hurry him along. But what he actually succeeded in doing, was throwing Wallace's balance off instead. He stumbled out the door and slid hard into the dumpster, shoulder first. Within a half-second, Ryan grabbed his arm, yanking him towards the side of the waiting van, pushing him through the open door, and slammed it shut with a grating bang. Two loud thuds hammered on the vans metal side, signalling the driver to pull away. The van jerked abruptly, causing Wallace to roll across the floor like a tumbling ball eventually crashing into the legs of the back bench, jarring his head. He got himself pushed halfway up, when the driver swerved to the left, throwing him down again. This time, he held onto the metal leg support to stop himself from skidding about.

Nitra, embarrassed by his antics, glared at him to get up off the floor. He pulled himself up by the armrest, "Who in the bloody hell is driving this thing? Mario Andretti? "

Brian laughed at the comparative joke, "No, it's only Steve."

"Hey there," yelled a friendly voice from the front as they turned another corner. All they could see from the back was a mass of red curly hair and a set of friendly green eyes in the rear-view mirror. "Sorry about the corners, but at this speed, I can't do anything about it."

Wallace had been looking out the window and noticed that they were on the other side of town, far from the police station, "Hey, we're goin' the wrong way boys."

Again Brian chuckled, "Wrong way for what?"

"The police station's the other direction." He looked at Brian for confirmation, "Does he know where he's goin'?" The lump on Wallace's head started to throb again. He massaged his temples to alleviate the stabbing pains, hoping to lessen the tight band of tension.

That remark brought a set of red eyes brows into an angry 'V' in the mirror. "Yah. I do know where I'm going ... do you?"

"Well, aren't we supposed to be goin' to the police station?" Wallace pointed to Nitra, then to himself.

"Ha! See, you don't know where you're going." With a sharp crank, he wheeled the van to the right, propelling Wallace sideways across the bench, slamming his large frame into Nitra. He yelled it over his shoulder, "For your information we are going to my house." His facial profile revealed Steve had a large Romanesque nose centered on a boyish face dotted with freckles.

Pushing Wallace off her, Nitra finally broke in, "Your house? Why your house? What on earth would we do at your house? Don't you think you should bring us to the station so we can get wired up? And where is Harry? Shouldn't he be part of this? This whole thing makes no sense at all, don't you think Wallace? And why aren't we being briefed about what's going to happen later tonight?"

221

With her hands firmly planted on her thighs, she was demanding the answers immediately.

Wallace counted them, eight in a row, a new all time record for her. "Now Nitra, these Lads know what their doin'. I'm sure they have their instructions. Right boys?" He looked at Brian with pleading eyes to agree with him, no matter how different the official answer would be.

It was as Wallace believed. They did indeed have their orders. Orders that were painstakingly designed long before Nitra Zupan ever moved to the town of Hamlin. This was the procedure that had been used in every threatening case such as hers. Brian had no patience with the civilians, "Look lady, we *do* know what we're doing. So why don't you just sit there and watch the pretty scenery go by." He turned towards his window, ignoring both of them.

Wallace gave Nitra a dirty look. She gave him one back before crossing her arms in protest at being talk to so nastily by a civil servant. Wallace was sure that Officer Brian was in for a blast at some point, but knowing her, she would pick a more opportune time and not a location within Brian's territory. Steve, sensing the tension, turned up his police radio.

Within seconds Harry's voiced called in, "Palmer to Keller. Over."

"Keller. Hi yah Harry, what's up? Over."

"Palmer. Where are you at? Time is a wasting. Over." Nitra rolled her eyes at hearing that annoying adage again. Wallace just grinned at it, and her.

"Keller. Be home in … say … sixty seconds." Steve wheeled the van into a driveway in front of a tiny bungalow. "Over."

"Ass hole! Out." A loud click indicated Harry had definitely signed off.

222

"Now you did it, Stevie. He's gonna be pissed." Brian jabbed his thick finger at him, "You keep me the hell out of this one. I took it for ya last time, but no more."

Steve turned around, "Yah, yah, whatever. You folks ready for this?" They both nodded. "Same order as before. Just follow Brian and everything will be fine." The door slid open with a grind ahead of Brian leaping to the ground. He waved at Nitra, "Come on, move your butt." She was next to jump down. He pointed to the rusted screen door. "Through there." She dashed to it, holding her hood so it wouldn't slide down, blocking her line of sight. Next was Wallace's turn. Brian pointed in the same direction, "Through that excuse of a door." He stuck his head back inside the van's cavity, "Man, when are you going to fix up this place? It's a fuckin' embarrassment to bring these people here." Slamming the door shut, he shook his head disapprovingly at Steve's laziness. In retaliation, Steve presented him with a full smile accentuated by a one finger salute as he pulled away. Brian grabbed the nearest thing handy, which happened to be one of the many empty motor oil jugs and whipped it at the escaping van, "Yah, you better run, you little jerk."

Inside the house, Nitra was attempting to locate a place to sit down as Harry's hand gesture suggested, but the whole lot was completely covered with tons of junk. Old magazines and newspapers were in stacks on the floor. She counted three different electric kettles in various places and by the look of the thick dusty coat covering each of them, none of them actually worked. Piles of hand written pages littered the couch, armchair, and on tops of their backs. She moved a pair of police issued boots off a chair, brushed off the dirty boot prints, and sat carefully on the edge as to not touch its greasy grimy back.

223

Visible filth covered every inch of the floor. It was all he could do to stop himself from compulsively sweep up the broken tiles, then scrub down every article in sight. With an appalled shutter, Wallace closed his eyes at the massive stack of slimy, dirty dishes molding in the sink.

Harry watched their disgusted faces, "Um, Yah, sorry about the mess. Steve's a good cop, but a lousy house keeper. Out of touch with his feminine side, I'd say." Realizing what he said, he apologized again, "No offense Wallace." He was untangling a knot of fine cables and miniature plugs.

Sucking in his robust stomach, Brian squeezed passed them both, his butt bumping a mound of newspapers, scattering them to the floor. Dense dust spewed into the air in a grey cloud. In the corner, something scratched its way out of a cardboard box and disappeared with a squeak. He wriggled his fat butt on the same bar stool the yellowing papers were previously stacked.

Nitra wiggled her behind to ease the strain on her lower back. "Harry, how in the hell did you get here so fast? Christ, we left my place long before you did." Then she sneezed three times in a row. The flying dust was aggravating her allergies.

"*Gesundheit*," Harry blessed purely out of habit. "Well, three things there. You drive pretty damned slow." He raised an accusing eyebrow at Wallace, "Like a good civilian should." Wallace looked away from him, avoiding eye contact with him. "You also where on the other side of town and further away than I was. Not to mention that Steve drove in a particular pattern that determined whether the van was being followed or not. It takes up time, but I created it for its efficiency. And lastly, you don't have flashy red lights or a siren, now do you?" He said the last sentence with a childish gleam in his eyes at being able to exploit that police privilege. Or was it that he finally got the knot disentangled. Without warning, Harry blurted out, "Now, strip off your shirt so we can get it on."

Nitra gasped wide eyed — Harry turned deep red — Wallace held in a giggle — and Brian switched his crossed legs with anticipation — and it all within a five second span.

He hastily back tracked, trying to undo the damage of his careless words. In a more cordial manner and kindlier voice, he asked her again, "I mean, let's see if we can secure this wire to your … uh … uh, person. And then we'll put one on Wallace's chest next."

She accepted the revised suggestion with greater grace than before. She indignantly pulled out her shirttails and hiked it up to the lowest edge of her bra, "You'll have to work with this." She narrowed her eyes at Harry, "And no funny stuff." Wallace gave a snort, which got him a death look for his efforts.

"Yes Ma'am." Harry was all formality after that point. Nitra turned her head, cooperating fully by doing what he asked, which was holding the lacy bra out from her cleavage enough for him to put the wire through. Careful not to hurt her, he pushed the wires of the mini-microphone up between the cups of her bra and taped that end down to the center of her chest. To ease the awkward tension, she asked a few questions she needed answers to. "Where did Steve go? This is his house, why isn't he here?" She winced as Harry yanked up the tape he had just pressed down and repositioned it for a smoother fit. "And how, in all God's cleanliness, could he live in this pig sty?"

"Oh now, be nice. He's a damned good cop, proud to have him on the force." Harry taped the wire around down to her ribcage. "It's just that he's a bachelor and don't know better."

"Yah, by the look of this rubbish bin, he's gonna bloody stay that way," was Wallace's comment on the filth. "He ain't bringin' home no Lass to this ruddy mess. Not if he wanted to keep her around awhile."

Brian had the next mini-microphone all laid out for Harry. Wallace didn't need prodding, he started by unbuttoning his shirt and pull out his t-shirt. "As for your other question, Steve's already at Quinn Street with Joey."

"What?" Nitra screeched it in his ear, making him jump back. "No cops. Christ Harry you heard her, she said no cops."

It was Brian who calmed her down, "Relax already lady." He handed Harry more tape. "Joey's a full-blooded Indian. He's famous for his vanishing abilities. He can hide better than anyone of us on the force." He smiled at Harry, "You remember that feller we caught from that robbery last year? Hell, he hid in the brushes outside that barn for nearly an hour. Then he crept up through his window and caught the guy sitting at his kitchen table eating his dinner." Brian's face winced with sympathy for Wallace when Harry ripped back a strip of tape pulling out multiple chest hairs. "Don't worry about Joey. Damn, we'll be lucky if we can find him ourselves without using the radio first."

Brian neglected to mention Steve, a detail that deeply concerned Nitra. "And what about your other officer? What about him?" She scanned the house with troubled judgment, wondering what type of discipline the officer held when he couldn't even keep his home clean and organized.

Harry answered her question with a question, "Which one, Steve, Toni, Andy or Ronnie?"

226

"There's three more? Jesus fuckin' Christ, Harry! No cops! We said no cops." She screeched it so loud, it made Harry's hands jerk, resulting in a few more dark hairs being yanked out of Wallace's chest. In a fatherly gesture, Harry rubbed Wallace's flesh to ease the pain — but soon realized who and where he was rubbing, and stopped immediately.

"God damn it Nitra, shut up," grunted out Wallace with a clench jaw. "Damn it."

Her blood was boiling, "No way Harry." She shook her head wildly, "We got to call this off. She'll recognize one of them and run." She hammered her thigh with her fist, "Or worse, someone could get hurt ... really hurt."

Again, it was Brian that shushed her temper, "She ain't gonna recognize any of them. They're from down south. Well, except for Steve, he's a local like me. But I'll be on the recording equipment, well hidden out of sight. That's where I'm going after we get you two wired up. Lucky for us, the guy across the street gave us full permission to enter and utilize his premises as we wish." Nitra's mind started to spin. Tom Harper's shop was situated on the same block as the warehouse. She wondered if it was him who gave his consent. If so, he was another person in her life that would be drawn into danger. The guilt knotted up, burning a hole where it sat inside her gut.

Tucking in his t-shirt, Wallace asked the question that was unclear to him, "Why from down south?"

"They're here on another investigation." Nitra raised her eye brows triggering Harry's immediate response. To emphasize the full secrecy of the situation, he placed his finger to his lips, "Official business, hush-hush police stuff." He put away the tape, along with the other items used in wiring them up, into what appeared to be some sort of preassembled law enforcement kit.

"So you're telling me there's absolutely no way she'll recognize any of them as cops?" Nitra narrowed her eyes at him, warning him that she wanted a direct answer, not a sidestepping explanation. "No bullshit."

"Not unless she's been in trouble with the law down there. And the odds of that happening are next to impossible." Brian handed him a thick envelope. Harry thumbed through it before handing it off to Nitra. "Ten thousand."

Her jaw dropped as she ran her thumb through the stack inside the envelope. There was, what she assumed to be, a hundred one hundred dollar bills. "How in the hell did you get this much money, so damned fast?"

"Christ, do you always need to know everything?" She persistently nodded yes. "Well this time, it's on a 'need to know' basis and you *don't* need to know." She frowned at his skirted answer, but he ignored her pouting and continued with his instructions, "Don't twist too quickly to either side or you'll tear the tape off your skin. And there's no good time to re-tape you once you leave here."

"Is it real money?" Nitra, still fixated on the money, lifted it to her nose and sniffed it, "It smells like its real money. It's got that 'dirty hand' smell. Are they marked? How do you mark them? Do you use special ink that glows under ultraviolet light?"

Wallace rolled his eyes at the ceiling in utter disbelief, then shuttered when he saw the long cobwebs hanging from a broken tile over the stove and attached to the dusty navy curtains. That's when he noticed that the daylight was fading fast. He point with his nose, "Lord, it's gettin' late. Look." Outside, the sky was slowly being swallowed by the dark shadow of night, turning its pale blue to a   bright crimson, streaked heavily in gold and lime green. "Delightful sunset for a shakedown, don't ya think?"

Harry was thankful for the distraction. It stopped Nitra's list of questions that police policy wouldn't allow him answer. Radio static made him reach for his handset, "Chief Palmer here. Over." He released the button with his thumb and waited for a response.

It was Steve checking in, "Hey Harry, what's shaking? Over."

"You are on police airways so knock it off. Follow proper procedures lunk head." He didn't let go of the button while he calmed his nerves. In his head he counted to twenty like his cardiologist told him he should. Early retirement was getting more and more appealing by the hour. "Just give me the site status. Over."

"Everyone's in position. Toni's on the street looking lovely, Andy's got wheels, and Ronnie's sleeping it off. Joey's vanished to where you wanted him and I'm Oswald. Over." It was all gibberish that Nitra didn't fully understand.

"They're on their way. Fifteen minutes, spread the good word. Chief Palmer. Out." He was about to hang it up when Steve came back on.

"Oh yah, Harry we've got one other issue you need to know about. The shop owner wants to stay during the take down. He claims he's a personal friend of Ms. Zupan and insists that he be allowed to stay or we can't use his building. Over."

"Shit!" Harry turned to face her, "Is that true Nitra? Do you know him?"

The image of Tom popped into her mind, causing her gut to ache again. Trying to appear unclear, she shrugged her shoulders, "I guess that depends on who the *him* is."

229

"Tom Harper." That's when Harry witnessed Wallace instantly straighten up, crossing his arms tight; a gesture of true male jealousy. Harry was truly going to have fun with these two. "That good looking guy who owns the restoration shop across the street from the warehouse."

"Um … why, yes I do … but …" Her face flushed fuchsia, then her words fell silent.

It was a first. Harry had never seen Nitra lost for words. "But … what?"

"But I don't know him that well. We only met the once." She examined her finger nails to avoid looking directly at Harry, "That and he did ask me out for a paper hunt … and dinner." She kept her face down, avoiding everyone's stare.

Her confession explained the arm crossing resentment of Wallace. It was then that Harry finally figured out what was — or wasn't — happening between them. *Boy wanted girl. Girl was confused about boy. And the other boy was really making a mess of the whole damned thing.* Harry examined Wallace, questioning why he was just standing there, not saying a single word. If he was Wallace McPhee and the object of his desire was the beautiful Nitra Zupan, he'd be jumping up and down, screaming his head off. Even he thought the Irishman was being a stubborn love sick fool that should be fighting like a crazy man for that girl. Deciding it really wasn't any of his concern who was courting who, he carried on with the radio conversation. With lips tightened white, he groaned out, "Yah, she knows him. And Steve, you tell him that he stays out of the way. No civilian ever gets hurt on my shift. Over."

"Roger that. I already threatened the hell out of him. You'd be proud of me Harry. I even used your '*I'll shoot you myself*' saying. Over."

230

That made Harry smile from ear to ear. At least one of his idiot-minded deputies had paid attention. "Roger that. Like I said, fifteen minutes and they'll be there. Chief Palmer. Out."

She noted the wording use by Harry, "You keep saying *they* will be there. You've said it twice now. Aren't you coming with us to the warehouse?" Nitra's face was getting paler with anxiety of having to go there solo. She calmed her heart rate down by inhaling precisely timed breaths.

It was Wallace who answered the question for him, "He can't. It wouldn't be safe. Chances are she seen him in his uniform. Maybe that day we went flyin' down the highway, drivin' like lunatics. She might have seen him out there bossin' about the other drivers."

That's when Harry put a fist on his hip, "And that reminds me. Weren't you supposed to meet me at my office the next day?"

Through a cupped hand Nitra coughed out, *Cinnamon Buns.* That made Brian snort. But not finding it so funny, Harry squinted at the Irishman for letting him and his stomach down.

"I … I … I was …" Much to Wallace's relief, the sound of a vehicle pulling into the driveway saved him from the wrath of Harry the Hungry. "Holy Hanna, it's your truck."

"Good, Ryan's here with your transportation." Out in the driveway was Nitra's pickup truck. Before a word was said, Brian sped outside, where both he and Ryan climbed inside another car that had arrived seconds later. They were gone in less than a minute. Convinced that all went as planned, Harry continued, "A few more quick instructions and you're out of here." Harry straightened tall, his hands locked behind his back, presenting himself as a proper officer of the law. "No heroes. There's no need to do anything except to have her repeat her extortion demands and hand her the money. When she leaves, the agents will arrest her. All the officers are primed in case something goes differently than planned. But I don't think there's much to worry about. She seems fairly harmless." His right eye flinched. Both Nitra and Wallace caught it, but said nothing. "And Wallace, I saw that knife of yours earlier. Do I need to tell you not to get in the way?" Wallace shook his head in agreement. "Good, 'cause as we all know, to be a martyr you generally need to be dead."

Even though the two men never had a true conversation about Wallace's past, he knew that Harry understood he was from Ireland and well skilled in the fine art of fighting hand to hand, "I'll be as meek as a mouse 'til needed otherwise." He patted his old friend tucked inside his jacket front. "And if need be, I have my wee helper here."

Nitra frowned at him, "Didn't you hear what Harry just said? No interfering."

"Yah and I said, only if need be. Christ Girl, ya need to pay attention." He reached out to give her a wee hug when Harry yelled, "NOOOOO!" but not fast enough. A high-pitched squeal fractured the air. Wallace clamped his eyes shut and she plugged her ears to reduce the shrill. Nitra shoved Wallace away with both hands and quickly stepped back while Harry ran for the knob, turning the volume down to a low whine. Nitra turned on the Irishman, "You idiot. You can't get that close to me. We're wired." Wallace widened his eyes, conveying that he didn't understand. "You can't put two mics that close together, they create feedback."

Harry made an attempt to back her up, but failed miserably, "She's right. You can't get that close." With a sinful little grin he added, "Well not chest to chest anyway, so no hugging or grabbing onto each other." He saw her eyes curse him again. "Oh Lord Nitra, you know what the hell I meant." Having enough of her female sensitivity, he hustled them along, "You two got to get going. Time's a wasting."

Nitra clinched her hands into hard fists, that adage had reached its peak of annoyance. With no reasonable explanation, Nitra blew up at him, "Are you fuckin' done?" She yanked her coat together and stormed towards the door. "Come on Wallace, we're out of here."

Wallace, knowing better, fell in line right behind her. He did manage to convey one of his "sorry" looks to Harry before exiting the door. Harry simply shook his head at his feeble apology for her behaviour.

Still infuriated at Harry's insinuation, she spun around and bellowed at him, "You driving or am I?"

It was time for him to take control or she'd get insufferable to work with. He stopped still and bluntly commanded, "I'm drivin' so get yourself in there. And don't be yellin' at me. I didn't do it." He stomped past her, "Get yourself together. We ain't got time for foolishness." He slammed the door, stressing his determination to have her calm down and focus on the situation ahead of them.

Under her breath, she called him a 'big stupid asshole' before climbing into the passenger seat, sitting down hard, crossing her arms and legs angrily.

Harry watched them through the window as they pulled out of the driveway. He could see the tense angry silence hanging between both of them. Shaking his head at their antics, he radioed ahead. His voice echoed the significance of the transmission, "Chief Palmer. All units be advised, prey is on the move. The estimated arrival time fifteen minutes. Confirm all units. Over."

One by one they responded from their locations.

A hushed whisper checked in, "Unit One, Roger."

"Unit Two, Roger," replied a muffled higher pitched voice.

Wind blowing against his headset made Steve's voice sound hallow and wispy, "Unit Three, Roger."

The next was the sound of a paper bag rattling over the airwaves, "Unit Four, Roger."

Classical music faintly played in the background, "Unit Five, Roger."

"Unit Six. Command post fully functional and waiting for arrival. Roger." Brian's voice came through the strongest.

"Confirmed all units active. Remember there maybe more than one, so keep alert. Blessings and bullets to all. Chief Palmer. Out."

There was a knock at the door. Gladys poked in her head, "Ready?"

Harry nodded, "Can you take this?" he handed her the black case.

"I brought ya a thermos of coffee. It's gonna be a long night for ya." She grinned at him, "Roy would've loved this one. It's completely wacky. Just the stuff he lived for."

"Yah, he would've. Lord I miss the good old days." He locked Steve's door behind him. Gladys backed her station wagon out into the street, where they sped off towards Quinn Street and the warehouse.

Chapter Thirteen

On the drive, Nitra talked non-stop, purely as a form of stress relief, something Wallace had become accustom to. "Hey, did you catch that slip of Harry's?"

"Which bloody one? The man's a walkin' mistake most of the time."

"True, but I'm talking about when he called them agents, then corrected himself by calling them officers after. His eye flinched too. Did you see that too? Wonder what that means? And what is the other investigation that's going on? Have you heard about anything that's going on in town that I don't know about? "

He cut her list short, "No and right now the last thing I'm worryin' about is somebody else's problems with the coppers. We've got enough of our own troubles, wouldn't you say Lass?"

"And what the hell was Steve babbling about?" She mocked his voice, *"Toni's on the street looking lovely"* … what was that crap? And what were the other ones?" She counted her fingers, "Oh yah, Andy's got wheels and

Ronnie's sleeping it off. And he's Oswald. That was some weird secret code they were using."

Wallace laughed at her, "Okay, the Toni part I don't get, but the others I do. He's '*Oswald*' means he's inside the buildin' across the street." Nitra shrugged her shoulders, saying she didn't understand. "Ya know, like Kennedy's assassinator — Lee Harvey Oswald."

She nodded her approval of his deduction process, "Huh, now it makes sense."

"And 'Andy's got wheels' probably means that he's in some kind of motorcar parked on the same block as the warehouse." He checked the rear-view mirror again, still no sign of Rosie or the grey sedan. "As for Ronnie's '*sleepin' it off*'... he's more than likely posin' as a drunkard lyin' about."

"And we know Joey's hiding where Harry wants him to be, which makes me more nervous than ever before." Since he was ignoring her and paying way too much attention to the mirror and the sight of the phantom, she decided to pull him back into the conversation, "I mean, what if I accidentally shoot him."

That caught his attention, "What are ya talkin' about? Ya have a gun with ya?" His focus was split between the road in front and her beside him, "Are ya crazy? You don't know how to handle a gun." He held out a flat hand in front of her and demanded, "Give it to me. And I don't want any argument. Hand it over, right bloody now."

She pretended to be stubborn and didn't move. Sitting absolutely still, she waited for more reaction.

"Now woman!" he shook his flattened hand at her, "I'll be damned if I'm lettin' you in that buildin' if you're carryin' a gun. You'll bloody go bonkers. Probably shoot me instead."

236

Still she didn't budge, she held her breath to stop her giggles from erupting. She was delighting in his face turning a bright angry red.

He yelled at her, and shoved his hand right in her face "Ni! The gun. Now!"

She tried to say no, but lost control of her humour and laughed like a lunatic. Her strained nerves were getting the better of her. She slapped her knee and poked him in the arm, "Sucker! That'll teach you for ignoring me while I'm talking to you."

His face went stern. With both hands returned to the steering wheel, he pulled the truck over into a parking space and shifted it into park. Turning off the truck, he sat quiet for several minutes, not moving, not talking; he just sat quiet with his hands white on the wheel while Nitra squirmed in her seat. She'd gone too far.

Finally calming his anger, he cleared his throat, "I'm disappointed in ya Nitra." He turned his head to face her, to look directly into her green eyes. She swallowed hard at the depth of worry she saw in his. His voice was low and stern, "This is serious. There's no room for error. One wrong move, one wrong word, and it can cost us … a life." He turned his face forward. Staring fixed out the front window. His tone was expressionless, "No more teasin' or ya go by yourself. Ya swear ya'll be straight, no more funnin' around. This is dead serious."

The words 'dead serious' repeated in her head. She reached out to touch his hand, stopping midway, letting her hand drop in her lap. Her voice was low and soft, but more than that, it was sincere, "I swear."

He twisted to read her face, to make sure she meant what she said. She nodded lightly that she did indeed mean her oath. She also added a thoughtful grin, letting him know she now understood that he was as frightened as she was. Without a word, he started the truck, pulling it back into the sparse evening traffic. The remaining distance was driven entirely in silence.

As they drove, they left behind the urban neighbourhoods and found themselves heading into the industrial section of Hamlin. Within two blocks, the landscape changed drastically. From urban houses with lush manicured lawns — to large square buildings of concrete, sheet metal and cracked pavement. The transformation from lively green to dismal shades of grey added to their already ominous mood. Night time was beginning to set in, along with the eerie feeling that this could be more dangerous than Nitra had first thought. Darkness would descend, impeding their ability to see. The knot in her guts lurched with the tension, she was sure she was going to throw up. For Wallace's sake, she swallowed down the bile, forcing it to return to her stomach. She slowly inhaled breath after breath, slowing down her heart rate and its thundering pulse. In a fast rhythm, she tapped two fingers on her legs — it was the form of meditation she used to calm herself down.

Wallace watched her out of the corner of his eye. The finger tapping signalled that she was preparing herself for what was about to happen. What that would be, neither of them were sure. For Wallace, the drive was pure hell. His mind raced with remembered violence of his homeland. Dangers that sat hidden in darkness, capable of taking life or limb, which either bullets or knives could rob you of. Of times pass, when a split second decision meant survival or death. Blood on his hands were stained forever in his mind. Those morbid memories now pushed his senses to a heightened awareness to all around him. His hands clinched the steering wheel, his knuckles turning white with the lack of blood flow. His eyes darted in every direction, at every moment, trying to take it all in, examining every dark corner and doorway. He feared doorways, hating their memory.

Nitra had been studying him, watching his demeanour slowly change. He went from confident to someone less than stable. His eyes were wild in his head, flitting back and forth as though they were going insane by their own means. She touched his forearm with her fingertips, "Are you all right? You seem like you're … freaking out. Are you sure you can cope with this?"

She saw through his tough guy act, discovering he'd become unnerved during the last ten blocks. Being on edge and told he was losing control, offended him. As always, no one called Wallace McPhee weak. Even though it was the truth, all he could do was deny it, then manipulate the accusation, "No Lass, I'm doin' fine. It's ya I'm worrin' about. Ya might tap your fingers off if ya keep on with that." She instantly dug her hands under the outside of her thighs, hiding their trembling. "Are ya sure you're ready for this?"

She hid her fears, not wanting to admit to it any more than he did, "Ready, willing, and stable." She grinned at her own witticism, a twist of a word and a stab at his masculinity.

He ignored her pun, hoping he wouldn't have to endure more of them throughout the night, "We're almost there."

As Wallace pulled around the corner, he began to spot the officers on the street, just as Steve had described them. "Without lookin', look on top of the hardware store, right beside the chimney. That dark blob would be Officer Oswald." As he past an off duty taxi, he nudged her with his elbow, "Looks like that cabby's got wheels."

239

Steve radioed from the roof top, "Unit Three to Unit Six. Pickup coming around corner. Prey is approaching. Repeat, prey is approaching. Out."

"Unit Six, Roger. Copy that Unit Three. Out." Brian's next radio message went out immediately, "All units. Be advised. Prey one and prey two approaching from south. All units stand by for go. Unit One. Are there additional suspects on location? Over."

"Unit One. None. Over." Joey's reply was a baritone whisper. All sounds made by him echoed through the cavernous warehouse. Silence was a must for his concealment.

"Unit Six. Copy that. Out" Each of the units heard the transmission — there were no others blackmailers at this point. Prey one – Nitra, and prey two – Wallace, would be visible within seconds. Time to act natural.

Nitra did her best to see without looking, "Wow, I never would have picked him out as a cop. He seems too young and pretty faced." She scanned the street hoping she would find the other two cops before Wallace did. Within seconds, she spotted Officer Toni and burst out laughing.

Her drastic swing in mood concerned him, "What's so bloody funny?"

"Toni." She couldn't get the words out, she was giggling so hard. Anxiety was making her overly emotional, so tears of hilarity filled her eyes, her cheek muscles burned from laughing so hard. The heavy tension she'd been holding in

240

her chest loosened with each giggle of laughter. She wiped the tears from her cheeks and tried to control her silliness.

"Toni? I don't see him. Where's he hidin' at?" he pulled the truck into a space across the street from the warehouse, its large windows black or broken.

Below the dash board and out of sight, she pointed directly to the bus stop bench thirty feet in front of the truck. She blew out a giggle to answer him, "Toni is a girl, that's why she's 'on the street looking lovely'. Fuck, they dressed her up as a hooker. Now that's a teasing twist. Definitely book worthy." As if on cue, the tall blonde standing behind the bench swished her hair over her shoulder, turned on her high heels and strutted her wares up the street.

"Lord, she's enough to make me do somthin' really bad just so I can get me self arrested. She'd use handcuffs, wouldn't she?" Out of instinct he jammed his body against the truck's door.

Nitra swung, but he had already got himself out of range, "Asshole!" It was infuriating to her that *she* had to swear she'd put a halt to her own pranks, but he had the right to act any way he wanted. And maybe she was a bit jealous too — but only a little bit.

Then Toni tapped on Nitra's window and sexily pivoted on her high hooker heel, waiting for her to roll it down. She leaned her six foot body into the hole of the window, pretending to solicit a date. The words were whispered, but definitely words of authority, not sexuality. "Evening, I'm Officer Bazzoli."

Wallace could barely hear her, but nodded hello and sent a flirty smile her way. "Good evenin' yourself. That's a fine costume you're sportin'. Did ya dress up like that just for me?' He scanned her up and down again, "That skirt

241

does wonders for your nice long legs." He waited for a response, but none came.

Getting a closer look at the true beauty of Toni, Nitra deliberately kept her comments, and her smile, to herself.

Toni ignored Wallace's unwanted behaviour, "None of us have seen any sign of her yet. And there's no one unaccounted for. But its eight o'clock now, so go inside and wait for her in there." She flung her hair over her shoulder and rocked back and forth on her red heels simulating how an authentic street walker acted. "Wait two minutes after I leave before you go inside, that way I'll be out of sight."

Nitra faced forward to avoid looking at her, "What I want to know is, how in the hell are you going to protect us from out here?"

Toni pulled herself out of the window and put a hand on her hip. Toni's body playfully swayed back and forth, while she waved a pointed finger at them. Visually it appeared as though Toni was defending herself from them, but in reality, her words were firm and direct, "Leave that concern to us. We've search through the warehouse and let's just say, we got the right man in the right place and you'll be in plain sight the whole time." She stuck her head high in the air, as though she had been insulted. Nitra thought the officer's acting skills were so superb that no one would have ever known who she really was. "I'm leaving. So like I said, wait two minutes before leaving the truck. Everyone's been listening so we're all aware of the next phase." Toni blew them a hand smacking kiss and strutted away before Nitra got the chance to ask any further questions, a fact that didn't sit well with Nitra. However knowing that all the officers were now listening, she crossed her arms and she held her tongue. She would mention it to Harry later.

Wallace was confused, "What did she say? Christ, she talked so low; I only caught a few words. I thought I heard her say we should wait ten minutes before we go to the warehouse. Did I hear it right?" He leaned forward to ogle after her, "Lordy, that girl's got great legs."

"No, Officer Bazzoli said *two* minutes." She remained cross armed as she watched Toni walk away. She decided right there and then, that when this was all over, she'd reveal the officer's true beauty secret in front of everyone as a payback.

Wallace checked his watch and the rear view mirror a hundred times before the two minutes was over. The street lights slowly flickered on, casting a blue tinge to their surroundings. He patted her knee, "Okay Lass, time to go."

Carefully they both climbed out of the truck, trying to avoid ripping out the wire — or any painful chest hairs. They quickly discovered that the faster they moved, the greater the chances of the tape pulling off their skin. Wallace met Nitra at the tailgate and positioned himself to her right, but one pace back, letting her guide the way. Her steps were short and hesitant, a sign of her reluctance to enter the unlit deserted warehouse. He sensed her opposition and held her by the elbow to direct her further along. A dog barking angrily in the distance, sounding the warning of the evils that prowl as the night fell. Except for the well placed officers, the street was empty. Long shadows crept across the pavement as the last of twilight vanished, letting the street light's replace its amber glow.

Halfway across the tiny parking lot of the warehouse, she stopped dead. Her fear had built up inside and now she felt the need to cry. It sat at the back of her mouth, making her lower lip quiver. Gulping air, she let the words out it one short burst, "Wallace, I don't think I can go through with this? It's too much." Her feet froze to the pavement where she stood. Her stomach churned and fear flooded to ever nerve in her limbs. She shook her head as she backed away, "I can't go in there."

"You don't have a choice Lass, it's a done deal." He watched her face pale with dread. "Breathe Nitra ... remember to breathe." Then an image of a scribbled phrase pinned to her writing room corkboard popped into his mind and he whispered it out, "What's that quote you like so much? *'When you're truly terrified, remind yourself how thrillin' it is.'* Well I don't know about ya Girl, but I'm excited as hell right now."

She remembered the truism that she had hastily wrote out many years before. She also recalled the immediate impact those words had on her viewpoint of the frightening events that happened in her life. They seem to give her permission to embrace the scarier episodes, to even search them out as adventures when needed. "Yah, you're right. This *is* damned exciting. I can't wait to write this all down." She sharply tapped her temple, "The plot line is all up here and the characters are spectacular. A novel in the waiting." Her happy expression faded, draining pale with fear again, "I wonder how it will end?"

That was Wallace's cue to get her motivated. He grasped her by the elbow and guided her towards the front door of the warehouse, "Well God damn it Girl, let's get the fuck going and find out."

Nitra hesitated, "Wait. I've never been inside there. Have you?"

"Only once. When I worked for Mona, I picked up a packet for her. If me memory serves me, the doors over there." He had pushed up on his tip toes to see over the abandoned shrubs, "Ya, the offices are on the front left hand side, next to the main entrance. I remember, I had to pick up the packet at the rear of the factory. I walked pass dozens of huge noisy machines, most of them grouped around the mammoth cement pillars. Most likely to save space I'm thinkin'. And at the very back, there are the two bathrooms, his and hers, on the left; and a wee dinin' hall on the right. The back entrance is in the middle of them. A set of big double steel doors that swung out. It's funny what the mind remembers?" He tugged her gently by the elbow, but released his hand after she pulled it out of his grip.

She nodded at him, telling him that she was fine now, that from that moment forward, she would continue on her own, "I hope they're unlocked."

He yanked on them. They were locked, "Damn it!" He snooped around for another entry point. Wait, there." He pointed to the hidden lower slider under the big picture window, "It's broken. I'll go first, then help ya through." She held back a stray branch, watching his large frame climb inside. Careful to not pull out chest hairs with the tape, he stuck his first leg through, shifting his weight completely inside, leaving Nitra alone in the night. It finally registered with her; the awful adventure was becoming reality. They were actually braking into the building and once inside, there was no turning back. That was the moment that launched it all. Overwhelming panic numbed her body; she stood lifeless, her arms dangling limply with the weight of fear. He stuck his head back out and whispered, "Come on, your turn."

The same dog started barking again, pulling her out of her numbness, without a thought she bent down to the window and dove in, head first. It was all Wallace could do to catch her, as she came through the other side. Although she didn't weigh all that much, her hasty impact made it difficult to catch her, preventing her from falling face first on the hard concrete floor. "Hold on tight Girl, I got ya." He slipped his arm around her waist, catching her in mid-air, scooping her upright, sitting her down on her feet. His hand felt every inch of her body, he was holding onto. There it was again, that heat he felt for her, that crushing urge to kiss her hard, feeling that electricity between them, to never let her go, to hold on forever. In his head, he scolded himself, *Wallace McPhee, get a hold on yourself boy. This ain't the time for that daftness.* He helped her balance herself then stepped away from her, placing a barrier of space between her body and his. But the unyielding ache remained tight in his groin and heart. He wanted to hold her, to protect her as she stood in the darkness, her arms wrapped around herself for comfort. He forced his mind out of its self-torment, moving on to the matter at hand, "Are ya all right? Did ya hurt yourself?" She shook her head *No* while she scanned the empty interior of warehouse.

The smell of heavy dust hung in the stale air, mildew covered the few window panes that were left intact, while the others not there, let shafts of light fall into the dimness. As they walked, fine dust particles lifted into the air, streaming and swirling through the rays, clouding their vision. They stopped, waiting for it to settle. As it cleared, their eyes adjusted to the half-light, allowing them to make out the surroundings. Wallace scanned every inch of the warehouse, trying to place walls and doors with those in his memory. The pale green machinery was gone, sold off long ago, leaving only the large cement pillars still standing in place. It was hard to get his bearings, but once he did, he knew exactly where he was headed. "Follow me." He grabbed her hand and towed her behind him.

"All I know is, that I'm gonna kill Harry when I see him. He should've given us a heads up as to what was inside here. Fuck for all we know, there could be holes in the floor — holes we could just stumble into."

They walked as lightly as they could to not disturb the layer of dust covering the concrete. Each step was cautiously placed, avoiding the debris that was scattered throughout the floor. A beam of light from an upper window highlighted the hazards it held. Cigarette butts and crushed beer cans, glass tubes stained with streaks of brown, discarded condoms, and bloody dirty needles were everywhere. They carefully stepped over them and skirted a mound of smashed liquor bottles. Neither of them had to say it, they knew they were in an empty drug house, and the dangers were still there, left behind by those who didn't care. He led them into the deep shadow and turned their backs towards the wall. From where they stood, they could see the entire warehouse.

Lying atop of the mezzanine, Joey watched them make their way through to the back of the warehouse. Wallace stopped Nitra no more than twenty feet from where he lay on his stomach, rifle in hand. He silently radioed in, announcing their arrival with a preset pattern. Three long held spaces of transmission. The secret language translated into, *"Prey one and two in place. Out"*

Out in the street, each office received the identical communication, "All Units. Suspect is approaching from the south. Activate all systems. Out." Brian's voice was calm, every word pronounced clearly so no one misunderstood.

Chapter Fourteen

At the far end of the block, a grey sedan gradually made its way towards the warehouse. As it passed the taxi, the woman slowed down to examine the driver. To her, he was reading a paperback novel, ignoring the world. The sedan continued down the street, parking behind Nitra's pickup truck. Turning off her car, she scanned the neighbourhood, ensuring there weren't any police to interfere with her plans. All that she saw was a cheap ten dollar hooker pacing her wares a hundred feet ahead. The taxi drove by, apparently in no hurry to pick up fares. Feeling satisfied that no police were near, she exited the sedan. That's when she noticed the arm movement in the alley; a drunk took a long drink from his bag wrapped bottle. *What a low life burden to society*, she thought to herself.

Ronnie's earpiece droned, "Unit Six, suspect on foot. Unit Four, initiate phase one. Roger." He lifted the paper bag to his lips, pretending to drink from the microphone hid inside it, "Unit Four, proceeding as ordered. Out." He

248

lowered the bag to watch Rosie walk across the street over its top edge. His orders were simple, once she had reached the building, he was to proceed to the front windows and observe from that position. Between him and Officer Wolf, they would have the clearest view throughout the warehouse.

At the rear of the building, Andy positioned the taxi in its designated spot. From where he sat, he could see both the street and the rear entrance of the warehouse. He parked the cab, lit a cigarette and using the taxi's hand set, radioed into Brian. "Unit Five to Unit Six. In location. Out."

Both Wallace and Nitra stood nervously waiting for something to happen. Their eyes had become accustom to the dim light, the darkest corner were now visible to them. Wallace leaned in, whispering in Nitra's ear, "I wonder where Joey's hidin'. I don't see him, do ya?"

"No and shut up about that. If she's in here, she could hear you." She swung her head up towards the window. A set of headlights sliced across the broken window, flooding the room with yellow moving light. "It's a car. Do you think she's here?" He didn't answer her. They waited motionless in the inky stillness.

An empty beer can bounced across the floor, producing an eerie tin rah-tah-tat-tat that echoed off the walls in every direction. Feeling the need for protection, Nitra jammed her body against Wallace's ribcage. He put his arm around her and whispered in her ear, "She's by the offices. That's where the sound came from."

"Are you sure? I thought it came from direction of the bathrooms."

249

"I'm not so sure now Lass. We need to be quiet and listen closer." It was his way of saying *"shut your bloody trap so I can hear where the hell she is."* That's when he saw it — a flash of a silhouette against the light from the street. She was inside the offices making her way to the main body of the warehouse itself. "Nitra, don't go crazy on me now, but she *is* here." He felt her body yank away from him, trying to bolt. He held tight, not letting her go. "Calm down Girl. Stay put."

She swallowed down the lump in her throat and tried to breathe, "Are you sure it's her? You know it could be someone else? Like a drug addict maybe?" Nitra amazed herself, she was actually wishing to see a drug addict instead.

"No it was her. I recognized her shape." Clicking footsteps came from the front; the lunatic woman had worn high heels to an extortion attempt. Then the sound changed, she was outside the offices. The sound was clearer with no walls to block the flow.

Nitra took in a deep breath. She whispered a low as she could, "Now what? What do we do now?"

"We stand our ground and get your page back. She can have the money." He said the last sentence louder so it would deliberately echo through the empty building.

Rosie's footsteps stopped. The building fell dead silent again.

Time was counted out in racing heart beats.

Neither party moved. The dog's angry barking added to the tension. Wallace, knowing the stages of battle, started this one. He bent down and whispered in Nitra's ear, "Say hello to the nice lady."

She didn't laugh at his joke. Instead she clung to him harder, digging her fingers into his side. He felt her inhale a deep expanding her lung full. "Hello." The timid word echoed through the entire building.

From the shadows came the large gaudy figure of Rosie, her lipstick glowing like a hideous beacon. "I'm here. Where's my money?"

He whispered to a frozen Nitra, "Answer her."

"It's right here … but you'll have to come get it." Nitra's voice boomed down the length of the corridor. She wasn't a street fighter like Wallace, but she knew the importance of a well positioned power play.

He whispered again, "Now wave the envelope at her. That'll get her here."

Her hand trembled as she pulled the envelope from her pocket. She held it at chest height at first, but Wallace pushed her hand high in the air. Taking her eyes off Rosie, she looked up at the envelope high above her. It was then Nitra made sure it sat in the beam of light from the window, a spotlight shining on the golden prize.

"That better be all in cash. Now give me my money. Bring it here." She reached out in front of herself, grabbing the air with her greedy hand.

Rosie's ugly greed flooded in Nitra's head, angering her in seconds. She let go of Wallace and stepped forward into the light shaft, "No. If you want it, you come here. And where the fuck is my page?" She banged the envelope against her flat palm. In between the slaps, she yelled, "No page, no deal." Then she remembered what Harry had told her. She'd have to get Rosie to repeat her demands; her incontestable prosecution depended on it.

Her leopard coat swung with her demanding greed, "Oh, it's not that easy. You see, this is just the first installment."

251

Nitra couldn't believe her ears, "What are talking about? Don't you remember the deal we made over the phone?"

"Sure do. A lousy ten grand for the most important page you need. It's not enough. I want more. I know you got lots of money and I want more of it."

Brian's called it in directly, "Unit Six to Chief Palmer. Suspect's admission recorded. Over."

In the back storeroom of Harper's Restoration, Harry responded to the transmission, "Palmer. Roger that Unit Six. Chief Palmer. Out." He turned to a very worried Tom Harper and gave a little jiggle, "We've got Rosie's confession on tape, she's going away for sure."

"But Chief, Nitra still in there with that lunatic. She's still in danger. Listen." He turned up the volume, something Harry didn't appreciate. Civilians were not to fiddle with the knobs of police equipment. Now he'd really have to tell him.

He looked him straight in the eye, "Tom, I think there's something you need to know. Nitra and Wallace are ... well, I guess you could say they're *involved*." He tried his best to say it delicately, yet resolute enough to make Tom understand the significance of his warning. "Wallace has fallen in love with the girl and well, I think she's starting to come around. Maybe it's best if you let them alone. Let them figure out what they're gonna do about it. Not to worry, right now Wallace is there hell bent on protecting her." He returned the knob back to its original position and bluntly ordered, "And don't touch my receiver again or I'll ship your ass out of here."

Tom's face went stunned. Harry wasn't sure if it was due to the Nitra-Wallace situation, or his warning about not touching the equipment, but his betting money was on Nitra. Finally he protested, "But she called me two days ago and … "

"Well, that was a whole two days ago. Things can change a hell of a lot in two days, especially with women and their hearts. Now shut up, I'm trying to listen to this."

A mixture of anger and fear swirled in Nitra's head, making it hard for her to think clearly. It was Wallace that straightened out her thoughts. He lightly kicked her in the back of the heel, bringing her out of her confusion, "How much more?"

"Another ten thousand." She held up the red lined paper in one hand and a *Zippo* lighter in the other. "Or I burn it." Confident that she had the upper hand, she walked towards Nitra, "And I don't give a fuck how you get it, but you better get it here fast. Or I'll …" For the first time she had gotten close enough that she saw Wallace in the shadows with Nitra. "What the fuck? I told you to come alone." At the sight of him, she instantly panicked. She dropped the lighter on the floor and reached into her pocket. Her leopard coat lifted, showing that she was holding a gun from inside the pocket. Wallace, recognizing the shape of the barrel, stepped out into the light. She pointed it at him, "Who the fuck are you?"

With steady hands, Joey shifted his body, aligning it with the barrel. He aligned the site of the rifle on Rosie's chest. One clean deadly shot. The urge was great, but he held his finger steady.

Ronnie's heart jumped. It wasn't expected to happen, yet there it was — a gun. He whispered into his wrist mic, "All Units. Suspect has gun. Possible hostage situation. Chief Palmer, advise. Over."

Harry ignored the frantic Tom behind him and calmly pressed the handset button, "Palmer to all Units. Wait for action. Use force only if necessary. We don't want anybody dead. Repeat, wait for action. Out." He twisted slightly in his chair, hoping to alleviate the tightness in his chest, but that didn't work either.

Wallace recognized the barely audible scraping noise from above. "Just a friend." He casually stepped sideways, intentionally placing a space between him and Nitra.

"You're no friend. You're her housekeeper." She scoffed at him, "So what's it like being bossed around by a rich bitch? Your whipped balls hurt much?"

Her vulgar comments about Nitra infuriated him. Keeping his head, he used her hate to his advantage. The old adage 'set a thief to catch a thief' slipped through his mind. "Ya got that right." With one hard shove, he pushed Nitra down onto her ass, "Who's gonna protect ya now? Well, ya don't pay me enough for this bullshit."

Nitra reached for the fallen envelope, snatched it up, she clutched it securely with her hand. "Wallace, what are you doing?" She couldn't believe what he had done, shoving her off to the side like that. And the switch in his attitude towards her, it was not normal.

He growled at Nitra, "Just shut up and stay where you are." Narrowing his eyes at Rosie, he demanded, "I want in on this. A wee breakin' away cash would be right handy." He side flicked his head in Nitra's direction. "I can finally get the fuck away from this one." He looked away from Nitra, hiding his eyes. He couldn't let Nitra in on the hoax; it was vital that she stay shocked, scared, but more importantly, cooperative.

"What the hell is he doing?" Harry straightened up from the radio, "This can't be happening. It's not like Wallace at all."

"So he's madly in love with her, huh? Sure sounds like it to me." Tom bent down closer to catch what was happening next. Harry just smiled to himself. Tom was absolutely right — Wallace did indeed love Nitra that much. He rubbed his upper arm, trying to ease the increasingly growing ache.

One step forward, one step sideways. Wallace was making his way to the other side of Rosie, positioning himself on the other side, away from Joey's aim. "Hell Love, let's make it a nice even fifty thousand and split it down the middle. That be twenty-five for ya and twenty-five for me."

She tilted her head at him, "Why the fuck would I do that? She's got ten thousand right there in her hand. Why would I let you in on this? What's in it for me?"

"An extra fifteen thousand, Love. *May as well be hung for a sheep, as for a lamb.*" He smiled as he said it, tormenting her with her own greed.

She looked at him sideways, questioning what other motives he might have. "So?"

"So, you'll need to have help, won't ya? I mean, whose gonna go get the money while ya got her held up here? You?" He nonchalantly paced around her, making her twist her head to follow him.

Rosie's eyes scrunched as she tried to figure out what to do next. She was finding it hard with him pacing around her and taunting her with numbers, big numbers.

"Twenty-five thousand dollars, Love. You could get yourself a genuine leopard skin coat with that kinda cash."

Nitra watched the confusion on Rosie's face and took advantage of it by walking in the circle Wallace was. Almost opposite to where she was before she saw passed Rosie's over teased hair at something above the rafters. The whites of Joey's eyes glinted against his blacked out skin. She looked away immediately. If Rosie had seen Nitra looking up at the platform and traced her line of vision up to Joey, it would destroy the whole setup.

"Come on Love. Twenty-five thousand dollars? Think of it? Sunny beaches and rich men. Rich men that will pay for everything, once you get them hooked on your sexy beautiful ways." He was laying it on thick, exploiting her emotions about her age. "Say yes and we'll runaway together. Oh, you'd like that wouldn't ya Love?" His stomach churned as he stroked her filthy coat with his fingers. "You and me in the hot sun … with lots of suntan oil."

Brian radioed Andy directly, "Unit Six to Unit Five. Status of location. Over."

"Unit Five. At the rear. Entering building through window. Requesting no further transmissions. Out." Brian thought to himself, *Stupid southern jerks. Always breaking the rules and playing superhero.*

Next he radioed Ronnie, "Unit Six to Unit Four. Status of location. Over." He had turned it off. He was now inside the offices, leaning against the inner wall waiting for his signal from Joey, a predetermined noise, which only a trained ear could distinguish from other normal sounds. Brian repeated the command, "Unit Six to Unit Four. Status of location. Over." He waited, but still no response came. "Unit Four, you dick head, give me your location? Over." Again he waited. With no response, Brian had no choice, but to radio Harry with the bad news. "Unit Six to Chief Palmer. Over."

"Palmer to Unit Six. What's up? Over." Tom was pacing behind him, trying to wear a hole in his floor.

"Unit Six. Harry, Unit Four isn't responding. I think Ronnie's got his radio turned off. And we ran the sedan's plate number, they're stolen plates. Over."

He whipped his note book across the room, "Fuck!" Tom scurried for a chair in the opposite corner. Harry's heart rate rose to the same level as the volume of his voice, "Palmer. You tell that southern son of bitch he's in so much trouble, he'd better hope he gets his ass shot just so I'll forgive him. Out." He tossed the handset down on the desk, "Fuckin' stupid bastard. He's gonna ruin it or get hurt in the process." Harry's face reddened with his high blood pressure. The word retirement sounded really good as he rubbed his throbbing head.

Tom quietly asked, "Do you think that Unit Four might actually be in trouble?"

Harry calmed himself before answering. It was Tom's fault that Ronnie was being such a jerk. Harry still held that civilians should never be included in stake outs; it made it too tempting to alter procedures. "No not really. Ronnie's notorious for turning off his radio if he thinks it's hazardous to be heard."

Tom didn't say much, he just nodded and sat quietly, while Harry paced the same ten feet back and forth.

In the street below Toni leaned against the hood of the grey sedan, twisting her long hair with her fingers, while she rocked her foot on the heel of her shoe, waiting.

Rosie smiled seductively yet suspiciously at Wallace. He had painted a delightful picture of him and her basking in the sunny tropics together. "So you'd go get the money then?"

He batted his brown eyes at her, hoping to confuse her with flirtation, "Sure."

"What would stop you from taking off with the money? Hell, you'd have fifty thousand dollars of missy pies money in your pocket." She wiggled the gun under the coat, "Why come back?"

He didn't have an answer for her. He hadn't thought that far ahead nor did he think she was smart enough to have thought that far in advance.

Nitra saw the blank hesitant look in his eyes. Recognizing that Wallace was at a complete loss, she decided to become a nuisance, distracting Rosie from his answer. She screamed it at the top of her lungs, "No, don't leave me. You can't leave me." She thrust the envelope at her, "Here, just take the money and leave. He's mine, you can't have him."

Wallace's heart ached, if only she meant what she was saying. If only she did love him that way. He knew what she was doing and played along with it. Without warning, Wallace took two long strides and did the unthinkable — he hit her. He slapped Nitra hard in the face, sending her across the floor again, "Just shut up." His stomach lurched at the sight of her sprawled on the floor, holding her face, tears running down her cheeks. Oh, how he wanted to hold her, to kiss away the sting of his slap, to tell her he didn't mean it. His heart ached for her pain. Instead, he shut off his emotions, ignored her sobbing, and turned his attention back to a somewhat shocked Rosie.

The action of Wallace hitting Nitra was so startling, that even Joey looked passed his scope, breaking the concentration of his aim; just to be sure it had occurred. To his sadness, it had actually happened. Nitra was on the floor holding her cheek, softly crying. He slowly aimed the rifle at Wallace's groin, holding it steady for a few vindictive seconds, then returned it back to Rosie's chest.

Ronnie then hiding behind a mammoth cement pillar, wasn't sure whether to stay in position or rush in to protect her. Instincts told him to stay put.

Brian immediately radioed Harry, "Unit Six to Palmer. Harry did you hear that? Over."

"Palmer. Yah, I heard it. Over." Tom was still standing beside the radio, staring at it, wanting to control what was happening on the end of it. Finally he backed away allowing Harry to get closer.

Brian questioned back, "Unit Six. So what do we do now? Over."

259

While Harry was busy talking with Brian, Tom quietly escaped down the back stairs. He was going to help Nitra, even if it meant injury or incarceration.

Harry turned around to check on Tom while talking with Brian, "Do you think he actually …" But he wasn't there, Tom was gone. Harry closed his eyes in disbelief. For all he knew Tom was down in that warehouse getting in the way. "Chief Palmer to all Units. Civilian in the vicinity, One Tom Harper's playing hero. Do not shoot, repeat do not shoot." In his head he remarked, *Leave that pleasure for me.* "If anyone knows his location, radio it in. And for Christ sake, stop him! Out." Harry's head hurt. This was the last thing he needed. It was bad enough he had the trio of southern idiots to deal with, but now Harper was trying to get his big dumb hero ass shot. His throbbing temples blurred his eyes slightly. He blinked hard to make both radios refocus into one single image again.

Andy carefully made his way through the debris of the lunch room. He positioned each foot exactly in spot. He heard the screaming, the slap. The sounds threw him off balance, tossing him to one side. His big black boot landed on top of a discarded crack tube, producing the crushing sound of broken glass. Instinctively he hissed and let out one long screechy meow, before standing completely motionless, listening for results.

From the back corner of the warehouse she heard a crunching sound, "What was that?" A cat hissed and yowled at being startled. She turned her head back, "Stupid street cats. They should shoot them all."

Wallace knew what it really was. It was an old diversionary trick he'd used many times himself. On the edge of his eye, he saw a crouched figure shift from one pillar to the next, silently hiding closer. He wasn't sure which one it was, but he was relieved that the officer was there. "Yah, shoot them all." At this point he'd agree with anything the old wacko said just to keep her occupied. If she was talking, they were getting closer to capturing her alive. "So, Love what do ya say, you and me in the Bahamas? White sand, blue skies and swaying palm trees."

She was about to reply to his tantalizing offer when heavy footsteps sounded from the direction of the offices. Grabbing his wrist, she swung herself around, pulling Wallace in front of her. She pushed up on his twisted arm, holding him in place as a human shield. She reinforced her position of power by sticking the barrel of the gun into his back. She yelled, "Who's there?"

Without warning, Tom jumped out from behind the office doorway and bolted directly at them. "You let her go. You got your money, now let her go." Aware that Wallace wasn't moving, along with where Rosie was situated, he realized the chances were she had a gun at his back. He stopped abruptly, "Just put the gun down. So no one gets hurt." Ronnie flattened his body tighter against the pillar and mentally cursed Tom out. The civilian was going to expose his concealed position, starting a sequence of procedures no officer ever wanted to carry out. The outcome generally ended in bloodshed.

Wallace couldn't believe it. The bloody fool had put himself in dangers way for Nitra, a woman he hardly knew. The man was crazier than Rosie was.

Tom took a short step forward, "What's your name?" He was trying to distract her in hopes of getting close enough to grab her and her gun.

"Never mind that, who are you? And how the hell did you know we were in here?" She yanked hard on Wallace's arm and whispered in his ear, "There better not be any more surprises." He felt the metal shaft jab in his back. He also felt the wire release from his chest, just dangling between his shirt.

Wallace let out a soft grunt at being jabbed. He said it loud so everyone could heard, "I don't know who he is, I've no met him before." He had told the truth. In reality Tom and Wallace had never actually met, Nitra was their only connection. And in all frankness, he didn't much care for the man who fancied his Nitra. "For all I care, ya can shoot the beggar." In the meantime, Tom had stepped another half pace closer.

A singular radio transmission came into Brian, "Unit Three to Unit Six. Over."

"Unit Six, go ahead Unit Three. Over." Brian tapped his pen on the table out of impatience and frustration with the officer. At this point, it was anybody's guess as to who was where, doing what.

His tone reflected his amusement, "Steve. Uh … sorry, I mean Unit Three. Tell Harry I have Harper in sight. I can see him from up here. He's talking to Rosie, who's got her gun at Wallace's back. Over." He was no longer concealed by the chimney, but now lying on his stomach, his site aimed right Rosie's head.

"Unit Six. Unit Three, I'd like to thank you for responding." It was a sarcastic dig at the other officers who

262

weren't following radio protocol. "Can you see where the other officers are? They've turned off their radios. Over."

"Unit Three. Dumb ass knobs!" he cleared his throat. It was windy, dusty and dry on the roof, yet the view was spectacular. "From here I see that Ronnie's hiding behind a pillar a hundred feet from the suspect. Andy's positioned in the lunch room doorway. Over."

"Unit Six. Do you have a clear shot at the suspect? Over."

"Unit Three. Roger that, suspect is within range and sited. Over.

"Unit Six. Shoot suspect if necessary. Repeat, shoot suspect if necessary. Will forward message to Palmer. Over."

"Roger Unit Six. Copy that. Out" With Steve's rifle site in line with Rosie's head, one pull of the trigger and she would no longer be an annoyance to anyone.

"Unit Six to Palmer. Over."

"Palmer here. Over."

"Unit Six. Steve's got Harper in the building talking to Rosie. Rosie's got Wallace in the back with a gun. And we've lost contact with his wire. Over."

Harry wiped the sweat from his upper lip, "Palmer. I knew it. Asshole civilians cause nothing but problems." He held on to the button while he inhaled deeper. The band of tension in his chest was getting tighter, making it harder to breathe. "Any sign of my guys. Over." Brian relayed Steve's information while Harry sat down, he was getting light headed. "Palmer. That's good news. Everyone's on the ball. Out." Harry hung up the handset. He laid his head on the desk and closed his eyes — he was exhausted.

263

"Stay where you are. Don't come any closer." She stabbed Wallace in the back with the barrel, "Tell him to back off."

Wallace flinched at the pain, "I keep tellin' you Love, I don't know him."

"Is that true?" she stuck her head around Wallace's tall frame.

"Never met the man before in my life." Tom shifted his hips, sliding his foot forward.

"So how'd you know we were here?" She was smarter than Tom thought.

The answers came easy though, "I own the shop across the street. I heard your voices." He shifted again, gaining another five inches. If he was going to dive at her, he would have to get much closer. "I thought you were junkies. I've been trying to clear them out of here for months now. They're ruining my business."

She twisted Wallace sideways so she could get a better look at his face, "So how'd you know about the money?"

That was the one question Nitra didn't want Rosie to ask. She shrieked hysterically to distract her, "Who cares how he knows, just take the money and go." She ripped open the end of the envelope and shook the bills at her, "Look at it, ten ... thousand ... dollars. All of it in hundred dollar bills. And it's all yours. All you gotta do is give me my page in exchange for it and leave with the money."

Wallace immediately encouraged Rosie, "I'd do it. Ten fuckin' grand. Go for it Love. Trade it and go." He widened his eyes at Tom to persuade her as well.

Nitra pushed the envelope her way and waved it again, "Here take it. Give me the page and take the cash."

Tom yelled at her, adding his directives to the confusion, "You want that money. Take it. Take it now."

Rosie's head whipped from one to the other. Her thoughts spun wildly. With all three nattering at her, it was difficult to concentrate on a decision.

"Give her the page and take it. Take the money." Wallace repeated it again, "Take the money for the page."

They were all saying it separately at once, confusing her to the point her head began to spin. It was Nitra that pushed her over the edge. She walked to where Wallace was and knelt down beside him. From her position of submission, she placed the envelope in Rosie's hand. She looked up from her knees and whispered, "Smell it!"

Rosie angrily narrowed her eyes at her. Nitra didn't budge, she coolly enticed her once more, "Smell it." She understood Rosie's kind and the life she lived. Knowing which buttons to push, Nitra used the one word that would strike Rosie to her core. "Freedom. It smells like freedom." She saw the impact of those words in her wounded eyes, eyes that had witnessed her own personal exploitations. Nitra pushed the woman further, shoving the envelope directly into her face, "Freedom from men. Men that abuse you, freedom from men who treat you like garbage. It's freedom Rosie, your freedom. Smell it."

Rosie's eyes brightened. They reflected her understanding of what Nitra was saying. Her anger eased and she did it, she sniffed at it. Then she inhaled its scent deeply.

Nitra held up her palm and softly whispered, "Rosie ... give me my page and go find your freedom." At that moment ten people held their breath, waiting for Rosie's reaction.

Her facial expression transformed from tolerant to serious. She nodded her agreement, but demanded a stipulation, "I'll take your fuckin' money, but only on one condition."

"Name it," Nitra's face pleaded.

"No one follows me."

"Wallace was the first to speak up, "Not me. Ain't anythin' in it for me. I'm stayin' put."

Quick thinking Nitra, grabbed her own foot, "I'm hurt. My ankles fucked thanks to that jackass." She sneered up at Wallace, blaming his push for her phoney injury.

"I'm staying here. Nitra needs protecting, and I'm the man to take care of her." Tom looked at Nitra as though she was a wounded puppy.

Nitra's blood boiled, she was no defenceless damsel and she certainly didn't need his testosterone laden salvation. She stifled her resentment and focused on the moment, "So we all agree to stay behind." She offered up an opened hand, hoping to either receive a hand shake or her page one, "Do we have a deal?"

Rosie hesitated for a few moments. Then, through scrutinizing eyes, she studied them all closely, deciding whether she should trust them. Deciding what she wanted, she sharply announced, "Deal." She handed the page down to Nitra, greedily she stuffed the money into the pocket of her leopard coat. She glared at Tom, "You. Stand over there." She pointed to a spot in a shaft of streetlight. When he had gotten to where she wanted him, she shoved Wallace in his direction, "Go stand with him." Next she targeted Nitra's head with her gun, "Get up. You're coming with me."

Adrenaline thundered in Joey's chest. He stiffened the grip on his rifle, aiming directly at Rosie's heart.

Steve held his breath to stop his rifle from jiggling. He'd have to shoot through the window and over Wallace's shoulder, but it was feasible. One shot straight in the forehead.

Nitra slowly got to her feet, terrified by what was about to happen.

"Now Love, you don't want to do that." Wallace forced his tone to be kind and concerned, "If you take her with you it'll be kidnappin'."

She stared at him for a second, processing his advice. Finally, she waved the concealed gun towards them, showing her where to go, "Fine, get over there with them."

Nitra limped to where the men stood. Together they waited for Rosie to make her next move. From within her pocket, she aimed the gun directly at them, "Stay there and no one gets hurt." She shook the gun in their direction, "I mean it." With it still aimed at them, she slowly backed away, each step getting her closer to the office door.

Above, Joey twisted his upper body, shifting the rifle in unison with his arms.

In the lunch room doorway, Andy slinked back into the shadows. He rose to his feet and stood, prepared to run if needed.

But it was Ronnie who was panicking. He was in the direct path of Rosie's retreat. He had only two choices, stay where he was and risk being seen, or to move to another location and risk being seen. The choice narrowed with each backward step she took; soon she'd be right on top of him. While deciding, she took a step backward and stumbled on a whiskey bottle, knocking her off balance. She tumbled forward, trying to catch her balance. That was Ronnie's chance. He tucked in his elbow and rolled to his left, stopping in a deep shadow, he pushed his body into a seated position behind a broken wooden door. He tucked in his boots, just as she took two more steps back — another two seconds, and she would have seen him.

Regaining her stance, she waved the gun at them and ordered again. "No one follows me."

"No one will," shouted Nitra, "Just go get your freedom." The phrase just popped into her head and she said it "Time is a wasting."

"Just shut up and stay put." She returned to the process of backing out towards the offices. "Better yet, everybody on your knees."

To show his cooperation, Wallace fell down on his knees first. Nitra did the same and slipped under Wallace's arm. He pulled her tightly to him. Tom frowned at the sight of her cozying up to her housekeeper, but knelt down nonetheless.

"Good boys." She didn't bother to correct her error of calling Nitra one of the boys, she was too nervous. She was having enough trouble walking through the debris that was scattered on the floor. Instead of stepping, she shuffled her high heels along the surface of the floor, pushing the garbage out of the way.

Wallace held back his laugh at the absurd sight. Right in the middle of all the dangerous commotion, Nitra had folded up her precious page one and was stuffing down the front of her blouse, being careful not to disturb her wire.

Once done, she quietly spoke into her hidden mic, "Suspect heading to office. Has cash. Is fleeing scene."

Rosie stopped her shuffling and yelled across the warehouse, "What did you say? Who are you talking to?"

Nitra's mind froze along with her body. Seeing the tendons in her neck knot, Wallace covered for her, "Me. She was talking to me." Then out of the blue, he pulled Nitra's face forward and kissed her long and hard. Pulling her away, he gazed into her eyes and pleaded, "Forgive me my love?"

The message in his eyes told the truth. Nitra didn't say a word, she couldn't. Her overflowing heart wouldn't let her. Unknown to the others, Wallace was in fact apologizing for his previous behaviour. To avoid crying, she lowered her face, avoiding his regret filled brown eyes. She still said nothing, but instead pressed her face into his chest.

Satisfied with his answer, Rosie continued on her way, shuffling her feet against the hard concrete floor. Reaching the next pillar, she instantly turned and lumbered through the office doorway. She reached the broken window, hiked up one leg and then the other. Losing her balance, she fell through its opening, crashing into the tall shrub. She tried to get up, but her coat was snagged on a branch. She carefully tugged on her sleeve trying to release it without ripping it. Then it occurred to her, why was she being careful with the raggedy old coat. She had ten thousand dollars to buy a new one. With all her might she yanked on the sleeve, ripping off a chunk of fabric. To Rosie, that shredding sound felt wonderful, purely pleasurable. She was rich now and could buy whatever her little heart desired. Back on her feet, she began to run to her car.

Halfway across the first lane, she noticed a tall blonde leaning on the hood of the car. She was watching Rosie run across the street. "Get off my car, bitch." She yelled loud and clearly so that Toni would hear it. But Toni didn't move — she was waiting for Rosie to get closer.

Through the front window of the warehouse, came each and every one of them. First was Ronnie then Andy, next was Wallace followed by Nitra and lastly, Tom made his appearance, steering clear of both Nitra and Wallace. Andy hustled the civilians around the corner of the building, far out of sight, and harm's way. Joey finally joined Ronnie, hovering by the shrubbery beside the warehouse's parking lot. They stayed hidden waiting for the right opportunity to charge on Rosie, capturing her without harming the civilians. The others couldn't stop themselves; they peeked around the corner, needing to watch it all go down.

Halfway across the final lane, Rosie yelled at the hooker again, "Get off my fuckin' car." This time the warning came with her holding up the gun inside her pocket. "Now get your whorin' ass off my car."

Within seconds, Toni charged her, grabbing her by the throat, attempting to twist her to the ground. But not willing to go down without a chance to fight, Rosie grabbed Toni by the hair and yanked hard, hoping to inflict enough pain to free herself. To Rosie's surprise — and Wallace's — Toni's blonde wig flung up into the air, Rosie fingers tangled in it, revealing Toni's buzz cut. Officer Toni Bazzoli was a man.

Wallace's stomach instantly churned. He wasn't sure if it was the adrenaline pumping through his body or the sight of Toni, the male hooker, but suddenly he felt the need to heave in the shrubs. It was Tom who yelled it out loud, "Oh my Lord, he's a *him*, not a *her*." His words distracted Rosie just long enough for Toni to get a grip on Rosie's arm.

In one hard shove, Toni had her face down on the pavement, his knee placed dead center of her back and one arm pulled straight into the air. He cuffed her right wrist and was bringing it down to connect it to the other one. They could hear Toni recite the memorandum to her, "You have the right to remain silent, anything you ..."

Nitra couldn't resist. Sweet as pie she pointed out to everyone, "Oh look, Toni's got handcuffs." She resisted the urge to giggle; instead she held it in, her face turning deep red with the pressure of not exploding into roaring laughter.

It was when Ronnie added the additional wisecrack in Wallace's direction that she finally lost it, "Yup that's my partner ... and yes, he does have nice long legs for that skirt." A round of chuckles burst out amongst the officers.

They had heard it all. Mortified, Wallace grumbled, "Fuck ya all. It was dark and I couldn't tell and ..." he stopped cold and switched his attention to a frantic Ronnie.

"Palmer, come in. Come in Palmer." His face drained white, "Come on Harry stop fuckin' around and answer me. Palmer, come in."

Nitra didn't like the urgency in his voice, "What's wrong?"

"It's Harry. He isn't answering. He always answers." His face went paler still, "Be honest lady, I'm worried."

Wallace couldn't believe he had to ask the question, but asked it nonetheless, "Good Lord boy, where's he at?"

271

It Tom who flew pass them, "He's up stairs in my office." Wallace chased after him with Nitra following right behind.

Inside, Tom bolted to the top of the stairs, flinging open the door. There on the floor by the desk, lay Harry. His arm stretched forward above his head, as though his hand was reaching for the dangling handset. His face was drained grey. Harry was unconscious.

Brian came over the radio, "Harry? Over." It clicked again, "Harry? Over."

Wallace rolled him over gently. Once flat, he listened for air. "He's not breathing. Without thought, he instinctively started chest compressions.

Nitra grabbed the handset, "Brian, its Nitra. We think Harry's had a heart attack. Radio for an ambulance. Over."

"Sure thing." There was a long pause in the air. "Holy crap, I was just talking to him and all of a sudden he stopped talking. Over."

She knew they'd want to know how long Harry had been out, so she confirmed the elapsed time with him, "How long ago was that? Over."

"Five minutes tops. Over."

"Brian, listen carefully. Shut up and call the damn ambulance. Harry needs you, now call. Out." She threw it on top of the desk. "Dumb fuckin' cops!" Ronnie had just reached the top of the stairs and frowned at her for the defamatory comment.

They both watched in amazement at the synchronization between Wallace and Tom. While Wallace pushed rabidly on his chest, Tom counted them out for him. And while Tom blew in the breaths, Wallace counted out

272

for him and listened to Harry's chest for any sign of air intake. All Wallace really wanted, was to hear a heartbeat.

This continued for what seem to be forever. With Wallace arms giving into muscular fatigue, Ronnie replaced him and then Wallace pushed Tom out of the way so he could monitor Harry's breathing.

Nitra recognized the sound approaching in the near distance, it was the ambulance. That same eerie feeling crept over her. Someone was injured and in dire need of medical attention. The excited wailing of its siren screamed that help was on its way. It was both a relief and a reminder of her time on the ground, waiting for the sound to come closer.

Tom pinched Nitra sleeve, pulling her off to one side. "Are you all right? It's been totally insane around here. Good thing I was there to get you through it."

Nitra took his male patronization as an insult and attacked his masculine ego directly, "You think that was insane? You do live a sheltered life, don't you? Up here all cozy in your little shop of old junk."

"Hey that wasn't called for. At least give me some credit for helping you out."

Her voice shot up four octaves with anger, "Helping me out?" She placed her hands on her hips, "How? By getting in the way, almost getting us shot."

He crossed his arms at her, "Well that's gratitude. I come to rescue you and you throw it in my face. Well, I'm glad I found out about this now."

"Ha!" The rest screeched out of her mouth, "Rescue me! Who the hell asked you to?" she stabbed her finger in his face. "I'll have you know, I can take care of myself. I don't need any God damned man to ..."

273

Ronnie yelled over her chastising, "Hey, do you two mind? There's a man suffering over here. Shut up already."

Wallace excitedly shouted over them all, "I got a pulse. It's faint, but it's there."

Footsteps thundered up the stairs, bringing with them two paramedics, a stretcher and one very brawny policeman. Joey insisted on lifting Harry from the floor and onto the stretcher. Nitra watched as the wiry young man laid the heavy man down as gently as a father would lay down a newborn, lovingly soft. It was then that she realised the true bond between the police officers, 'The Family' they called it.

The paramedics did their work under the scrutiny of everyone. Harry's eyes fluttered as the hissing mask did its job of filling his blood stream with well needed oxygen. He lifted his hand up no more than a quarter inch, before the paramedic leaned down to listen to his words. His head bobbed as he listened to the mumblings of his patient. With a rather confused expression, he repeated Harry's words, "He wants to know if you got the Lipstick Lady?"

Nitra stooped down beside him, to look him in the face, "Yah Harry, we got her. Congratulations, you got the bad guy … um, girl." Through his steamed up mask, she saw his faint smile, Harry was happy. He released the tension in his body, letting go, melting into the blanket. She slapped the side of the stretcher twice, "Now get out of here old man. Time's a wasting." The phrase was starting to grow on her.

Standing beside Nitra's truck, they listened to the siren fade slightly as it made its way to the hospital across town. Tom slammed the door and locked the latch.

Nitra snorted at him. She'd let that argument slide, old dogs sometimes can't be taught new tricks. She blew out a tense breath and let her body go limp. The strips of her flesh where Toni had removed the wires still stung under her clothing. Yet the pain was somewhat eased by the memory of Toni telling Wallace to take off his shirt, he needed to strip him. Watching Wallace's intimidated red face was a great pain killer. The preliminary statements were taken with the promise of a thorough affidavit to follow the next day. "They say, he'll be fine. We got to him on time. Should we go first to the hospital to see Harry or to the station?"

"How about goin' home instead? I'm thinkin' a wee shot of whiskey would be lovely about now." He pulled the door open for her to climb in. "That's if ya left us a drop or two."

Chapter Fifteen

At the house, she finally allowed herself to relax. It was over. The whole terrifying ordeal was finished. The Lipstick Lady was in custody, leaving Nitra Zupan to her quiet writer's life. Her stomach growled — for the first time in days, she felt hungry. The aching knots of stress were completely gone. Wallace was putting the little table back into the living room, removing the final traces of the last evening's encounter. Gemma was in tow, meowing wildly for any sort of attention she could get. Instead of bothering Wallace to make dinner, she sipped on her tulip tumbler, savouring each drop of the 18 year old scotch. Wallace kept referring to it being a 'single malt whiskey', particulars she knew very little about. Looking through it while turning it in her hand, she made a mental note to definitely find out more about the amber liquor. Its strong flavour was like a slap in the head, but the hot buzz it left in the mind, was worth its spiteful burn. She swirl the golden liquid, "Yes, I need to know more." The comment wasn't just about the whiskey, it included Wallace as well. If she was going to go completely, ridiculously, head over heels for the man, she

276

should learn more about him. The thought of him and her being one of those couples that had loved each other forever, but never knowing it, made her smile. Feeling a slight pinch of pain, her hand went directly to her face, to where her cheek still stung. It was bruised from where Wallace had hit her, a slap so hard it left more than an outside injury. She stared out the kitchen window, wondering what it all meant.

Wallace watched her from the living room doorway. Gemma slipped between his legs, following the human that fed her. Seeing Nitra hold her cheek, churned his stomach with guilt. He had hit her, a cowardly act that Wallace McPhee never did. Hitting a woman was the sign of a weak man, a wretched beast that couldn't control his temper. He understood that it would take time to make it up to her, to reassure her that it was part of the moment and not an action he would purposely do ever again. The healing of that slap would take time and tenderness to mend. He walked towards her, wanting to start that healing tonight. The phone rang, breaking his stride.

Without a question of who should be the one to answer it, he did as she watched. "Hello?" He sat on the tiny chair and listened. "Uh-huh." Nitra widened her eyes at him, pleading for more information. "So it was a heart attack." He pointed his finger in the air, halting her impatience. "Yah, we'll be there first thin' in the mornin'." He rubbed his chest, massaging the bands of pain where the tape had ripped out his hair. "Uh-huh. Well, I'm sure you wanted to get it a better way, but just the same, congratulations! You'll do a great job of it." He looked up at Nitra, his eyes big with delight, "Yah, she must be fine. She's already in to my whiskey." She flipped him a finger. "Uh-huh." He flipped a finger back in her direction. "Yah, okay. See ya then. Bye."

"Well, who was it and what did they say?" She nervously pranced around him, anxious of what the answers might be.

He took his time in answering her; payback for not telling him about Toni before he made a complete ass of himself. At the china cabinet, Wallace took out a tulip tumbler for himself. "It was Brian. He called to let us know that Harry did have a heart attack. He's out of surgery and is stable. The ICU nurse told Brian that if it wasn't for me and Harper doin' what we did, he'd be a dead man." He poured a tall ounce into the glass. "So it looks like Brian is Hamlin's new Chief of Police. Harry's retiring." He chuckled out, "Funny how it took a scrape with death to do it." He took a deep swig then shuttered a tiny bit as the liquor seared its way down his throat. "Remember that gun Rosie had in her coat? Turns out it was just a piece of copper pipe and not a revolver at all. Apparently, she's pleadin' and beggin' like a crazy woman." He saw Nitra's face fret. "Not to worry though, Brian assures me that she's not goin' anywhere. They're not givin' bail at all. I didn't know Judge Heath is an old friend of Harry's." He grinned at her, "Life's grand that way, ain't it?" She held out her glass for more. He frowned at her, but poured her another half tumbler full. "So my dear literary lady, now you know how the novel ends."

Her eyes went huge, "Christ, you're right, I do." A blank expression cloaked her face. She walked right passed him as though he had suddenly disappeared. Wallace recognized that distant gaze in her eyes. She was a writer plotting a mind full of twisted thoughts. A trance induced spell that only can be broken by the powers of pencil and paper.

The ideas thundered through her head like hailstones on a tin roof. A sense of urgency overtook her. She had to write down each of the thoughts, both warped and

278

inspirational, before they were lost. She ran for her pad of red lined paper. Time was of the essence, it had to be done now or they'd be lost forever. She ran for the notepad, opening her brief case. There tucked inside was Mara's manuscript, the one she to meant sent to William. "Oh Christ, William!" she blurted out. In all the commotion of her life she'd neglected poor William. "Oh Wallace, what have I done, he'll be worried. I've got to call him right away."

She immediately picked up the phone, but admiring the manly stature of Wallace holding his tiny glass of whiskey, she changed her mind. This was one phone call she wanted to make in private. She returned the receiver to its cradle, "I think, I'll make this call from my office. I have to tell him the news … well, the whole story actually, considering the fact I haven't let on that there was a problem in the first place. So it looks like I'll need to grovel a bit. I'll need that deadline pushed back. I'd prefer to do that in private if you don't mind."

Wallace held the living room door open for her, "Say hello for me would ya. Tell William he owes me a bottle of whiskey for saving your bloody life … again."

In protest to his teasing, she let the door swing shut in his face. Right to her room she went, closing the door tightly behind her. She placed the manuscript on top of the writing pad. Another layer added to the already mounding stack. She dialled the numbers and ran her finger over Mara's novel while she waited for an answer. "Hello William. How are you?" To her relief the poor man was frantic about another problematic situation that didn't pertain to her at all. "She's gone? Just like that?" She listened to his fast paced words as he explained the circumstances to her. "So she just up and left with her boyfriend." He corrected her use of words, "Okay ran away with him. Don't worry you'll get another house keeper. It'll take time to find the right one, but you'll find one." She held the receiver back from her ear, he was hysterically screaming on the other end. From that arm length distance, she caught the phrases, 'hosting dinner party for European clients' and 'less than one week.' She yelled at him, "William slow down, I can't make out what you're saying."

She nodded as she listened to dilemma, then a smile swept across her face when an image of Katie popped into Nitra's head. She cut off his ranting, "How's your patience with the Irish, Billy Boy? 'Cause I've got the gal for you. I met her while I was picking up one of my missing pages." She winced at William's vocal reaction. "You see I lost my manuscript in a windstorm and offered twenty dollars a page for those returned to me." Once he stopped yelling, she continued to tell him her full adventure of the last few days, its places and its people.

In the kitchen Wallace was preparing Nitra's favourite feast. The 'writing plate' he named it. On one of her writing frenzies, she'd command food before she imprisoned herself in for the night. And since eating with a fork and knife couldn't be done while scribbling manically on paper, she generally preferred a plate of finger held tidbits. It consisted of her favourites — slices of salami, chunks of extra old cheese, hands full of grapes and olives, wedges of apples and pears alongside a mound of crisp whole wheat crackers. Gemma begged for a morsel of beloved human food. Wallace indulged her with a thick salami slice. He arranged the food stuffs in a manner that each colour and texture balanced out against the other. Satisfied with his efforts, he started to bring it to her, then remember the pitcher of water and her favourite glass, the one with a heavy flat bottom that wouldn't tip over, spilling on her hand written papers.

When he reached her door, he gently shoved it open with his foot and whispered between the crack, "Nitra. I brought you a wee somethin' to nibble on."

"Just a minute William." She slipped her hand over the mouth piece. "Wallace, what do you say, you put on a fire tonight?"

"Can do Lass." He held the tray up to her, "Where do ya want me to put this."

"Can you put it out there by the fireplace? I'll be out once I'm done talking to William." She batted her eyes at him, "Please."

Her actions puzzled him for a moment, but she slipped a seductive smile on her lips which promptly cleared up his confusion, "No problem. See ya in a bit then." Gemma slipped inside making herself comfortable on the window seat.

She wheeled her office chair across to the door, slowly shutting it quietly as she watched him place the tray on the coffee table in front of the sofa. *He is a worthy man ... and handsome too,* she reminded herself. Maybe it was time for this to happen. "Now where was I ... oh yah, so this manuscript of Mara's its really good. Juicy as hell. Not to mention the super-twisted plot line. Right up our reader's alley. I'll send it to you along with my first draft and chapters one and two." She tapped her pencil on the writing pad as he praised and promised. "Well, since you mentioned it, you can return the favour right away. I need

281

help with some traveling arrangements." She scribbled on the pad. A big loopy *N* intertwined with an *M*. "Oh no William, it's not for me. It's for Wallace's mother. He hasn't seen her in years and I thought that it might be nice if she came for a surprise visit at Christmas time. It'll be my secret gift for him. Will you help me?" She squealed out her excitement, "Oh, thank you, thank you. I'll let you know more details later. Oh and I've got an idea about a cookbook too. It involves Wallace and his cooking, but that's for later on as well." She drew a heart around the wishful initials, "Yes, I promise that I will. I'll talk to her first thing in the morning. Don't worry; I'm sure Katie would love to work for you. In fact, I can almost guarantee she will." She added the little arrow ends to the heart shape. That did it, she couldn't hold back any longer, "Listen William, I've got to go, Wallace is waiting for me. I'll talk to you soon. Bye." Nitra didn't wait for his goodbyes, she hung up the receiver and hurried to the door.

She pulled it open slightly. Through the crack she watched Wallace fuss with the fire, the muscles of his back were taught and strong as he put on another wedge of wood on the already crackling fire. Gemma rubbed up against her leg. Talking to the cat she whispered, "Who knew that a few freckles could be so God damned sexy on a man." The cat meowed and disappeared up the stairs. She couldn't believe that she had missed it all this time. They'd lived under the same roof for years, but she never saw it. She smiled at her own lack of observation. It was laughable, the writer not seeing her own life.

When he straightened, he saw her peeking at him, and smiled, "Hell of a chill in the air tonight. You know that old saying *'autumn steals summer like a thief.'*

282

She made her way to where the tray was and sat on the sofa behind it, "Wallace would you like some? Come sit with me."

Her behaviour was truly odd. Normally she'd be elbow deep in scribbled notes, pacing the floor. "But aren't ya gonna start on your next book?"

She raised her eye brows, "It can wait 'til the morning." She gently padded the space beside her, "Come sit beside me."

It was the sultry tone of her voice and the sparkle in her dark green eyes that made her intensions perfectly clear. "Come to think of it, I've been rather starved lately." He gently sat down next her, waiting for her to give him the next clue. It took no time at all for him to get the hint. One enticing smile and she slid in beside him. "Tomorrow, eh? That leaves your evenin' fairly free to do something else then."

A sinful little grin slipped across her lips as she lost herself in his eyes. Unable to suppress the emotions in her heart, she embraced them and released her true feelings on Wallace. She threw her arms around his neck and kissed him wildly, pushing him backward onto the overstuffed sofa.

Her sudden rush of passion stunned Wallace at first, but her powerful persistence told him to go further. He drew her on top of him, her body melted into his arms, "Oh that be better." He kissed her gently, finally letting his emotions for her free to flow through his heart. He kissed her lips then her cheek, ending with soft full kisses behind her ear. This was the moment he had been craving for so long, it was easy to get lost in the dreamy romantic rush, but the man that he was, needed to know for certain, "Nitra, are ya sure this is what ya want?"

283

Against his cheek she nodded her commitment and kissed his neck tenderly, sealing it with her devotion. Her loving hands gingerly turned his head so she could gaze directly into his eyes. She understood that Wallace needed her blessing — it was the kind of man he was. "Yes, I am sure." With a hint of amusement in her hushed voice she whispered softly, "Well, it's like that adage you always say, *"One today, is worth two tomorrows."* Her eyes then smiled, "And after all ... time is a wasting."

Be sure to
look for
Kay's previous book,
Life on the Lawn
now for sale

This is the story of four, life long, best friends - Fran, Pearl, Ruby and Violet - who attend the auction of Henry Phillips, the husband of their late-friend, Virginia. Henry, no longer able to take care of himself, is forced to leave the farm life behind and retire into a nursing home. With his unwanted transition, comes the selling of his remaining possessions in a simple country auction.

Treasures and heirlooms that his greedy children do not care to inherit. As the sale proceeds, these elderly Southern ladies share with each other the memories and adventures that are connected to many of the items up for auction. Tales of apple pies, lost loves, and murder. Many of the local folk and neighbours gather to bid on the household items at hand, but it's Emmett, the worldly auctioneer, who is downright curious about the quiet outsider. Why is someone as sophisticated as him at a small town auction? Who is this unknown wealthy Frenchman? And why is he watching the four ladies so intently?

This is the story of one simple day,
at a not so simple auction.

285

Keep reading for an excerpt

from the upcoming book by

Kay D. Johnson

MARKED

January 2017

Chapter 1

George Oscar Dack loathed his life.
It was dull, predictable and uneventful.
And that night, he was going to put an end to that.

George had a plan.

His inspiration first came to him while working in his bookshop. He observed a customer, glowing as purple as the ten dollar bill she paid him with, had an abnormal and abrupt change in attitude.

He noticed immediately that the bill had been vandalized. Stained a crossed its front, were the curse words, 'WHORING BITCH'. The slur was accompanied by a thick blue arrow pointing to the head of the stoic Monarchy. The customer herself was impatient and unbearably rude. That was until she released the bill into his custody, then as if a switch had been flipped, she became pleasant and calm.

After she left, George took the old bill from the register and studied it closer. The quietness of the bookshop allowed his mind to envision and wander to places it normally wouldn't. As his mind searched the bill's energy, questions formed in his head. Was there a connection between the meanness of the lady and the scribed dollar bill? Was she nasty all the time or was she influenced by the bill's permanent blue scars? Could that be possible? And more importantly, could he recreate the identical effect with his powers?

But tonight he would start the first phase of his experiment in finding the answer — he'd been preparing his method for weeks.

Unfortunately, he still had to get through his regular work day, before he could execute his meticulous plan.

For George, each day was the same and that morning was no different. His alarm always went off at ten to seven. To save time, he brewed his coffee in his lonely one-cup coffee maker while he had his daily shower. There, he paid particular attention to his long brown hair, in his opinion his finest feature. He made his own special conditioner in his own shop; a blend which allowed each strand to gather power from light, both solar and lunar, that made it shimmer with vibrant energy. Energy that he used in daily life to ward off unwanted darker powers wield by others. He also carefully shaved away his facial stubble, admiring his smooth kissable skin in the mirror — even though there was no one to kiss it. His was always the same monotonous routine.

He hastily ate his cinnamon toast over the kitchen sink while attempting to stroke his cat Darius good-morning ... he was ignored as per usual. Pulling his long hair back, he used a simple black hair band, locking it in a plain ponytail. Someday, he would leave it loose, letting its long tendrils move freely over his square sturdy shoulders. Someday, he would show everyone the real him; the true George that lived inside him. The parlour clock bonged the quarter hour, announcing that he was running a little late. He grabbed his black leather backpack and dashed through the front door, stopping only long enough to make sure it was completely locked. He didn't want anyone pilfering his things. He had spent years accumulating his eccentric collection of curiosities. Some were considered extremely rare and irreplaceable. It would be a shame to lose them after all the searching he had done to finally be with their true owner. Not to mention the financial sacrifice to procure those fragile curiosities. Spinning on his heels, he scurried down the sidewalk toward Main Street.

His shop was seven small-city blocks from his apartment — a short twelve minute walk for his long legs. Each morning was a mini-adventure for him. George was an observer. He watched everything, the seasonal scenery, the church where he worshiped, the old houses, the animals both domestic and in nature, however what intrigued him the most, were the people. He watched them interact with each other, or in some cases, not interacted. He watched how they changed from week to week, year to year. Babies growing into children, puppies turning into full grown dogs that barked their hellos to him on his way home from the shop. Sometimes their glowing auras changed too — sometimes for the worse, sometimes for the better.

A current situation he was studying, concerned him greatly. It all started the previous spring when Mr. Hamlin, the senior who had lived there as long as George could remember, failed to wake up one cold February morning. Subsequently his apartment was taken over by a young couple that April. George noticed the changes right away, when they replaced the dull brown drapes with vivid red ones. A single pot of tiny flowers and a new door mat were placed out front, making the once subdued building, cheery and youthful.

George also took notice of her — the slim redhead that glowed brightly from head to toe. Ivy shimmered in shades of violet, indigo and electric blue. He marveled at the vast number of variations her aura would transform into. Some mornings she was solid violet with tinges of indigo on the outer edges, while other times, she was surrounded by swirls of all those three aura colours. But lately, he had noticed blackness creeping in. Black was a sign of upheaval, a disturbance within the normal balance of a being. That worried him. He decided to keep an eye on her, just in case she needed rescuing.

Through George's eyes, most people glowed in some way or form. Ivy was different from the rest — she made *him* glow. He had never seen or experienced his own aura before meeting her. Mysteriously, his own aura would only react when she was nearby — vanishing when she left. As long as he could remember, he only saw others glow.

George could still remember the exact moment he knew he was different. He was nine when he discovered that other people didn't see what he saw. Paul and him were playing chestnuts in the school yard when Amy Weller walked by. Paul inhaled a whistle and announced under his breath that she was *hot looking*. George merely commented that he liked the particular shade of green she radiated. Paul immediately straightened up and wanted to know, '*What the hell are you talking about?*' By the quizzical look on Paul's face, George realized that what he had just saw and said, wasn't normal. To avoid an awkward explanation, he quickly changed the subject to a recently injured baseball hero.

290

From that day forward, he talked to no one else, but his Mother about their special gift. In his life he'd seen hundreds — no thousands — of people who glowed. Shopping malls and grocery stores were full of them. Each one was different from the rest, unique to that particular individual and their current state in life. Their health, sleeping habits, stress level, eating habits, substance abuse, and spirituality — all factors affecting their energy flows.

George unlocked the front door of the book store with three minutes to spare. Not that it mattered; no one ever came in until at least eleven o'clock. His clientele tend to stay up late and therefore, woke later in the day. He closed the door behind him and flipped over the sign pronouncing the *'Grapefruit Moon'* open for the world to enjoy. He was proud of his little shop with its book stacks overflowing with old and new books alike. The shelves were filled with items such as candles, earthenware, and happy little chachkas. To the average person, these things appeared to be simply gift items, displayed in random vignettes to entice the eye.

But to his regular clients, these were the essentials of their craft. He searched far and wide, sometimes for years to find the exact item that fit his specific criteria. After a four year search, he discovered a small candle company in Manitoba that not only manufactured a wide variety of styles and colours, they also used wax from their very own bee hive. This allowed them to maintain its purity, a great plus to his trade.

What really hooked him, was one particular type of candle – the 9" onyx black, six sided, pillar candle. That was what he needed to complete his collection of required elements. Solid black through and through. Hard to find in today's economy driven world. It cost him

291

three times what the cheaper outer coated candles cost, but they were worth it. That also meant his customers had to pay a premium price. No one complained though, instead they paid the price and praise him for having the opportunity to purchase such a fine quality product. Crystals, mortar and pestle, candles, shimmering orbs, and tiny glass bottles were displayed throughout the shelving and amongst books. He was providing the finest quality products that his type of clientele preferred. He kept the elements simple and discriminating, yet fulfilling the magical aspects his clients desired.

Walking to the back of the store to flick on the lights, he heard a noise he hadn't heard at that time of morning in many years — the entrance bells above the door. George turned to see a hunched over elderly lady, limping her way to the blue bucket chair nearest the books shelves. Her body slapped down hard against its leather surface. He flicked on the last switch and called out to her, "I'll be with you in a minute."

"No hurry, young man. I've got all day," she yelled back to him in a kindly manner.

Making his way to the front, he made small talk, "Looks like another beautiful day?" He studied her face for a few moments. In a bewildering way, he felt as though he had met her before, yet couldn't quite place her in his memory.

"Oh my, yes. They're calling for a high of 87°F this afternoon. That's much too hot for me, I like it cooler. Actually, it's quite pleasant in here." She wiggled in the chair, squeaking the leather as she made herself comfortable.

"Climate controlled." He nonchalantly added as not to raise any suspicion. "For the older books."

She simply nodded her understanding. From her tattered purse, she pulled a crumbled list, "They tell me you have these things. They say you're the one to come to." She offered the pale blue paper up to him.

"I'm flattered, but who exactly are *they*?" George examined the list and immediately recognized the ingredients for a particular potion. Quickly glancing at her, he wondered how old she really was.

She politely cleared her throat, "It is not my place to tell such tales. Discretion is the utmost importance amongst our kind." Her green eyes twinkled with secretive exuberance.

"This is true." For a split second, an image of his Uncle Thaddeus flashed in his mind. "Give me a few moments to gather what you have on your list." He waved his hand in the direction of the book shelves, "Please feel free to browse through some literature while you wait." She nodded her understanding. "Now, if you will excuse me." He disappeared through the black velveteen curtains that led to the hidden back storeroom.

But instead of reading, she closed her eyes and inhaled deeply, breathing in the aroma of old books and exotic scented candles. She felt very much at home amongst them. As she waited, her breathing became shallower, a calmness washed over her body.

From various coloured jars and sectioned drawers in the elements room, George measured out each ingredient precisely to the amounts listed on his ancient scales, placing each one in its own small white paper bag. Soft violet leaves, fragrant whole sage, and coarse magnetic sand were labeled with his stylish script. In turn, all the ingredients were put in a larger double

293

handled violet bag. He wrote out the bill and tucked it inside the bag. Stepping through the curtains, he noticed her closed eyes and wasn't sure if he should wake her or let her rest some more. He stood by the chair and quietly waited.

"It's alright George, I'm not sleeping." Her abruptness made him jump. "Taking time for peace is important for ones soul." She opened one eye to examine him. "Nervous? Valerian tea will take care of that. Oh, but of course you already know that, don't you George?"

"Yes Ma'am, I do." An odd sensation rushed from his feet up toward his head. She was searching him. He blocked her before she reached his mind, "Now, now, there will be none of that." He smiled approvingly at her, "But good try."

"He was right. You are perceptive." She smiled up at him, "So how did you manage with my list? Is everything in there?" She slid forward making the leather creak and groan.

"Only one thing left." He walked to the shelf that displayed a wide array of small bottles of various hues, forms and sizes. "You need to pick out your own vial. You tell me which one you'd like and we're all set." While he waited for her to choose, he wondered who she was referring to, but decided not to ask.

Her long finger pointed directly at it, "Well, the choice is obvious, the pink one."

He took it from the shelf and admired it, "Longevity and true love, very appropriate for a potion such as yours. Do you have the witch-hazel or will you need that as well?" It wasn't on the list, yet he knew she would need it to concoct the potion.

"Goodness, you *are* good." She slowly hoisted herself from the chair, creating more leathery sounds.

"No, I have plenty of that. But you know, I've been eyeing that pewter mortar set in the front window. Please add that to my bag George."

As she slowly made her way to the counter, George wrapped the mortar and pestle in Violet coloured tissue. Not wanting to crush their contents, he gently placed the heavy package on the bottom and placed the white bags on top. Totaling the handwritten bill, he rang the prices through the nickel plated antique register, "Eighty six dollars even."

"Even? How odd?" They exchanged smiles. He'd given her a break on the price and that pleased her. All she said as she dug through her purse was, "Thank you young man. Now, let's see?" She counted out the bills on the counter, "Twenty, forty, sixty, eighty and three two dollar bills ... since I know you're looking for two's." Those she placed directly in his palm.

Again her probing rushed through him, and again he blocked her. "Why yes I am. But how did you know that?"

Her eyes twinkled at him, "Oh, you may be good ... but I'm even better!" Instantly he felt a light tickle behind the block he held in his mind. She only grinned up at him and patted his hand, "You are so adorable." She wagged a thoughtful finger at him, "You know what? I'm going to teach you all that I know. We will start in two days time." With that, she snapped up her purple bag and looped her purse over her arm. She called behind her as she hobbled towards the door. "Until I see you next. And I like oolong tea. Bye George." The door closed behind her, leaving him standing, staring at the door with only the sound of bells chiming through the air.

He uttered one question to himself, "Who was that?" Shaking his head to loosen her faint yet effective hold, he heard a voice warn inside his head, *Be Careful!* Then, as if on cue, the bills in his hand began to warm, reminding him of their presents. He switched his focus from her to them, examining them closer. Unfortunately, none fit his requirements.

To his nose they smelled foul, and their glow was the wrong colour. Blues and greens would simply not do. The bill he was searching for would have to glow a true orange, indicating its abilities of strong motivation. He was almost relieved that his two dollar bill didn't come from her and the strengths she held. He shoved them along with the twenties into the till and slowly closed its drawer.

George went about his morning routine — restocking shelves, changing displays, and checking inventory for tomorrow's orders. His favourite duty was reading the new books that came in; after all it was important that he knew exactly what he was selling. Unfortunately, there was no time for that today. He opened the mail when it arrived. Paid the bills, sent off correspondence, and filed invoices.

Same as every other day – then two o'clock happened.

Chapter 2

George was knee high in price tags and new books, when the small group arrived. Nine women came in at once, all of them examining everything simultaneously. Nine — a number of significance — and of worry. He straightened from his work and greeted them with a cheerful smile, "Welcome, to the *Grapefruit Moon*." He un-stickered his fingers and placed his full attention their way. "Is there anything I can help you ladies find today?"

The eldest of the group spoke first, "Good day to you sir, my name is Roma." She locked her hands together at the waist of her dark blue robe, not offering a friendly hand shake. "I was told you carry a large library of older publications. We are looking for a particular doctrine."

"*The Nine Moons of Sister Mountain*," interrupted the taller one, "And not a recent copy. It *must* be a first edition." Her knitted eyebrows emphasized the importance of that singular fact.

The shorter one blurted out, "And money is no object."

A collective grunt came from the group. The tallest one elbowed the shortest one, "Shut up, Manta."

To save the situation, Roma quickly jumped in, "What she means is ... we are open to negotiations on the price." She flashed him a sweet grin, hoping it would smooth over the blunder.

"Do you have it?" The tallest one's voice was overly eager, "A first edition? Do you have one?" An indication of neediness he was delighted to hear.

He knew precisely where he kept it in the shop, yet George took his time walking to the furthest bookcase. To build anticipation, he tapped the spines of several books, shuffled a few others, returning one to another lower shelf. Believing they had waited long enough, he pulled the book from the top shelf. He puckered up his lips and blew away its fine layer of dust. "*The Nine Moons of Sister Mountain* – First edition." He announced, just loud enough for them to hear.

They rushed him. Within seconds he was surrounded by nine very excited, very grabby women. To avoid having the book damaged, he held it high above his head. "Hold on, hold on." He wriggled himself from the middle of the group and dashed to the front till, positioning the counter between them and him for protection. "Ladies, ladies. This is an extraordinarily ancient and sacred writ. It is fragile and delicate. Please, one at a time. Also, I will remind you of my shop's policy, '*If you break it, you take it!*'" He looked directly at the Elder for confirmation. "Understood?"

Almost in unison, they nodded their heads in agreement. As though prearranged, all but Roma backed away from the counter. Confirming George's suspicions, she was indeed their Elder. "I will determine its authenticity." She gently patted the counter, "If you please Sir."

George lowered his arms and placed the thick sky blue book on the countertop, "It's over 1100 years old. Be careful." With the last two words, something tickled in the back of his mind. To his disbelief, the old woman was still in there. "Please turn the pages slowly as to not tear them."

As the Elder prepared herself, George became aware of the black haired one in the group. He felt his ponytail react to the increased flow of her energy. She was staring into him, into his mind. The longer she stared, the larger her eyes grew. He felt her creep along his block, inch by inch, looking for away in.

Still watching her, he bluntly ordered, "Tell her to knock it off. It won't work."

With both hands on its top, absorbing and reading its power, the Elder was so fully mesmerized by the book she had no idea what was happening around her. "What?" She turned to sense Suki's probing. He felt the Elder connect with the underling, "What are you doing? Who gave you permission to do that? Did *I* say you could do that?" She slapped the top of the wooden counter. "Stop it! Immediately!" The loud crack scared Suki out of her probing, her legs let go from beneath her.

Fortunately, Manta caught the girl before she hit the floor. Standing once more, she apologized for her disobedience, "Sorry, Roma."

"No one is to do anything until I say so. Is that clear?" All nodded again. Roma send back a hard nod of satisfaction and returned to the task at hand.

Through the silence came Suki's muffled voice, "He is strong. Beyond what I can rule."

MARKED

January 2017

www.ingramcontent.com/pod-product-compliance
Lightning Source LLC
Chambersburg PA
CBHW020343180626
46812CB00001B/323